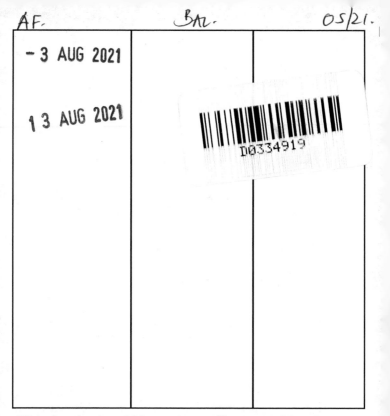

Double Blind

Also by Edward St Aubyn

The Patrick Melrose novels
Never Mind
Bad News
Some Hope
Mother's Milk
At Last

On the Edge
A Clue to the Exit
Lost for Words
Dunbar

Double Blind

Edward St Aubyn

Harvill Secker
LONDON

1 3 5 7 9 10 8 6 4 2

Harvill Secker, an imprint of Vintage, is part of the
Penguin Random House group of companies whose addresses
can be found at global.penguinrandomhouse.com

 Penguin
Random House
UK

First published by Harvill Secker in 2021

A CIP catalogue record for this book is available from the British Library

penguin.co.uk/vintage

ISBN 9781787300255
TPB ISBN 9781787300262

Typeset in 10.2/13.87 pt Sabon LT Std
by Integra Software Services Pvt. Ltd, Pondicherry

Printed and bound in Great Britain by Clays Ltd, Elcograf S.p.A.

The authorised representative in the EEA is Penguin Random House Ireland,
Morrison Chambers, 32 Nassau Street, Dublin DO2 YH68.

Penguin Random House is committed to a sustainable future for
our business, our readers and our planet. This book is made from
Forest Stewardship Council® certified paper.

MIX
Paper from
responsible sources
FSC® C018179

For Sara

PART ONE

1

Francis ducked into the sallow copse that had sprung up on the land next to his cottage, pushing aside the pliant branches when he needed to and weaving through them when he could. As the slippery mud of the lane gave way to firmer ground among the trees, his tread relaxed and his attention expanded to take in the October air, already cool but still soft; the scent of growing fungus and sodden moss; the red defiance and yellow lethargy of decaying leaves, and the crows rasping in a nearby field. He felt the life around him and the life inside him flowing into each other, some of it in a tangle of sensation – when he touched the branch it also touched him – some of it in similes and resemblances and some, on the outer edge of his awareness, like a network of underground streams, or the pale mesh of roots under his feet, known without being seen. He felt this confluence of mutual life, although it was hard to hold in mind, was the fundamental background to all the sharp particularities that tried to monopolise his attention, like the robin that had just landed briefly in front of him, making him mirror the tiny, abrupt movements of its neck and then inviting him to follow the loops of its descending flight through the trees, to the rustle of its arrival among the leaves. Each form of life was bringing its own experience into the world; sometimes tightly overlapping with others, like the Purple Emperor cocoon he had seen stitched to one of these sallow branches last May; sometimes briefly interpenetrating, like the robin that had paused on a similar branch only a moment ago, and at other times radically isolated, like a streak of bacteria hidden in an Antarctic rock, but still embedded in its niche of whistling wind and perpetual frost.

Later today, Olivia was coming to stay with him for the first time. It was a bold move for two people who knew each other so little, but neither of them had wanted to end the last weekend with vague promises to meet in a future of crumbling enthusiasm and growing diffidence. At the conference in Oxford there had seemed to be some subterranean attraction that connected them before they were introduced. They felt something more like recognition than discovery. Olivia was certainly pretty, her dark brown hair set off her pale blue eyes in an obviously striking way, but it was the clarity of the eyes themselves that got to him. He had the sense of someone who would not just hold his gaze, as she did when they first met, long past the fading smiles of routine sociability, but someone who would also hold the gaze of an unsettling experience or an inconvenient fact. It was a kind of moral seduction that lent inevitability to her physical appeal. They had only spent one night together, but it had the tentative intensity of a love affair rather than the practised abandon of hedonism.

What would it be like for her to be on this walk? Would she, like him, feel part of a web of living experience? Francis couldn't help wondering how Olivia's relationship to the natural world had withstood her training as a biologist. So much biology consisted of killing animals, during or after performing experiments on them, it was an education that cried out for dissociation from the rest of nature. It had never been a good time to be a 'model organism', a fruit fly, a mouse, a dog, a rat, a cat, a rhesus monkey or a chimpanzee. As an undergraduate, he had done more than enough vivisection, dissection and deliberate infection of laboratory animals to drive him to specialise in botany as soon as possible. Why did every generation of biology student have to amputate the legs of living

4

frogs and spectate on the beating hearts of crucified mammals, as if they were trying to join a tough gang whose rite of passage was a random murder? At the peak of his rebellion against this tradition, he had come across a remark by Wittgenstein, not especially eloquent in itself, but striking at the time, because it seemed to vindicate his unease about the way he was being taught: 'Physiological life is of course not "Life". Nor is psychological life. Life is the world.' He might not have made the grade as a lethal biologist, but he remained a naturalist, trying to appreciate the last of those three short sentences as deeply as he could. Being a naturalist wasn't a bad tradition; after all, before neo-Darwinism there had been Darwinism and before Darwinism, Darwin, a man writing about earthworms and making detailed observations of living creatures and joining pigeon fancying clubs and gardening and corresponding with other naturalists, without treating their testimony as 'merely anecdotal'.

Francis came to a halt. After eight years at Howorth, he had grown to know the mushrooms scattered around the estate, identifying the woods where he might expect to forage giant puffballs, or porcini for lunch, as well as the meadows and pastures where the flimsy and modest-looking liberty caps hid their psilocybin charge, like jewels sewn into the lining of a refugee's tattered overcoat. Right now, he had almost stepped on a chanterelle. It was evidence of a vigorous mycorrhizal network under his feet, the product of a symbiotic association between fungi, foraging for nutrients in the soil, and the roots of these young trees. In some ecosystems, the nutrients were transferred from favoured plants to struggling ones, but in any case, the whole network was supposed to take much longer to establish. It was exciting to see new knowledge emerging from the wilding experiment that was taking place on the land around his cottage. Ten years ago, his landlords had noticed that the old oaks at Howorth were sickening and beginning to die back; they had lost their bloom and some skeletal branches were sticking out of the canopy like bare antlers. They called in an expert who told them that the oaks were dying from the constant ploughing that churned up their roots and from the pesticides and artificial fertiliser being showered on the soil. Trees that had withstood the demands of shipbuilding, the Industrial Revolution and the timber quotas of the Second World War were being killed by improvements in farming. George and Emma made the radical decision to abandon intensive agriculture and turn over their estate to wilding. The monotony of wheat was replaced by Red deer and Fallow deer, Tamworth pigs, English Longhorn cattle and a herd of Exmoor ponies, acting as proxies for animals that would have roamed Britain in the past – aurochs, tarpan and wild boar – in a landscape that was gradually turning into a kind of English savannah of open grassland dotted with trees and shrubs.

Francis, who had arrived at Howorth two years after the wilding began, was given the job of monitoring the resurgence of species and taking visitors on tours of the estate. He found himself living in a world of growing richness, a hotspot for nightingales and turtledoves, a place that might help save a species from extinction and where scientific knowledge was being advanced. The Purple Emperor cocoon, for instance, that he had seen ensconced on the branch of some scrubland sallow in the middle of a field, disproved the established view that the Emperor was a woodland butterfly. Agriculture had simply eliminated isolated sallow before the observations were recorded in scientific literature. There had been one clear-water pond on the estate in the agricultural days, less polluted by nitrate run-off than the others, where the rare water violet led its happily neglected life. Now, the violet had spread to the other ponds and, radiating around them, there was also a series of 'scrapes' – shallow indentations made to collect rain. Sometimes in the early summer, before they dried out, Francis had seen animals gathering around these ephemeral watering holes in a density that seemed more African than English; deer and cattle drinking, ducks and moorhens swimming, swallows and dragonflies dipping, and the cries of nearby skylarks piercing the chatter of all the other birds twisting through the air above the water and the reeds.

The flat land around Howorth, with its heavy clay soil, set in one of the most densely populated parts of the country, was quite different from the Somerset village where Francis had been brought up, on the edge of the Quantocks, the first Area of Outstanding

Natural Beauty to be designated in England. The village contained a house where Coleridge had lived for a couple of years. About thirty miles away, on Exmoor, was Ash Farm where he had been writing 'Kubla Khan' before he was interrupted by the 'person from Porlock' – a coastal village which Francis often visited as a child, scanning the beach for the vandal who had done such a disservice to poor old Coleridge. Francis's father had dreamt of becoming a vet, but there had not been enough money to complete his training and he had taken up a job in the Taunton branch of Lloyds where his parents' small dairy farm had its debts. It was supposed to be a temporary measure, but between the mortgage and the costs of bringing up a child, there had never been time to go back to his vocation and so he led his life as a reluctant banker, specialising in agricultural loans, which at least allowed him to drive around the countryside to visit clients who appreciated the astute and compassionate gaze he brought to their herds and flocks.

Francis's childhood home was full of animals: the brilliantly intelligent sheepdog, Balthazar; a tank of tropical fish; a tortoise slowly exploring the garden, and a nervous albino rabbit, Alphonso, who died by nibbling voraciously through an electric cable. Without sheep to work with, Balthazar practised herding the hens that Francis's mother kept, until she finally asked his father to put up a fence between them. Although Francis was only six, he was invited to help.

His father took to the hammer with uncharacteristic ferocity, frightening Francis with his strange atmosphere. After a few violent blows, he apologised, explaining that the bank had repossessed a farm belonging to a family he had known all his life: they had fought so hard to keep it and he felt guilty about his failure to protect them. 'Let's measure out the fence,' he said, in a calmer voice; 'you can cut the wire.' By Sunday afternoon they had completed the job: half a dozen willow stakes, connected by three rows of gleaming wire, curving across the end of the garden. At first it all seemed rather stark and new, but then in the spring Francis saw the bare stakes, which had appeared to be old timber, coming back to life; they were sprouting and turning into willow trees. This early experience of regeneration had a strong impact on his imagination and connected the landscape at Howorth with his own deep past, making the differences between his current home and his childhood home less important than their shared regenerative power.

He belonged, like Olivia, to a generation that felt it had been born on a planet irretrievably damaged by human greed and ignorance. The previous generation had perhaps been preoccupied by the prospect of nuclear annihilation, but for Francis, who was only five when the Berlin Wall came down, there was clearly no need for a war to lay waste to the biosphere; all that was needed was business as usual. In his first conversation with Olivia at the megafauna conference, perhaps already exhilarated by their meeting but not yet prepared to express it directly, he couldn't help noticing the strangely cheerful, almost rivalrous way they had discussed the inevitable death of nature. They agreed that the Anthropocene Age was more likely to mark the downfall than the triumph of its brash protagonist; or rather, that they would both be parts of a single event, like a property developer cutting the ribbon on a looming skyscraper that bears his name, only to be buried moments later under its tsunami of rubble and dust. He told Olivia that during his adolescence, the weight of ecological doom was sometimes so great that he had felt the pressure of misanthropy and despair. When he read that the acidification of the oceans through the absorption of excess carbon dioxide would lead to the loss of thirty per cent of marine life, the scale of the crisis invited a sense of impotence equal to his sense of horror. He felt that if each soldier killed in a war deserved to have his name inscribed on a monument, an entire species wiped out by hunting or the destruction of its habitat must deserve to have its name recorded as well. After admiring endangered species in captivity, a Hall of Extinction would provide a solemn and natural finale to a day at the zoo. In his early twenties the antidote to his sense of dread was to join other eco-warriors in clandestine operations, releasing beavers into Devon rivers in the middle of the night. The excitement and camaraderie were sometimes outweighed by an angry assumption that the rest of the human population was made up of 'consumerist zombies' who regarded nature as little more than a recreational facility, a virtuous alternative to watching television on a cloudless afternoon. In Francis's experience, ecological angst was in fact almost universal, but most people found it hard to know what to do other than eat and drink around the clock in a conscientious drive to fill as many recycling bags as possible.

When he moved to Howorth and started to participate in the wilding project, he found himself transformed by the transformation taking place around him. The paradox of forcing a landscape to become wild was no longer a paradox in the Anthropocene Age, which was bound to reverse man's absorption in nature's rhythms and force nature to mimic favourite human narratives. Wilderness, after being exiled from paradise, could find salvation in national parks and conservation areas. It was too late to let it be itself, but it could be legally exempt from exploitation, placed beyond the reach of utility and, as a place of 'Outstanding Natural Beauty', like the Quantocks, acquire some of the glamorous self-justification of art. The lost paradise had of course not been one of bloodless harmony, but of self-regulating abundance and predation, before the devastating advantage of machines fell into the hands of a single species. The passenger pigeon, once the most numerous bird in North America and perhaps the world – with one flock, observed as late as 1866, a mile wide and three-hundred miles long, with three and a half billion birds in it – was extinct by 1914, without the assistance of an asteroid or an Ice Age.

In the Yellowstone National Park, the reintroduction of wolves had rebalanced the entire ecosystem, breaking up large herds of grazing animals, keeping elk away from favoured pastures, leading to the regeneration of aspens and cottonwoods, and to an increasing number of eagles and ravens, which were able to feed on the carcasses of wolf kills, and so on: a 'trophic cascade' correcting the extermination of the wolves initially endorsed by the Park authorities. Wilderness enthusiasts argued for the reintroduction of wolves and lynx in Scotland, but they ran up against the opposition of livestock farmers and sporting estates. Instead, a hundred thousand deer had to be culled each year to prevent them from overgrazing and impeding forest regeneration.

Wilding was not a fantasy of returning to a primordial land, emptied of traffic and filled with extinct species, but an attempt to understand the dynamics of an unmanaged landscape and relaunch them in the modern world. One reason Francis had gone to the conference was to look into the historical question of how ecosystems had achieved equilibrium in the past. Had Britain been an almost uninterrupted woodland before the dominance of human influence, the need for fuel, building materials and agricultural land, or had megafauna prevented the emergence of unbroken forest by knocking over and trampling trees, together with smaller animals that inhibited tree growth by damaging bark and feeding on saplings? Fascinated as he was by the rival visions of ancient wilderness presented at the conference, Francis soon found that he was even more fascinated by Olivia. On the second day, they drifted away from a discussion group dedicated to portraying the life and environmental impact of the giant sloth before its extermination by Native Americans – or murderous newcomers, from the giant sloth's point of view – and started discussing their feelings for each other instead. Catching up the next day, Francis was relieved to hear that the conference had come out in favour of the kind of landscape that was emerging at Howorth.

Francis's thoughts were interrupted by a series of short, multiplying caws. He turned around just in time to see dozens of rooks launch themselves from the shaking branches of a tree. They made him think of the drops of ink flying from his fountain pen as it twisted through the air in his Finals. The whole episode had seemed to take place in slow motion – at just about the speed of these flapping and circling rooks in the distance – induced by the spellbound terror that his pen might land on its nib in the middle of his life's most important exams. The association was so strange, but so intimate, showing his imagination and memory were forming their own combinations in parallel to the guided tour he seemed to be compulsively preparing for Olivia.

Her train would be arriving in a few hours and it was time for him to head home to change the sheets and get the remaining ingredients for dinner. He had come to the green lane that had once been used by drovers to take sheep and cattle from the South Downs up to London for sale and slaughter. Now he could cut back along it, walking the straight edge of his semicircular path. He set off rapidly under the midday sun, his longing for reunion uneasily combined with the feeling of how little he knew Olivia, and by the stress of so many specific novelties: her first visit to his cottage, the first time he had cooked for her, the first time he had bought the barely affordable red wine recommended by the local wine merchant, and then there was the potential for disappointment that surrounded all these novelties. Francis stopped for a moment, interrupted his anxiety, took in his surroundings again and burst out laughing, realising that everything was perfect just as it was and that it couldn't be improved by speculation.

2

Lucy took up the window seat that Jade had booked for her, a little pod that extended into a narrow bed. She was taking the day flight from New York to London, but she was shattered enough to risk the circadian havoc of going to bed first thing in the morning. Before switching off her phone, she sent a text to Olivia. She tore the plastic cover from the blanket and broke the seal on the little black bag containing a miniature toothbrush, miniature toothpaste, miniature lip balm, miniature moisturiser, night socks, eye mask and earplugs. She took out the last two items and stuffed the bag into the pouch beside her. Jade had asked Lucy for her seat preferences, her dietary preferences and, for her stay in Hunter's seldom used but fully staffed London flat, her favourite coffee, her favourite newspaper and her breakfast preferences. She was being so solicitous that Lucy was bracing herself for an email about her blood type, her favourite position and her political inclinations. Jade was Hunter Sterling's vibrantly efficient personal assistant and had clearly been told to treat Lucy with great care.

Lucy had sat next to Hunter at a dinner party three weeks earlier, and so impressed him with her background in science and business that by the time they were sipping their fresh mint tea, he had invited her to double her salary and head up the London office of *Digitas*, the digital, technological and scientific venture capital firm he had founded after selling his legendary hedge fund, *Midas*, only a few months before the collapse of Lehman Brothers. She had been persuaded to make the move from *Strategy*, the consulting firm she had been working for, partly because of the excitement of a new opportunity, but also because of the collapse of various aspects of her personal life. Hunter was so eager for her to get to London that he had thrown in a fortnight in his apartment in St James's Place while she looked for somewhere reasonable to live. It was a generosity that would inevitably lead to an anticlimax. The floorplan of the penthouse duplex, sent by Jade in an email with enough bullet points to start a civil war, made it clear that Lucy would be falling off a cloud when she eventually moved into a flat she could afford. Still, it was a kind gesture, as was this luxurious seat, and the limo to the airport, and all the rest of it. She tried to feel spoilt, but she was too bewildered to be entirely convinced.

Lucy was accustomed to attracting favours and special treatment and she always reciprocated with her own forms of generosity. Her need to magnetise a certain level of protection was rooted in the drastic uncertainties of her childhood: when Lucy was five, her mother had been sectioned after a manic episode and had been taking drowsy Lithium ever since; and by the time she was sixteen, her handsome father had drowned in a whirlpool of alcohol. There was no doubt in Lucy's mind that her parents were loving and well-intentioned, but they had been incapacitated by their afflictions. Seeing them was like watching someone you love climb aboard the wrong train and then having to run down the platform trying to warn them of their mistake as the train draws out of the station. For much of her childhood Lucy had been forced to look after the people who should have been looking after her. She had developed a penetrating sensitivity to the moods of anyone she was close to and a longing for a level of security that would put her beyond the corrosive financial anxiety of her childhood. In a sense her whole life had been a rather fraught dialogue between her resolute drive for independence – her 'shield maiden' persona, as she thought of it, in honour of her mother's Swedish ancestry – and her effortless ability to find a granite harbour – as it had become in this extended Viking metaphor – by attracting the protection of powerful men.

Lucy told the flight attendant that she wouldn't need any breakfast but would love a Bloody Mary. She was impatient to get airborne so that she could try to get some sleep. As she buckled her seat belt she felt a weird spasm clutching at the muscles of her right leg, like the cramps that sometimes attack the arch of a foot but spread over a much larger area and more spasmodic. She sat up slightly in her seat and gripped the armrests until the sensation subsided. This had happened twice before in the last few weeks and she had taken the view that it was a panic attack. It was certainly frightening but hardly surprising that some kind of symptom had emerged from what was probably the most stressful and sleep-deprived month of her adult life. After her visa renewal had been unexpectedly rejected, *Strategy* had offered to transfer her to London, but she had decided to accept Hunter's offer instead, leaving her not only homeless and switching continents but also starting a new job. And then there was Nathan.

During the last four years in New York she had been living with Nathan, her rich and handsome American boyfriend, whose close-knit family had grown to treat her as one of their own. Nathan's parents, with their waterfront compound on Long Island and their large brownstone in the West Village, and their three grown children all living in charming apartments in the same neighbourhood, had given Lucy, through their warmth and inclusiveness, free from the stresses of poverty and mental illness, a radically different experience of family life from the one she had been brought up with. When she discovered that she had to leave the States, Nathan had said that the obvious solution was for them to get married. She would acquire American citizenship and become further integrated into his splendid family. Their relationship had gone on for so long, and Lucy was so well liked, that there was a collective assumption in Nathan's family that the two of them would end up together anyway, so why not now, when it was useful as well as romantic. For Lucy, Nathan's proposal had made her realise that she didn't want to spend the rest of her life with him, or indeed any more time at all. The sudden pressure had forced her to recognise that their relationship had long depended on the trance of habit and the fear of loss. At first, he argued against her rejection by invoking his passion and the depth of their history, but when she persisted in refusing him, it became clear that he found it impossible to imagine a woman from such a fragile background turning down such an advantageous offer.

'But don't you want this life?' he asked, waving his hand towards the vast lawn and the private beach in one direction and then back towards the monumental house, designed by Philip Johnson and featured in so many books about masterpieces of American architecture, and the guest house beyond it, in perfect harmony, and the studio, like a high-windowed church, ready to accommodate any artistic impulse, however slight, in a space large enough to work on fifteen Jackson Pollocks simultaneously; not that there was room in the house for any more Jackson Pollocks. Beyond the cluster of buildings was a swimming pool and a tennis court and a driveway that led to two gatehouses occupied by some of the adorable staff of whom it could truly be said that they were part of the family.

'It's not the house that's proposing to me,' said Lucy, uncontrollably irritated by Nathan's question. It was traumatic enough to be rejecting someone to whom she had been so close, without being bribed to change her mind. She knew that she wanted to achieve something of her own and not have her ambition crushed by a boa constrictor of complacency. Of course, she was susceptible to the offer of so much security, but she was also deeply suspicious of her susceptibility. Her true enemy was not her lack of security, but her longing for it. There were greater things to strive for than the appeasement of her childhood fears.

'Thank you,' she said, accepting the Bloody Mary from the flight attendant.

Her leg ached after the cramp and felt strangely useless. She massaged her thigh while she drank her premature cocktail. There had been a time when she used to have an uncontrollably fluttering eyelid, after spending ten or twelve hours a day in the library, week after week. She didn't need Martin Carr, Olivia's dad, to psycho-analyse why the flutter had moved from her eyelid to her leg: she was making too many journeys at once. The shield maiden was leaving the granite harbour of Nathan's family and setting off on another adventure, but she was out of practice and needed to get back into shape.

At least this turbulent and confusing part of her life meant that she would be seeing Olivia again. They would be meeting in London in a few days and later in Oxford, where Lucy had to introduce Hunter to lots of heads of departments during his lightning tour of Europe. It would be useful to have Olivia around since the pages of her own Oxford address book were a bit foxed after six years. It was difficult to know who Hunter might *not* want to see, given the breadth of the *Digitas* portfolio. She was particularly intrigued by the biotech division but had already made a study of its other holdings, including an AI and robotics division, *Brainwaves*, run by a guy called Saul Prokosh. Hunter had told her that *Brainwaves* had a project, nicknamed Happy Helmets, that was 'going to be huge'. They were still looking for a marketing name that didn't make it sound like a children's toy. There was also some military stuff that Lucy was going to keep well away from, although Hunter had told her that his 'ethical position' was to provide protection and not to develop weapons. Her science background had been recognised at *Strategy*, but only so that she could work out more efficient ways to deliver antibiotics to cattle that should not have been taking them in the first place, or to calculate the patient population of a disease, so as to tell a drug company whether one of its products was an 'orphan medication', or whether some of its side effects could be repurposed for a new market. Moving from consulting to entrepre-neurial science would stretch her talents for the first time in a while.

She couldn't wait to tell Olivia that *Digitas* had acquired a controlling interest in the start-up founded by Olivia's old nemesis, Professor Sir William Moorhead. *YouGenetics* was a medical company based on data harvested by several generations of gradu-ates working under his guidance. The correlations, however small, between thousands and thousands of genetic variations, deletions, duplications and mutations and the propensity for and the outcomes of hundreds of the world's most popular diseases were locked in the data banks of *YouGenetics*, and might well remain locked there since they had given rise to so few useful treatments. The science might be limited, but Lucy knew that the company could make money. Moorhead had been too lofty to feed the endless public fascination with genetic ancestry. Lucy was not so prudish. It was not at all clear how a person's ability to pay her mortgage or love her children would be enhanced by the discovery that one per cent of her genes were Haplogroup R-DF27, or that she was descended from Genghis Khan (a startlingly common fate, showing that if the true purpose of human existence was to disseminate genetic material, raping and pillaging was the way to go), but there was a market for it. She intended to offer an especially expensive version of this pointless surrender of data, making a huge fuss about the genealogy of the company itself, founded by the paterfamilias of antique genetics. With this new income, she could reform the company and make it cutting edge.

It was great that Olivia was having her book published soon, but she would be lucky to sell six hundred copies and get a review in *Current Biology*. Lucy wanted to help change things on a larger scale. Only last night a colleague had been telling her about the seeds from cotton plants that had been attacked by beetles, giving rise to a new generation of plants more resistant to beetle attack. Basing the development of seeds on epigenetically acquired characteristics would be a revolution in agriculture, using nature's own defences rather than the violent crossbreeding of standard genetic modification. GM had produced few successes and met with enormous resistance. Monsanto, too enterprising to rest on its laurels after *Agent Orange*, had gone on to formulate 'terminator' seeds, but their popularity had never extended beyond the company's own boardroom and had ended up being banned.

As they started to taxi away from the gate, Lucy looked out of the window at the parked planes, the busy push-back tugs and the brake lights bleeding across the wet tarmac. She felt a sudden tightening in her body, as if a forgotten companion she was roped to had lost her foothold and was dragging her backwards just as she was about to reach the summit. Nostalgia, she didn't do nostalgia, but right now it was pulling her into a free fall of inexplicably poignant detail: the green and white tiles in Nathan's shower, the energetic tedium of his mother's conversation, the diner on the corner where she had drunk enough insipid coffee to fill that refuelling truck; the jetty where Nathan's little sister told her she had lost her virginity the night before; the great gilded adequacy of her old life; the family that had adopted her and would now never speak to her again.

As the plane took off, she could hear her friend screaming like a jet engine and then it was as if Lucy took a knife out of her belt and cut the cord and the screaming faded as her friend fell. She couldn't go there. She just couldn't go there. She needed another Bloody Mary to help her sleep and to soothe the weakened muscles in her leg.

3

Olivia sat on the crowded Friday afternoon train trying to check her proofs. After reading the quotation she had chosen from Svante Pääbo – 'The dirty little secret of genomics is that we know next to nothing about how a genome translates into the particularities of a living breathing individual' – she put down the proofs and surrendered to the daydream that had pursued her from Oxford to London and had now caught up with her again on the journey to Horsham.

Thrilled and apprehensive about being on her way to spend the weekend with her new lover, she stared out of the train window at the stammering suburbs, the football fields, the back gardens, the industrial estates, the little patches of wood aspiring to rural life, some bulbous silver graffiti on a brick wall, the double speed and double clatter and sudden intimacy of a train passing in the opposite direction – it looked as if London would ramble on until it finally had to be drowned in the sea. She had to recognise that she was crazy about Francis, mad about him: it was hard to find a phrase that made it sound like a good idea. Crossing over into another person's subjectivity, if such a thing were possible, was always fraught with excitement and danger. For a start, there had to be a person on the other side, not just an assembly of fragments, occlusions and self-deceptions; and then it was essential not to leave too much of oneself behind in the hectic rush towards the shining lake that all too often turned out to be a mudflat shimmering with excited flies. Even without the hazards of confusion and anticlimax, it remained a logically impossible transition. How could one ever truly enter into another subjectivity? And yet the impossibility seemed pedantic in the face of the imagination's capacity to sense another way of being. She often felt ephemeral connections spring in and out of existence between her mind and other minds, but it was not often a temptation to turn those rainbows into more durable bridges. Her desire to do so now, on so little evidence, was like a kind of seasickness, pitching her between groundless bliss and groundless despair, between a fantasy of happiness and a fantasy of losing the happiness she didn't yet have.

She picked up her proofs again. Her book on epigenetics suddenly seemed like a refuge rather than a chore. Since the millennial utopianism that had greeted the completion of the Human Genome Project twenty years ago, the search for the genes that corresponded to every desire and disease, every inclination and physical feature, had been, with a few exceptions, a failure. When Svante Pääbo had been in charge of the chimpanzee genome project, he had expected to find 'the profoundly interesting genetic prerequisites that make us different from other animals', but ended up, after the chimpanzee sequence was published, admitting that 'we cannot see in this why we are so different from chimpanzees'. Not only did we turn out to share almost all of our genes with our fellow primates, but with far more distant relatives as well. The homeobox genes, which determine the position of limbs and other body segments, were almost identical in flies, reptiles, mice and humans. Where most variation was expected, there was least change. Nor was the quantity of human intelligence and self-regard reflected in the quantity of its genes. When the human genome had been sequenced, it turned out to contain twenty-three thousand genes, about the same as a sea urchin's, but drastically fewer than the forty thousand in rice.

Ah, yes, here it was, the key paper in *Nature* on missing heritability (Manolio, et al.), that ended with the sublime sentence, 'Given how little has actually been explained of the demonstrable genetic influences on most common diseases, despite identification of hundreds of associated genetic variants, the search for the missing heritability provides a potentially valuable path towards further discoveries.' In what other field of science would something be demonstrable 'given how little has actually been explained'? In what other scientific field would lack of evidence be described as 'a potentially valuable path', except in the sense that all paths that had no actual value could only be 'potentially' valuable? It was amazing that a journal which stood for the highest standards of scientific rigour would publish such an incompetently devious sentence. A more honest version would have been, 'After decades of research, we've found almost nothing, but we've devoted our careers to this fruitless field, so please give us more money.' Of course, some evidence might turn up in the future but one of the most valuable contributions made by genetic studies was to show that so far there was no purely genetic influence on the formation of all but rare monogenic diseases, like Tay-Sachs, haemophilia and Huntington's, known to be caused by a mutation in a single gene; and there was the extra copy of chromosome twenty-one that produced Down's syndrome, but after these simple certainties, 'polygenic scores' and 'multifactorial' explanations had to be brought in to prop up the plausibility of the genetically determined story.

However familiar it had become, she was still irritated by the phrase 'missing heritability', implying that genetic connections might turn up one day, like a favourite family cat, if only enough posters were put in shop windows or stuck on neighbourhood trees. For something to be 'missing' it had to have been there in the first place, but as far as the experiments showed, the correspondences were mostly non-existent, and only got upgraded to 'missing' by a doctrinaire refusal to revise the original hypothesis. It was a phrase from the same semantic playbook as 'side effect', which tried to pretend that among the range of pharmaceutical effects caused by a medicine the undesirable ones were somehow incidental. A patient suffering from blindness or liver failure after taking a medicine might well find the experience just as central as the intended effect. Would a depressive who had spent years feeling cursed by having the less active version of the SLC6A4 gene feel that she was on a 'potentially valuable' path when its connection with depression turned out to be 'missing' and that she had been waiting for a cure that could not exist, while losing out on those that did? As the daughter of two psychoanalysts, and the sister of a clinical psychologist, Olivia was especially pissed off that so much money had been spent and so many papers had been written pretending that this 'candidate gene' was the cause of depression; money that could have been spent on helping depressed people – for instance – or mending potholes.

Ironically, it was Professor Moorhead, the most ardent champion of the old neo-Darwinian model, who had catapulted her into the exciting new field of epigenetics. After graduating, she had initially been thrilled to be given a place in his lab, only to discover that he was a serial seducer of his female students and that working under him was a proposition that he took, like so many others, all too literally. Since Moorhead assumed that human nature was entirely mechanical, as he explained with an irresistible combination of smugness and impatience in his masterwork, *The Insatiable Machine*, she had assumed that his advances could be mechanically rebuffed, but this particular machine seemed to have a mind of its own, or at least someone else's mind programmed into it, since it wasn't strictly speaking entitled to one of its own. With whatever mysterious quantity of free will he brought to the task, Moorhead turned out to be a pest, writing Olivia a thirteen-page letter endorsing his amorous claims with a list of notorious symptoms, including insomnia, starvation and a renewed interest in poetry. Luckily, his unwelcome flattery coincided with her growing interest in epigenetics, a subject that Moorhead regarded as a passing fad, or at least a waste of his graduates' time, which should have been spent dragging blocks of data across the desert floor of his genetic fundamentalism to erect a mausoleum fit to entomb his reputation. Olivia could still remember when any mention of Moorhead had lowered her mood, fleetingly but irresistibly, like the eclipse she had seen on a field trip in Indonesia, when she stood on a hilltop watching the edge of the moon's shadow race across the forest, silencing the wildlife with its perplexing darkness. At the time of his repulsive advances she had sidestepped a confrontation by changing the subject of her DPhil. Since then, she had been waiting in vain for what should have been his inevitable downfall, but instead had been forced to watch him leap, like a supercilious chamois, from one improbable perch to the next. He had gone on to acquire a knighthood which had led, by all accounts, to a further decline in his chivalry. Despite her contempt for him, Olivia's objective had never been to lodge a complaint, but to defeat him in his own field, and to overthrow the oppressive and strangely popular influence of his scientific ideology. In the meantime, she had become a Research Fellow, without teaching or lecturing to distract her.

Olivia saw her phone light up on the corner of the table. She had only left it there as a salute to the sense of potential emergency fabricated by the technology itself. What if Francis had a flat tyre? What if her mother had dropped dead? She leant forward and saw that it was in fact her brother Charlie who was calling. For a moment her deep scholarly habits pushed back against the distraction, partly because she welcomed it so much, but then, just as she changed her mind, the call ended. She felt annoyed with herself for putting up a struggle, but moments later he called again – it was so like him to assume, to know, in fact, that she really wanted to talk to him.

'Hi, C,' she said.

'Hi there,' said Charlie. 'Is that the clatter of a train I can hear?'

'Yes, I'm on the way to Sussex.'

'Because you met a tall magnetic stranger at a party, and he invited you to spend the weekend.'

'Well, actually, it was a conference. The rest is terrifyingly accurate.'

'I'm psychic,' said Charlie. 'At least when it comes to you.'

'It's only with your patients that you don't have a clue what's going on in their minds.'

'It's for them to make that discovery,' said Charlie, 'to find the gold mines that were hidden in their psyches.'

'Or the potato fields,' said Olivia. 'I feel that's more like the sort of discovery you would inspire ... Hello? Hello?'

Charlie called back.

'I was thanking you: potatoes are much more nutritious.'

'Hmm,' said Olivia, 'of course that's what I meant. Hello? Oh god. Hello?'

'Hi, I'm here,' said Charlie, 'this connection is hopeless.'

'Let's talk when I'm back in Oxford; I must do some work. I have to finish my final edit.'

'Don't worry,' said Charlie, 'nobody is going to read your book anyway!'

They both had time to laugh before the signal died again. Charlie had been one of the most ardent advocates of Olivia turning her thesis into a book and she knew that he was really ringing to cheer her on. They had spoken a few days earlier about a challenging new paper she was determined to include, even at this late stage. Trying to find the right place for it was keeping her editing fresh. The experiment consisted of administering electric shocks to mice each time they were exposed to the sweet orange smell of acetophenone. It was hardly surprising that the mice, electrocuted five times a day for three days, started to become 'reliably fearful' from exposure to the smell alone. What was challenging to the standard view of inheritance was that the offspring of those mice still exhibited fear in the presence of acetophenone, without being given any electric shocks themselves. Indeed, the effect lasted into a third generation. The mothers of the new generations were of course unexposed, in case they passed on their fear *in utero*, and a further control was introduced through artificial insemination, eliminating the risk of rumours spreading from mouse to mouse through other forms of communication. Nobody understood how the fear of acetophenone had produced chemical changes that altered the expression of genes in a way that entered the sperm of the electrocuted mice. The orthodoxy of random mutation claimed that an organism's complement of DNA was fixed from the moment of its conception. In this view it was impossible for a learnt aversive response to write itself into the DNA and be stably inherited by the offspring. It was just this kind of challenge to the conventional view of inheritance that made epigenetics such an exhilarating field.

Olivia looked up at the display of the stations that lay ahead. There were still three stops to Horsham. She knew she didn't have the concentration to read any more but promised herself that during her stay with Francis, or at the very latest on the return journey on Sunday, she would find a place in her pages for the subversive, paradigm-challenging, reliably fearful mice. What she really needed to do was to get any texts and emails out of the way before she became absorbed in her torrid weekend. She ran through the new messages with the efficiency that could only come from deciding to postpone all the complicated ones, delete the intrusive ones and deal exclusively with Lucy's confirmation of their dinner on Tuesday with a simple, 'Can't wait. Xx'.

Lucy was flying in from New York this evening. It would be lovely to have her back after her six years in the States. They had been so close as undergraduates and had both stayed on at Oxford but Lucy, unlike Olivia, had grown sick of academic life and had gone on to work as a corporate consultant in London and later New York. It was all very well for Olivia to say that she wanted to pursue pure knowledge, but she also knew that Lucy had no back-up, no inheritance in the pipeline, whereas Olivia's parents had slowly acquired their large house in Belsize Park over decades of hard work. It was now preposterously valuable and would one day be coming down to her and to Charlie. It was naïve to underestimate the psychological impact of that difference. They had kept closely in touch, inter-continentally, but it was exciting that Lucy was now going to be fully back in her life.

Olivia finally switched off her phone, packed the proofs in her rucksack and took her overcoat down from the ledge overhead. There was no way for her to be more prepared without loitering by the carriage door and getting in everybody's way during the next two stops. She sank back in her seat, turning slightly sideways so she could raise her knee and tuck it against the edge of the table.

She gazed across a field, enjoying the complicity between the colours of the autumn woods and of the fiery evening sky stretching behind them, but soon her attention folded back on to the volatile thrill of imagining herself so close to someone she hardly knew.

4

'Everything happens for a reason,' said Saul, holding the silver straw delicately between his thumb and forefinger, 'but unfortunately, when it really matters, we don't know what the reason is.'

Saul had always spoken rapidly, but on that Monday morning he was sprinting to the next full stop like an athlete trying to break a record.

'For instance, the exact nature of the correlation between electro-chemical activity in the brain and the experience of being conscious is entirely obscure, and since everything we know depends on being conscious, the description we give of reality, however coherent it seems, hangs over an abyss.'

He leant down and sniffed up the softly gleaming powder; perfect cocaine with the texture of crushed pearls, its curving lines like claw marks across the glass surface of a silver-framed photograph of Barry Goldwater. All the presidential candidates, Democrat and Republican, going back to Nixon's failed contest against JFK in 1960, had given Hunter's father signed photographs. He hadn't had to wait for Wall Street to teach him about hedging his bets, he just used to totter into the library and read all the warm messages inscribed to his father by America's bitterest rivals.

'An abyss ...' Saul repeated. 'God, this stuff is *really* good ... Where was I? Oh, yeah, I mean, experience accuses science of being reductionist and authoritarian, while science dismisses experience as subjective, anecdotal and self-deceived. We have an absurd situation where the first-person narrative of *experience* and the third-person narrative of *experiment* shout insults at each other from either side of an explanatory gap, that huge, huge explanatory gap.'

He threw his arms apart to give Hunter some idea of just how huge this explanatory gap was, and then sank back into his creaking wicker chair, puffed out his cheeks and stared from the rosewood deck at the interlocking golden hills of *Apocalypse Now*, Hunter's ranch in Big Sur, sloping steeply down to the silent Pacific. Out at sea a fog bank drifted towards the shore, swallowing the lazy glitter of the swell, but however thick the fog grew, Hunter knew that it would never reach the house, only generate a sea of hoary mist beneath his feet.

'Looking at this view,' said Hunter, 'I'm having a complex experience of perceptions, reflections and memories. What I'm not experiencing is neurons firing, even though none of this could take place without firing neurons—'

'It's a tormenting question,' Saul interrupted. 'I mean, what is the matrix that transforms one into the other? I'm a materialist, don't get me wrong—'

'I'm pleased to hear that,' said Hunter. 'Maybe developing *Brainwaves* can help reduce your torment.'

'Sure,' said Saul, 'but materialism still has a lot of explaining to do, not just about consciousness but about a ton of other things as well ...' He trailed off, overwhelmed by pleasure. 'God, I feel so high without being wired. Can I buy some of this off you? Sorry, maybe that was inappropriate.'

'It was,' Hunter confirmed.

'Are we cool?' said Saul nervously.

'Well, one of us is cool and the other isn't,' said Hunter, with a guffaw.

One thing Saul Prokosh was not and never would be was cool. He and Hunter hadn't really been friends at Princeton, but at least Hunter never gratuitously insulted him, unlike some of their more lock-jawed contemporaries whose grandfathers still sighed longingly at the memory of the golden days when Jews were not admitted to the best hotels in New York and Palm Beach. Saul was now *The Lafayette Smith and Bathsheba Smith Professor of Chemical Engineering, Artificial Intelligence and The Realisation of Human Potential at The California Institute of Technology*, as it said on his unusually large business card. Currently, he was scanning the brains of people in various allegedly desirable states of mind in order to reconstruct those states in other volunteers, using trans-cranial magnetic stimulation. It was proving fiendishly difficult to reverse engineer these correspondences and replicate the effects in the minds of others, who seemed set on having their own thoughts, even when the scans of their brains, after trans-cranial stimulation, showed many similarities to the original neuroimaging. There were no completely clear results up to now, but Hunter had been so impressed by the addictive potential of this new technology that he impulsively offered to make Saul a Senior Vice-President of *Digitas* and put him in charge of *Brainwaves* and New Projects.

'Maybe I'm a visionary,' said Hunter, texting 'Wagyu Ragu' in answer to his cook's lunch suggestions, 'or maybe I'm suffering from survivor's guilt, but I've decided that it's time to give something back. Perhaps "back" isn't exactly the right word. I'm not talking about refunding the investors who bought my hedge fund for $1.6 billion a few weeks before the stock price tanked; and I'm not giving the five hundred former employees of *Midas* their jobs back.'

'It sounds like "back" is definitely not the right word,' said Saul, looking longingly at Barry Goldwater.

'In any case,' said Hunter, 'I want our products, *Brainwaves*, *YouGenetics*, and all the other great ideas we have, to be based on intellectual property that makes a fundamental contribution and wins all the science Nobels across the board.'

'We gotta leave them some of the prizes,' said Saul, like a lawyer pleading for clemency.

'They can have Peace and Literature,' said Hunter.

For some reason, the two men just cracked up and couldn't stop laughing.

'Peace and Literature,' said Saul, trying to control himself. 'Why is that so funny?'

'We're stoned,' said Hunter.

'I know, but it's still just inherently …' He couldn't go on, except to howl 'Peace and Literature' one more time.

'You've pretty much nailed the *Focus* and *Relax* programs,' said Hunter, 'but we've gotta do more work on the *Bliss* algorithm and then, once we've got a global craze on our hands, we'll release the *Nirvana* helmet.'

'Totally,' said Saul. 'In fact, I should head back to Pasadena; we're scanning Matthieu Ricard's love, joy and compassion this afternoon.'

'The French lama—' said Hunter.

'Right,' said Saul. 'This guy is phenomenal. You could waterboard him and his vital signs wouldn't shift, he's so deep in the Alpha State.'

'Here, have one for the road,' said Hunter, handing Saul a signed photograph of Ronald Reagan on which he had been chopping a couple of long lines. 'We shouldn't really have carried our weekend into Monday morning, but when you're brainstorming, you're brainstorming.'

'Definitely. Brainstorming,' said Saul, snuffling up one of Ronald Reagan's trouser legs.

'You'd better go scan your lama. I've gotta make a call to Lucy Russell, the new head of *Digitas* in London.'

'How's she working out?'

'We'll see, but you know me – easily bored – and I'm not bored by her. Most people are falling over to agree with me, but she's not afraid to point out if I've missed a beat,' said Hunter, snorting his way up Reagan's red tie, across his creased and grinning face and into his incongruously inky hair.

The two men parted with back-slapping hugs and Saul set off on the six-mile drive from Hunter's ranch down to the meandering ribbon of road along the coast.

Left alone, Hunter returned indoors and after cleaning the photos with screen wipes, hung Senator Goldwater and President Reagan back on their hooks against the oak-panelled walls of his magnificent study, which looked entirely traditional, except that two of the walls formed an arrow head of thick glass pointing out to sea, making the masculine gravitas of the room seem to float in air and light. He was fired up and ready to talk to Lucy. The call was scheduled for fifteen minutes' time. He took up his position in a red leather chair opposite the gleaming scabbard of a priceless samurai sword, cradled among the bookshelves on the other side of the room.

Saul and Lucy and the rest of the team were his *consiglieri* as he laid claim to the crucial neighbourhood of human endeavour known as science, so often neglected by the billionaire community in favour of art, animals, opera, Mars, orphans and famous diseases. It was hard to make a splash when Bill Gates already had malaria and the Metropolitan Museum was growing more philanthropic wings than a mutant fruit fly, but he had endowed a Foundation devoted to finding scientific solutions to the world's manifold problems. The trouble was that whenever he came across a good idea it somehow ended up in *Digitas*. Still, for a man as rich as him to show his face in society without a Foundation would be like a construction worker not having a hard hat on a building site. At the dinner party where he had met Lucy, he had mentioned his Foundation, quite casually, only to have her say, 'To a foreign eye, America has so much philanthropy and so little charity. Most people have to kill themselves to prove that they deserve ordinary kindness, while a tiny group of people never stop boasting about how generous they are – as long as it's tax-deductible.' That's when he'd decided to hire her.

Eight minutes left and he was beginning to feel the encroachment of that old catastrophe: comedown. He glanced up at Jimmy Carter (it was his turn) but realised it was too late to organise himself and he would screw up the call. Punctuality and control mattered to him immensely – perhaps because part of him was so out of control. He had been living this way since he was a teenager; now only in occasional bursts, but with the threat always there in the background. When he had first become vaguely aware of Saul at Princeton, Hunter invariably wrote his essays through the night, just before they were due. The exchange rate was about twenty lines of writing for one line of coke; writing that started out with declamatory confidence and degenerated into convoluted confusion. He must stop. It was no way to carry on for a man in his late forties, but despite all the therapy, there was something he couldn't reach, a bomb he hadn't disposed of, a part of him that wanted to smash everything up. He thought of using these last painful minutes to check the stock market on his phone, or check the schedule Jade emailed him each morning, but instead he glazed over, looking bleakly at the perfection of his surroundings until the digits on his clock finally flicked to the right number. He punched his fist into the palm of his other hand and brought himself back before he tapped Lucy's number.

'Lucy! How are you doing?'

'Hi, Hunter! I'm loving your flat. Are you looking forward to your visit?'

'I can't say I'm looking forward to it,' said Hunter, 'except for seeing you and the great schedule you've lined up. I spent twelve years on those damp islands, until I managed to graduate from Westminster to Princeton. Returning to the States was like going to a Super Bowl game after visiting your grandmother in her twilight home. We moved to London when I was six. When my father gave me my first five-pound note, I thought they'd named the currency after my family – five pounds Sterling. Shrinks always love that: early signs of narcissistic grandiosity.'

'You've still got a *little* bit of that in you,' said Lucy, tentatively exploring the boundaries of a new relationship.

Now that he was on the call, Hunter could hear the coke speaking through him, but there was nothing he could do to stop it.

'You know, Lucy,' he said, 'the world is divided between the mediocrity of committees, the paralysis of checks and balances, and the merciful megalomania of the rich. Everybody else is just shouting in a bell jar while the air gets sucked out – however close you lean in you can't make out what they're saying: "I'm sorry, what was that? I can't hear you!" Historical "process" is for human debris, drifting on the tides of fashion and fate. I believe in extraordinary individuals, Lucy; I believe in game-changers and I hope you're one of them, because that's the only type of individual I want working on my team. So, what have you got for me?'

'I've set up all the meetings you were interested in,' said Lucy, 'with the heads of most of the Oxford science departments. The Psychiatry department have a promising psychotherapeutic virtual reality program called *Avatar*, which apparently is helping people with schizophrenia—'

'I'm not interested in schizophrenia,' Hunter interrupted her. 'It only affects one per cent of the population and most of them are poor.'

'Most of any population is poor.'

'You should see my address book!' said Hunter.

'I can't wait,' said Lucy impatiently.

'The higher your socio-economic status,' said Hunter, 'the more likely you are to be diagnosed with "bipolar disorder" than with "schizophrenia", while exhibiting the exact same psychotic symptoms. Not that I'm hostile to *Avatar* and a human-machine synthesis: internet contact lenses, the world's knowledge in just one blink. Forget verbal dictation, what about *thought* dictation? Straight from the synapses on to the screen, we've got a sensational start-up that's making real progress with that, we're calling it *SignApps* – patent pending. Anyway, your schizophrenia thing is too specialised, but if it works for bipolarity, we could look into it.'

'Everything in science is too specialised,' said Lucy. 'People assume that scientists are intellectuals, but very few of them have an overview, or a critical approach to their methodologies, they're just too busy securing funding or tenure or zapping individual cells in the *Caenorhabditis elegans* nematode worm with laser beams – this is a one-millimetre worm, so we're talking about precision work – looking for that single-cell death-inhibitor.'

'A single-cell death-inhibitor – do you know the guy in charge of that research? I want to meet him. Get it on the schedule.'

'What time shall I meet you?' asked Lucy, with strenuous neutrality.

'The plane lands at Farnborough at seven a.m. – isn't it strange the way people more often say "my plane lands" when they've rented a seat on a commercial flight and more often say "the plane lands" when they own it?'

'Amazing,' Lucy confirmed.

'Meet me there. The driver can pick you up on the way.'

Before Lucy could say anything, she realised that Hunter had ended the call.

'What a wanker,' she said, chucking the phone on to the cushion beside her – on to Hunter's cushion. Staying in his flat made her anger more inhibited and more compelling at the same time. Her pulse was throbbing in her neck and wrists. He had been so seductive during the recruitment period, making her feel that her science background would be put to better use, that she would be bringing all sorts of benefits to the world and, of course, by offering to double her income. That combination, and the severance package, if she were dismissed for any non-criminal reason, made her ignore all the warnings she heard about Hunter's 'colourful' past and his 'explosive' character. Now she was living under the tyranny of his whims and his threats … Oh, Christ, it was happening again.

The signs were subtle for the moment, but she knew with absolute certainty that she was starting to have another panic attack. She managed to sit down next to her discarded phone just as the heaviness took over. Gravity seemed to have suddenly been multiplied in one place, dragging her attention to the right side of her body while the rest of her looked on helplessly from above, like a mother watching her child screaming to be released from the adhesive wall of the spinning barrel in a fun fair. Then the spasms came, slowly at first, but picking up pace as the attack reached its peak. Midway through, she felt an alien effervescence rushing down the right side of her body, as if a soda syphon had been discharged into her lower back. It was over in a minute, but Lucy was left feeling dazed, with an enfeebled and shaky leg and a foot that remained numb for several minutes.

If this was a panic attack, thought Lucy, it was really working. She was in a total fucking panic. As soon as she had recovered enough, she rang her kind, clever doctor friend, Ash, who immediately offered to come over. He ran some tests, making her push her legs against his hands, and also asking her to walk in a straight line, and to stand on one leg at a time. Lucy succeeded in all these tasks and her reflexes responded to his rubber hammer in the expected way.

'Listen, it's almost certainly all the stress you've been under,' said Ash, 'but, since the attacks keep showing up in the same place, I'm going to call in a favour from a neurologist I know and see if we can get you an MRI tomorrow, in case there's any nerve damage affecting your leg. I'll give you a Zopiclone to make sure you get a good night's rest.'

After Ash had reassured her, Lucy felt much better and since she almost never used sleeping pills, she soon fell into a deep, long sleep.

5

Olivia was in far too good a mood to really mind, but she couldn't help wondering why Lucy had chosen to meet at Noble Rot for such an early dinner. It was a dry, clear evening and Olivia had decided to walk from her publisher's office. It had been tough negotiating for the inclusion of the intergenerationally traumatised mice, but her editor had totally seen the point and had agreed to the disruption of the proofs. Her weekend with Francis had stretched into four nights and she had only been able to focus on the mice that morning, her feet interlaced with his under the table on the train until they were wrenched apart at Victoria station. She had gone to her parents' house and Francis had set off to a meeting of the Soil Association. Now, after nine long hours, they were converging on Lamb's Conduit Street.

Driving home from the station last Friday, Francis had warned Olivia that his cottage was off the grid, at first tempering his confession with an apology, but soon admitting how pleased he was to be able to quit the hive mind of the internet and wander away, like a rogue bee, from the buzzing subjugation of the colony. They sank back for a while into the familiar hammock of ecological catastrophe, until Francis started to describe the counter-proposal being made by wilding and also conjectured that Gaia, a collective planetary intelligence, or at least an intelligent way of thinking about the planet as a whole, was beginning to have her revenge and would soon shrug off the human infestation that was poisoning the 'critical zone', that faint blue ring of air and water in which all complex life occurs. A few ancient families of bacteria, viruses, fungi and insects would no doubt survive, as unimpressed by the Anthropocene Age as they had been by the lumbering passage of the dim-witted dinosaur. Olivia wasn't so sure about Gaia. She felt that the craving for domination and convenience was enough to consume its devotees, one drone delivery at a time.

'With or without Gaia, we're talking about the same basic angst,' she said, as Francis drew up into the parking space on the far side of his cottage.

Instead of replying, he turned to her and smiled disarmingly, as if they both knew that these big topics had only been needed to enliven the journey from the station. Now that they had arrived in a place beyond the reach of tracking cookies, where the microphones and cameras on their devices couldn't be switched on by invisible supervisors, a place with the timeless banality of simply being where it was, without advertising its location on the world wide web and provoking a cascade of Bayesian data mining, self-reinforcing behaviour patterns and tailored news, now, at last, they could give up working out precisely which great extinction they were taking part in and get down to the real reason for their being there in the first place.

Going straight to bed without taking her luggage out of the car, or being 'shown around', dispersed the expectations of awkwardness or unbridled passion that had been running through Olivia's mind since she accepted Francis's invitation. What she could not have imagined, along with the thick sky-blue and cream stripes of the wallpaper and the worn elm of the beams and the window frames, was the depth of trust she already felt for Francis, or spontaneously felt – it was hard to tell, since their only previous encounter had taken place in the kind of haze that can make impulsiveness look like spontaneity, and drunkenness feel like destiny.

When he had taken her upstairs in his cottage soberly and silently, they had soon cut through any lingering fog associated with that evening in Oxford, meeting face to face, holding each other's gaze, not distracted by shyness or fantasy, smiling effortlessly at the delight they found in each other. And then, as they lay side by side, entangled but still speechless, not bothering with compliments or professions of bliss, because they both knew what had happened; in that vibrant stillness, her mind seemed to have obliterated all impressions except for her awareness of the vibrancy and the stillness. They started to kiss again, like two people who change their minds after taking a few steps across the burning sands of a tropical beach and decide to dive back into the breaking waves. They had too much to tell each other to go on talking. Words would only multiply distinctions that were being abolished by something that permeated and surrounded them, like a magnetic field, drawing iron filings into the shape of a flower.

Conversation returned when Olivia came downstairs after a bath. Her thick socks blunted the sensation of walking over the cool, uneven flagstones of the kitchen floor. Francis greeted her through the steam rising from the potatoes he was pouring into a colander. He was preparing dinner with what struck her as impressive calm. Her own cooking was a combination of monotony and panic, always making the same meal without losing the conviction that this time it was going to go wrong. She seemed to remember a distinction Steven Pinker had made in one of his immense books between 'blending grammar' and 'analytical grammar', or something of that sort. Cooking and painting, amazingly enough, turned out to be in the 'blending' category and she wasn't any good at either of them.

'That's all the cooking I can do for the moment,' said Francis, as he transferred parboiled potatoes to a pan, shook them around, blending them (grammatically, she supposed) with the olive oil and rosemary and then sliding the pan into the oven. He invited her into the sitting room, where they stretched out on the big sofa, with their heads cushioned at the far end, looking at the fire, smouldering and crackling on a soft pile of ash and embers.

'God, I love it here,' said Olivia.

Anticipating the rush to self-revelation that inaugurates every love affair, she had decided during her bath that she would tell Francis that she was adopted, unlike her brother Charlie, who was Martin and Lizzie's biological child. And so, she let him know the bare facts and how her parents had told her when she was sixteen.

'Do you think that's why you became a biologist?' he asked.

'Probably, but it took me a while to work out. My father was very restrained in not interpreting my choice of A levels: Biology, Chemistry and Sociology.'

Francis laughed and held her closer.

'I had certainly worked it out for myself by the time I was an undergraduate,' said Olivia. 'I was totally invested in refuting the idea that the most important contribution to my formation was a genetic inheritance handed down to me by a couple of strangers.'

She had chosen not to track down her biological mother, feeling that it would be a betrayal of her real parents in favour of the outsider who had chosen to give her away. It was only when she was twenty-six and a friend of hers had her first baby, that Olivia's resolve was broken. She was allowed to hold her friend's newborn child in her arms and felt the encircling tenderness that sprung up spontaneously between them in the few minutes before the baby's mother reached out to take him back, craving, despite her exhaustion, the need to comfort and protect her child. The experience inflamed Olivia's imagination, making her wonder about her mother's motives for giving her away, and so she finally set about arranging to meet Karen Hughes, as the culprit turned out to be called.

On the day of the visit, Olivia woke at four in the morning in her parents' house, bathed in sweat. She was in that superstitious state of mind in which everything seemed overloaded with metaphor and meaning. She wanted to stay at home, the home she actually lived in with her loving family, not the home she might have had in the meaningless dimension of a conditional past tense. She left Belsize Park far too early and was so preoccupied on the Underground that she overshot her stop by two stations. She decided to work her way back to Karen's neighbourhood, exchanging so many texts and calls with Lucy and Charlie that the battery on her ageing phone went flat. She would have to ask someone the way – although she certainly wasn't going to ask that hollow-cheeked man who was being dragged towards her by the rolling gait of his bulldog. The grey tower blocks across the road were darkened by patches of rain and so densely studded with satellite dishes that they looked to her like the tentacles of an octopus. At their centre, a balding patch of grass was planted with bushes that discouraged vandalism, not only with their ferociously serrated leaves, which stuck out like a gargoyle's tongue, but also through their perfect ugliness, which it was impossible to enhance. Two of them had taken the further precaution of dying. Olivia was disgusted by her attitude to her unfamiliar surroundings. Bloody psychotherapy, it ruined the random discharge of negative emotion. The mixture of terraced houses and blocks of flats was typical of dozens of areas she had walked around in London, but now she was projecting her fear of meeting a treacherous parent on to some rain-soaked buildings and a man walking his dog; and her fear that it might turn ugly on to some neglected plants.

She told Francis that her paranoid state of mind had been temporarily dissolved by a friendly passer-by who told her that Mafeking Street was, 'Second on the right, can't miss it', but that it rebuilt itself as she approached the turning. Her pace slowed. What, in the end, did any of this have to do with her? A sense of hysterical reluctance weighed down her steps. Whatever reservoir of genetic information lay inside Karen's house was already, for what it was worth, inscribed in her own body. She suddenly felt that she must turn back, but then the front door opened and a tired, but kind-looking woman with thick, loosely stacked grey hair was standing in front of her in an old sweater and a pair of jeans.

Karen led her into a little sitting room crowded with books. They were on the shelves and on the tables, but also on the floor beside the armchair. The room was quite dim apart from the pool of light around the armchair and the glow of an electric fire, which lit up some black and orange logs with the brazen fraudulence of what would have been kitsch, if the rest of the room hadn't pointed towards austerity and indifference. In the first awkward minutes

Karen poured some tea and Olivia turned down a biscuit. Once Karen was sitting in the armchair, a tortoiseshell cat jumped into her lap and she began to stroke it with an emphatic haste that seemed to have more to do with her own state of mind than any needs the cat might have.

'There was an unframed photo lying flat on one of the lower bookshelves,' Olivia told Francis. 'It looked to me like a younger Karen holding a baby in her arms. Is that burning?' she interrupted herself.

'Oh, fuck,' said Francis, jumping over her. 'I was too caught up in your story. Tell me what happened over dinner,' he said, opening the smoking oven and salvaging the unusually crispy potatoes and chicken.

She did tell him the rest of the story over dinner and felt even closer to him than before. They stayed close for the next three days until they were forced apart that morning. Soon, mercifully, they would be back together.

As she approached Noble Rot, Olivia could see through the big glass windows that Francis had already arrived and that Lucy was there also, but at a separate table. It was strange to see two people she knew so intimately sitting in the same room, alone and unknown to each other, waiting for her arrival to create a new compound, like a clear liquid suddenly swirling with colour as a third solution is poured into it. At least, she hoped that's what would happen. Francis got up while she was still outside, as if he had already seen her, or sensed her in some other way, although he had been reading when she first spotted him. He opened the door for her and kissed her hello. Lucy was slower to notice her arrival, but soon came over and gave Olivia a big reunion hug. After Olivia had introduced her friends to each other, they were all led to a table at the far end of the restaurant, where Lucy sat down in the corner with her back to the wall, facing Olivia and Francis.

'I love this restaurant,' said Olivia, leaning gently against Francis, 'but I thought you said Hunter's flat was in St James's.'

'It is,' said Lucy, 'but I had to go to the Neurology Hospital in Queen Square.'

'Oh, no, are you okay?' said Olivia.

'It's probably just stress, but I've been having these muscle spasms. I had a particularly strong one last night, so I called Ash – remember him? – and he arranged for me to see a neurologist this morning, Dr Hammond. We marvelled at the body's capacity to somatise psychological states. "Those poor men who came back with shell shock from the First World War: truly astonishing cases. Neurologically speaking, it made no sense," he said. Still, he arranged to fit in an MRI for me "just to tick that box". That's why I booked a table here because they gave me the last slot at the scanning centre around the corner.'

'When do you get the results?' asked Olivia.

'Next Tuesday, after my very long weekend with Hunter, The Boss Who Never Sleeps. That starts on Thursday when my alarm goes off at five in the morning.'

'It sounds like you've got enough alarms going off already,' said Olivia.

'If it isn't stress, it might be nerve damage from that accident I had when we went cycling in Ireland.'

'Oh god, that was terrible,' Olivia explained to Francis. 'I was behind Lucy and half-saw her flip over a gate further down the lane. At first it looked like a perfect somersault, and I almost expected to find her standing in the field, like a gymnast, with her feet together and her arms stretched out. Then I heard a scream and it was all ambulances and X-rays and crutches.'

'Oh dear,' said Francis, 'that might well be it. How was the MRI? I've never had one.'

'They were all very friendly and upbeat,' said Lucy, 'dressed as if they were about to go running, in sportswear and trainers, even though they spend most of their day filling in forms and pressing buttons. I felt rather calm and cosy in the scanner. When you work for Hunter it's quite a treat to be able to lie down and do nothing. So, I just closed my eyes and lay in corpse pose.'

'You make it sound like a spa treatment,' said Olivia.

'It was a bit on the high-tech side, but I was taking a spa approach to the earplugs, and the juddering and the squawking that sounds like an evacuation alarm but signals that you have to lie absolutely still. After a while I could just make out, over the muffled racket, a female voice saying, "We're just going to pop you out of the scanner for a moment." She told me they wanted to inject me with some contrast fluid. It felt cold, spreading all around my body as they "popped" me back in for another fifteen minutes.'

'Do they always give people contrast fluid?' asked Olivia.

'That's exactly what I asked the Australian nurse who took the cannula out. She said, "Oh yeah, we do it all the time. It's just so we can see certain structures more clearly." "What kind of structures?" I asked her. "Well, structures," she said, and I got the impression that I wasn't going to get anything else out of her. She stayed very cheerful, taped on a bandage and said, "Okey-dokey, you have a good evening now." It was late and I felt they were all keen to get to their spinning classes, or to have a drink in the Queen's Pantry, the pub on the corner of the square, named after the building where Queen Charlotte kept special provisions for George III when he was mad with porphyria.'

Olivia could tell that Lucy was shaken. She was talking rapidly and seemed to be overflowing with impressions.

'Talking of pubs, let's have a drink,' she said.

'I looked at the wine list when I arrived,' said Francis, 'and you can order small glasses of lots of different wines. It gives an educational atmosphere to getting incrementally drunk.'

'That's right,' said Lucy, '"compare and contrast". Let's do some of that.'

As the three of them worked their way down the list of red wines, vacillating between Portugal and the Rhone, Australia and the Veneto, Burgundy and Bordeaux, Lucy seemed to relax and put her taxing day behind her, and Olivia also relaxed, realising that Francis and Lucy liked each other both for her sake and independently. As Francis had predicted, the number of glasses was beginning to outweigh the size of the samples and they all agreed that they should have just one more. Lucy decided that such an important choice required her to google the comparative merits of the Californian and Chilean wines that they hadn't yet tried. When she looked at her phone, Francis and Olivia expected her to embark on reading the hilarious list of random objects: blackcurrant leaves, saddles, long notes, cigars and ripe cherries that make wine prose into a cryptic branch of literature that can only be deciphered by drinking the wine it fails to describe, but instead they saw Lucy's face contract into a frown.

'Sorry, there's a message I should respond to,' she said.

Olivia assumed that Hunter was making some further ludicrous demand on Lucy's time.

'Dr Hammond wants me to come in first thing tomorrow,' said Lucy.

'I'll come with you,' said Olivia immediately.

'Thanks,' said Lucy. 'Jesus.'

'It's probably the nerves that got torn in that cycling accident,' said Francis.

'Or "structures",' said Lucy. 'Structures.'

6

In the consulting room, Olivia reached out and put an arm around Lucy's shoulders.

'I feel like someone dropped a car battery in the bath,' said Lucy. 'I've never felt like this before: these waves of terror coursing through me. Can I have some Xanax?'

'I don't think that's a good idea,' said Dr Hammond.

'If this diagnosis isn't a good reason to prescribe tranquillisers, what is?' said Olivia.

'All right,' said Dr Hammond, 'but don't take too many at once.'

'If I wanted to die, I'd be asking you for a bottle of champagne,' said Lucy.

Dr Hammond's face remained solemn.

'I'll give you a prescription for fourteen Xanax; that should tide you over until you see Mr McEwan, the surgeon. I am also prescribing a drug called Keppra, which will stop the seizures.'

'When will I be able to see Mr McEwan?'

'Early next week, when you were supposed to see me.'

'Oh god, I can't wait that long, I really can't; I'll go mad. Sorry, but my brain – I recognise that this may be about to change radic-ally – has always been my main asset, my only asset really, and the more knowledge I have, the better. My new boss is flying in from America tomorrow and he absolutely *cannot* know what is going on, but that means that I absolutely *must* know what is happening to me – as well as stifling it with Xanax – by the way, can I have some right now?'

'I'm afraid you'll have to go and collect the prescription,' said Dr Hammond.

'Shall I ask Francis to get it?' asked Olivia. 'My boyfriend,' she explained to Dr Hammond, 'he's in the waiting room.'

'That's fine,' said Dr Hammond, handing it to her. 'I'll try to have a word with Mr McEwan to see if he can fit you in any earlier.'

Francis was trying to relax as best he could in the strange circumstances, fixing his gaze on a mid-point between a heap of wrinkled magazines and the silent, subtitled television news. Although Olivia told him nothing, which made him like her even more, she looked too distraught, when she asked him to collect the prescription, to disguise the serious nature of the diagnosis.

He went outside into the pale radiance of the morning. The fading leaves in the gardens and the fluorescent ambulances parked around the square both pointed to mortality in their more or less strident ways. He saw staff hurrying in to work and neurological patients with complicated walks making their way towards the central hospital. On a bench in the gardens a man repeatedly tried to eat a croissant but more often than not missed his mouth, his overcoat scattered with the debris of his failed attempts. Francis tried to irradiate him with strength and calm, but only realised how little he had of either.

After leaving Noble Rot, they had all known, more or less, that it was probably bad news, while hoping they were wrong. Olivia invited Lucy to stay at Belsize Park, in Charlie's old room, which Lucy knew well from the years when they'd gone out together in their twenties.

'You won't find it changed much,' she said, 'as you know, my parents aren't really into interior decoration. They're too busy moving the furniture around in people's psyches.'

'God, I could do with some of that,' said Lucy, switching off the intercom in the taxi.

They arrived at the Carrs' house, where both of Olivia's parents had consulting rooms, Martin's in the basement overlooking the garden, and Lizzie's on the top floor. Olivia left Francis in her bedroom and went downstairs to give Lucy a chance to talk to her alone. He took in the impressive surroundings that his new girlfriend had been brought up in and couldn't help wondering whether she thought of Willow Cottage as 'cute' or 'cosy'. The solidity of her background, with two parents who were still happily married, was at odds with the disturbing adoption story she had told him over the weekend. It turned out that Olivia's ultra-Catholic father, Henry, had threatened to kill Karen if she had an abortion. He called it 'God's justice'. When it turned out that Karen was pregnant with twins, he had put up no resistance to Olivia's adoption, but had insisted on keeping her brother, Keith. The photograph that Olivia spotted on the bookshelf was of Karen holding Keith in her arms when he was an infant. Was Olivia's adoption a crack in the foundations of the upbringing she had received in this substantial house, where he was now sitting on the edge of her bed, or was it almost entirely irrelevant, given that it barely constituted an experience? She had battled against genetic fundamentalism for years and felt that victory might have been secured by the 'reliably fearful' mice that she told him about over the weekend. And yet, if their inherited characteristics came neither from the standard model of genetic transmission nor from any contact, Francis wondered if Olivia had liberated herself from one kind of legacy by arguing for a more subtle transmission of intergenerational trauma. She seemed so well; perhaps she would only find out when she had a child of her own.

Early the following morning, they had accompanied Lucy to her appointment with Dr Hammond. Francis had hesitated to come along, but Olivia seemed to want his support as much as Lucy wanted Olivia's.

'The name of the patient,' said the pharmacist suspiciously, seeing the supposedly enviable tranquilliser listed on the prescription.

'Lucy Russell. She's with Dr Hammond across the square and I've been asked to pick this up for her.'

'And you are?'

'A friend,' said Francis.

'A friend,' the pharmacist repeated, as if this were the name of a famous terrorist organisation.

'Listen, I think she's just been given some bad news,' said Francis impatiently, 'can you please give me the fucking medicine?' He immediately regretted swearing and realised how disoriented he was by the situation.

The pharmacist pointed at a notice saying that abuse of the staff would not be tolerated.

'I'm sorry,' said Francis, 'I was abusing the news, not you. I know you were just showing due diligence.'

He had wanted to say 'absurd pedantry', but managed to swerve at the last moment. If only the pharmacist could appreciate how little he envied Lucy's Xanax, let alone whatever reason she had for needing it. The offended party dawdled before returning with the half-empty box of Xanax and three full boxes of Keppra.

'Thank you,' said Francis, taking the blue and white paper bag and heading back towards Dr Hammond's room.

On his way, Francis spotted a fig tree hanging over the railings of the garden square; he had to cross the road to have a closer look. It was his thirty-second holiday on his way back to Lucy's panic. He was as bad as the pharmacist, dragging his feet, except that he wanted to bring something from the ripeness of autumn back into the consulting room, from a tree that was pushing nutrients into its fruit and not just retracting them from its leaves. He reached up and touched one of the fig leaves, itself like a splayed hand reaching into the air and the light. He ran his fingers over the veined under-side of the leaf, imagining for a moment the particular niche of life occupied by the fig tree. The fleshy sacs, usually thought of as themselves the fruit, in fact contained the hidden flowers and the hidden single-seed fruit of the tree: he felt the infolded richness of the plant, its reserves of sweetness and fertility. He also felt how he longed to return to Howorth. Much as he was infatuated with Olivia, he was rather stunned by the pace at which things were moving and he needed some solitude to take it all in. He was at Lucy's obviously harrowing consultation fourteen hours after meeting her, adding

48

another kind of precipitous closeness to his ever-expanding weekend with Olivia.

When he got back, he knocked gently on Dr Hammond's door.

'Here are the meds,' he said to Olivia.

'Thanks,' she said. 'We might have to see another doctor. Hammond has gone to check.'

'I might go for a walk.'

'I'm sorry,' said Olivia. 'Maybe you want to go back to Howorth. You must have things to do.'

'No, no, I'll stay. Just text me when you've finished. I won't go far.'

Olivia went back inside, gave the paper bag to Lucy and walked over to the basin to fetch some water. It had been a savage and bewildering morning. When they first arrived at Dr Hammond's, Lucy had left no time for platitudes or courtesies; her anxiety made her sound impatient, almost angry.

'Please just tell me what's going on,' she said, as she was sitting down. 'I've been awake all night.'

'Well,' said Dr Hammond, speaking slowly and clearly, knowing that the information was itself impairing. 'I'm afraid the news is not good. Your scan indicates that you have a tumour in the left hemisphere of your brain that is affecting the right side of your body. The spasms you've been having are what we call "focal motor seizures". I know you must be in shock right now and I want to make sure that you're taking in what I'm telling you.'

'Yes,' said Lucy, repeating verbatim what she had just been told. 'Is it cancerous?'

'Yes. I believe this is a low-grade tumour, so after a biopsy, we'll discuss whether to follow up with chemotherapy and radiation.'

'Can it be operated on?' asked Olivia, seeing that Lucy was having trouble absorbing so much devastating news.

'That's for Mr McEwan to decide,' he said. 'Would you like me to turn the heating on? I can see that you're shivering.'

'No thanks,' said Lucy and then, after a silence, 'Does this mean I'm going to die young?'

'It might shorten your life, yes.'

'Holy shit,' said Lucy.

And that's when she had asked for the Xanax.

Olivia handed the water to Lucy in a frail plastic cup that dented at the slightest touch.

'Why me?' said Lucy, swallowing two Keppra and a Xanax. 'Why *not* me? Both questions make as little sense as each other. Somebody has to get a brain tumour, or they wouldn't exist. It's just the intimacy of the shock.'

Olivia watched Lucy build a cerebral defence against her brain tumour, as if it were a puzzle that could be solved.

'It's like being raped while you're in a coma and only finding out when you see the CCTV footage,' she went on. 'It's in my *brain*, but I never knew about it. Is it my brain that now knows? Don't get me wrong, even though I'm questioning the relationship between my brain and my mind, I'm not filing for a divorce.'

Dr Hammond came back into the room with a brief, serious smile.

'I've spoken with Mr McEwan and he can squeeze you in as soon as he gets through his current consultation. Is there anything else you want to know from me before you see him?'

'If you got this diagnosis,' said Lucy, 'and you had unlimited resources, what would you do?'

'I would have any surgery done here. Mr McEwan is really the top in his field. I would let him operate on me, or any of my family, without hesitation.'

'Okay, thanks,' said Lucy, getting up and shaking Dr Hammond's hand.

After letting the receptionist know, the two friends went outside for some air. They paced the pavement in silence, until a man appeared before them, with his head and face swathed in gauze, except for a gap around his eyes. He was wearing a T-shirt, underpants and some knee-high circulation socks, visible through his open dressing gown. He seemed to be in his thirties, but his legs were rigid, and he moved forward with great difficulty.

'Jesus, that poor man,' said Lucy, after asking to go back inside.

'Don't worry, we won't let you out of the hospital looking like that,' said Olivia.

'Promise?'

'Promise.'

'At least do my dressing gown up.'

'You got it,' said Olivia.

They had barely sat down on one of the black, steel-framed sofas in the reception area, when they heard Lucy's name being called and saw, across the hall, a smiling man in blue scrubs, leaning out of his office door.

Mr McEwan welcomed them into his room. He was in his fifties with buzz-cut hair and eyes that matched his scrubs. He sat at his desk and swivelled his computer screen so they could all see.

'So, I have the images from your MRI here.' He pulled up a file that contained numerous black and white pictures of Lucy's tumour, shot from many angles. He scrolled through them for a while, seeming to be so fascinated by the penetrative power of the technology that he forgot that there were other people in the room. On every image, a large white blob appeared at the top of the skull. McEwan eventually turned his chair away from the screen to face Lucy, like someone looking up from an engrossing novel to deal with a practical enquiry.

'What I ask myself when I look at you is why you look so healthy and why you're in such great shape? Why are your physical symptoms not more severe?'

'I don't know what to say,' said Lucy. 'You seem to be giving me a compliment and a death sentence in one blow: how can I seem so well considering how unwell I really am. Is that it?'

'The border is very well defined,' said McEwan. 'If it were a glioblastoma, it would probably have bled out more into the rest of the brain and produced much more severe symptoms by now, but there is no way of knowing unless we do a biopsy. Also, you see the vascularisation here at the centre?' He pointed with his pen towards what looked like two tiny clouds that were more brightly lit up than the rest of the tumour. 'That makes me worry that it could be higher grade.'

'So, what would the biopsy entail?' asked Olivia, who could see that Lucy was close to tears and unable to speak.

'We would drill a small hole in your skull and go in with a computer-guided needle to take a sample of the tissue that we can then analyse.'

'Can I stay awake during the procedure?' asked Lucy. 'I'm terrified of not waking up, so I would rather not go under.'

'Yes, you could,' said Mr McEwan. 'We frequently perform awake surgeries, but this is not a risk-free procedure and you should think very carefully before going ahead. The risk of death is less than one per cent, but there is also a chance of bleeding on the brain and having a stroke. That could leave you paralysed on the right side of your body. It's not very common but it does happen.'

'Jesus,' said Lucy.

'Also, these are not very detailed images,' McEwan went on. 'All we can see is that you have a lesion in the left frontoparietal area in the paracentral lobule. We need to do a functional MRI to understand what neural tissues surround or are inside the tumour. Hopefully, we won't have to go through any key functional areas in order to get a sample, but there is a risk of damaging healthy tissue, which would leave you with certain impairments, depending on our approach.'

'I see,' said Lucy, closing her eyes.

'Is there a case for just monitoring the tumour?' asked Olivia.

'That's possible,' said McEwan, 'but I must emphasise that if this is a high-grade tumour, you will want to know as soon as possible so you can begin treatment to extend Lucy's life expectancy.'

'My life expectancy,' said Lucy faintly.

'After the fMRI, I am going to present your case to my colleagues. There's a weekly meeting where sixty of our most senior doctors and researchers at Queen Square get together and discuss all new cases. I suspect they will all recommend the biopsy route since, without it, there is really no further treatment we can offer you.'

'Well, I guess I don't have much of a choice then.'

'You should feel no pressure. This is entirely your decision.'

'Assuming I want to proceed, what are the next steps?'

'My assistant would book you in for an fMRI next week. And I might also send you for a cognitive evaluation with one of my colleagues in the Neurology Department. So, we are looking at a surgery date within the next two weeks or so.'

'Okay, let's do it,' said Lucy, standing up. 'Thank you for squeezing us in,' she added, shaking Mr McEwan's hand.

7

Hunter was frazzled, even by his own prodigious standards. He had stopped over in New York and reconvened with Saul before the two of them set out independently, Hunter to England to see what initiatives Lucy had come up with, and Saul to Paris to check out a Frenchman who claimed to have created a ceramic armour that was cheaper and more effective than those being developed by DARPA in the US or by the various Ministries of Defence around the rest of Europe. Before the two men could converge on Italy to explore further projects, Saul had dashed up to Edinburgh to meet John MacDonald, one of the world's leading experts on inorganic life.

Hunter's apartment was on the top two floors of a sudden, isolated skyscraper that had been driven, like a spike through the heart of Manhattan, well below the tall buildings of the Upper East Side and well above the tall buildings of the financial district. When Saul arrived, he had made some suggestive remarks about feeling tired out by his journey from California and his many meetings around town, expecting the usual line or two of coke, but instead Hunter asked him if he'd ever tried freebasing, snapping open a red leather briefcase, which turned out to contain two glass pipes and a small blowtorch embedded in red velvet moulds.

'Wow!' said Saul. 'I'm not sure I'm ready to go down that road. Isn't that like the most addictive thing in the world?'

'The most addictive thing in the world is power,' said Hunter, 'if you have it, freebasing is just kidding around; without it, you can get addicted to stale doughnuts or rubber underwear.'

'Or freebasing,' Saul insisted.

'Sure,' said Hunter. 'But when we finish with the pipe later tonight, I might go for a couple of months without even glancing in this direction again, because we're brainstorming here, Saul.'

'You're the expert,' said Saul, disinclined to argue openly with his overwhelming host. 'Although Richard Feynman said that science is belief in the ignorance of experts,' he couldn't help adding.

'That would make Donald Trump the world's greatest scientist,' said Hunter.

'I guess he was thinking of people who have pushed existing knowledge to some kind of limit,' said Saul, 'rather than the ones who have turned their backs on it.'

Hunter loaded the pipe with a little pellet of paste.

'Okay, okay, I'm sold,' said Saul.

Although he had only taken the most tentative sip of the smoke lingering in the stem of his glass pipe, Saul felt remarkably reinvigorated and eager to tie together the many strands of conversation that he and Hunter had initiated since forming their alliance a year ago. Fatigue was a delusion he could hardly believe he had been taken in by, now that everything seemed to be edged with vibrant light. Hunter, who had taken a more voracious approach to his pipe, was staring fixedly ahead, perhaps at Francis Bacon's smear of warped human anguish hanging above the black marble fireplace, or perhaps into the infinite space of an unfocused gaze, Saul couldn't tell, but he was determined to take advantage of the wave of lucidity that was breaking over him.

'I guess the thing I've been trying to get across to you over the last year is that if science offered a unified vision of the world, it would be a pyramid, with consciousness at the apex, arising explicably from biology, and life arising smoothly from chemistry, and the Periodic Table, in all its variety, emerging inevitably from the fundamental forces and structures described by physics; but in reality, even physics isn't unified, let alone unified with the rest of science. It's not a pyramid; it's an archipelago – scattered islands of knowledge, with bridges running between some of them, but with others relatively isolated from the rest.'

Hunter let out a long trail of thin smoke.

'We should be backing the bridge-builders,' Saul continued, 'people like Enrico, who is organising the scan of the Blessed Fra Domenico in Assisi, so we can nail the Catholic market with our *Capo Santo* helmet—'

'The guy I want to back is the guy who builds the fucking pyramid,' Hunter interrupted.

'What I'm telling you is that that's not going to happen,' said Saul, 'some things are just not reducible to each other or built on each other. Nothing they discover at CERN is going to shed light on E. O. Wilson's seminal account of life in an ant colony, let alone the other way around.'

Hunter gave Saul another pipe and lit it for him.

'Hold it in,' said Hunter.

Saul really sucked the smoke into his lungs until he couldn't fill them any more. The tingling sensation that ran down the sides of his body from the crown of his head, like an overflowing fountain of electricity, was the prelude to a sense of gargantuan well-being and authority. He sank back in his armchair, exhaled and closed his eyes. He was now in territory he had never visited before. His mind was a far more powerful instrument than he had ever dared to imagine. It was like a great Alaskan river after a spring melt, but instead of flowing with churning brown water, this river flowed with mercury, the brilliant mirror of its surroundings reflecting the sky and the trees and the clouds, but also endowed with a penetrating intelligence that knew them for what they were. A few droplets scattered like scouts on to the banks of the quicksilver river could decipher the atomic structure of the rocks on which they landed and, joining together again, trickle their knowledge back into the imperious flood. If he could just get the world's fifty top scientists and make them feel what he was feeling now, they could join into a single super-mind, they could build the pyramid, they could make all of human knowledge spring out of the desert in a perfect, monumental geometry.

'Pyramid,' he whispered.

Hunter clasped his hand and hoisted him out of the chair.

'What did you say?' he asked.

'We can build the pyramid,' said Saul, unclicking his eyelids and looking fervently into Hunter's dilated pupils.

'Yes!' said Hunter, raising his free arm and bending it with a clenched fist, like a boy inviting admiration for his biceps. '*Yes, we can!*'

Things had gone downhill from there. They had stayed up all night, which had not been part of the plan, and although Hunter had been given an extremely high-dose vitamin C and mineral drip, a vitamin B shot, enough antioxidants to annihilate all the free radicals in New York City, and had managed to pass out during a four-hour session with Ocean, his favourite New York masseuse, he still felt like shit when he got on the plane. He ensured a heavy night's sleep on the journey, but it was too short and as they approached Farnborough he popped an orange Adderall, the strong one, so he could be resolute and attentive at all those meetings Lucy had set up with a succession of supposedly brilliant scientists.

Lucy sat in the back of Hunter's Maybach, behind the driver, naturally, where the leg room was ample but not the length of a child's bed as it was on Hunter's side, with the passenger seat moved fully forward. She had a pint of latte in a cup holder couched in the diamond-patterned white leather of the armrest next to her and an ignored file on her lap, page after page of bullet points. Bullet points and soundbites were made for a man like Hunter, whose combination of aggression and inattention needed bites and bullets to keep him focused. She had intended to revise these pages so as to be emphatically on top of everything, but since yesterday everything had been emphatically on top of her, even though the Xanax gave her a little shelter from the catastrophe, like one of those fragile enclaves in a collapsed building, where an earthquake survivor waits for rescue in the dust and the dark.

After leaving Queen Square the previous morning, Francis had apologised and said that he had to return to Sussex for work, but that he would see her soon. He gave her a heartfelt hug, in the most literal sense that she felt a pulse of strength and sympathy from his heart to hers, a transfer of energy that was palpable and astonishing, although Francis behaved as if nothing had happened.

'Thank you,' she said. 'And thank you for coming along,' she added, in case she had been imagining the whole thing and was making too much of the embrace. On their way back to Belsize Park, she said to Olivia what an amazing person Francis was, partly to please her, but mostly because she couldn't think of anyone else who could have handled with such unobtrusive but deep engagement meeting a stranger who is almost immediately diagnosed with cancer.

Since they both worked at home, Martin and Lizzie Carr often had a break in the middle of the day and so Lucy asked Olivia, in case they ran into her parents, not to mention the tumour. Much as Lucy loved the Carrs, she needed time to adjust before deciding on the right balance between discretion and confession. She wanted to spend some time alone with Olivia, but as they slipped into the house, Lizzie happened to be in the hall and of course invited them to join her and Martin in the kitchen. She was so affectionate and welcoming that Lucy couldn't refuse.

Martin also greeted Olivia and Lucy with great warmth, but immediately plunged back into the flow of the conversation he had been having with his wife. He was well known for being one of the rare psychoanalysts who was prepared to take on schizophrenic patients. They were referred to him, without the usual preliminary consultation he would have had with a private patient, at the mental health clinic where he worked once a week for free. He had been sent a new patient the day before and was complaining, as he often did, about the limitations of psychiatric approaches, which treated the disordered language of schizophrenics as a symptom that needed to be suppressed rather than a communication that needed to be understood.

'The intelligent patient I saw yesterday had bought the Oxford University Press *Very Short Introduction* to schizophrenia, written not by one but by *two* professors, because he was trying to research his illness. And this is what he got for his pains,' said Martin, opening a little green book at a page he had marked with a torn piece of kitchen towel. Olivia smiled at Lizzie in recognition of Martin in full flood.

'This,' he said, 'was an IQ test for naming as many animals as possible in three minutes:

> *The errors of patients with poverty of speech and action tended to be of omission. These patients often failed to respond in the time permitted. For example, on a verbal fluency test one patient could name only three animals in three minutes. He commented, 'The only one I can think of is cheetah.' In contrast, the errors associated with the disorganization syndrome tend to be of commission, that is patients fail to inhibit inappropriate responses. For example, another patient performing the same verbal fluency task produced the sequence, 'emu, duck, swan, lake, Loch Ness monster, bacon ...' In this example, the word 'lake' is closely associated with the word 'swan', but should not have been given since it is not an example of an animal. The word 'bacon' is also inappropriate, and why the patient produced it is difficult to understand, but this inexplicable conjunction of words is typical of the incoherent speech sometimes associated with schizophrenia.*

'"Inexplicable conjunction of words",' gasped Martin. '"Cheetah"! Perhaps the patient felt that the examiner was a cheater, making him do an IQ test while he was psychotic, perhaps he cheated on someone, or someone in his family was a cheater, we don't know, but we know that it's a communication. As to lake turning into Loch, what could be more explicable? Of course, the mind of such a person contains monsters that may be real or may not be, like the Loch Ness monster. Perhaps he thinks he's a monster for eating bacon, the flesh of another animal, or he comes from a tradition in which pork is forbidden, or he feels like dead meat. We don't know, but it's a communication that could be deciphered by someone who is prepared to pay attention.'

'Of course you're right, darling,' said Lizzie, 'but it's easier to just give them more anti-psychotics.'

'To cheat them like the cheaters that we are.'

'Are you all right, Lucy?' asked Lizzie.

'Not really,' she said. 'I had a brain scan yesterday and the results came in this morning.'

'Oh god,' said Martin, 'and I've been ranting. What's going on?'

'I wish the evidence from my scan was being as outrageously misrepresented as the evidence from those IQ tests, but it turns out I have a brain tumour.'

For the rest of the day, the Carrs helped to look after Lucy in their loving and generous and sane way. Lizzie said that although it was against the recommendations of psychotherapy for them to talk formally, given how well they knew each other, she was of course available as a friend, and could guide her towards a colleague, if Lucy wanted professional help. After a quick sketch of Hunter's personality, they all agreed that keeping her medical news private was essential to spending the next few days in his company.

That decision was one of the only firm reference points in Lucy's mind as she arrived at Farnborough airport to pick up her boss. She waited, making every effort to work up some enthusiasm for their days together. Before long, she saw Hunter striding across the tarmac in a pink shirt, blue jeans, cowboy boots and, despite the cool morning, a brown suede jacket hooked over his shoulder. At six foot four, he was an indisputably big presence, with his square jaw and his broad shoulders. After his passport had been glanced at and his luggage loaded in the boot, the two of them settled in the back of the car and set off for Oxford.

'I remember you saying that you used to live here,' said Lucy, with mechanical brightness.

'One thing you should know about me, Lucy, is that I'm a present tense kind of guy,' said Hunter, 'more tense perhaps than present at this precise moment but, in any case, not lost in beachcombing my memories.'

'You can be present to your memories,' said Lucy, 'they're not time machines.'

'That's true, although I've heard that some people can catch a ride on a madeleine,' said Hunter, 'but the French already have the patent on that low-tech time machine and anyhow it's headed in the wrong way. The only direction I want to travel in is towards the future.'

'I don't think we have any choice about that,' said Lucy, 'annoyingly enough.'

'So far!' said Hunter, with a sudden laugh. 'Anyhow, it's great to have you on the team, Lucy. I want you to select bulletproof projects to protect me from charlatans and snake-oil salesmen. I don't want to be the Citizen Kane of science funding, hiring an opera house for my squawking, tone-deaf wife to caterwaul on stage, while the opera lovers heckle from the stalls.'

'Absolutely,' said Lucy. She decided that she would just let Hunter wash over her, agreeing now and again to whatever he said. In a way, Hunter was a very simple person, who just wanted to be right all the time. It was easier to play along while she sheltered in her little enclave of rubble. He spoke unstoppably all the way to Oxford. Occasionally, she would slip in a smile, an expression of wonder, or an approving comment. Hunter was sometimes charming, sometimes needlessly confrontational, but nothing he said or did could possibly compete with the horror of her existing situation. Still, on the surface of her mind, she could remember wanting him to like the visit she had organised.

They were due to make an affable start by having a breakfast meeting with William Moorhead. Moorhead was a known ally and a business partner and despite his remark to Lucy – 'In my opinion "Breakfast" and "Meeting" are two words that should never be seen side by side' – he had of course agreed to come. Hunter was extremely genial to begin with, but when Moorhead said that the reasons for *YouGenetics* not having yet made a profit would 'require at least two PhDs in biochemistry' for Hunter to understand, there was a rapid shift in mood.

'You know, Bill,' said Hunter, 'there are a hell of a lot of professors crowding this little planet of ours, and I could have landed a meteor of money in any one of their backyards and watched them fall to their knees to thank me for saving their children from eating another can of dog food for dinner, but I chose you, because Saul assured me that you were the guy with a database we could turn into a great company. And yet all you can think of doing is to insult my intelligence. Well, guess what, Professor? I bought half the fucking company! Don't patronise the patron, Bill. In fact, read the contract. You didn't want me to have more than fifty per cent, but as CEO of *Digitas* I control *YouGenetics* and since you can't monetarise the data, I've given it to Lucy to run.'

Hunter seemed to calm down after his explosion and began again in a gentler tone, albeit with a frighteningly accurate impersonation of a pompous English accent.

'Now, if you want to wait for the next "tranche" of spare change to come in from your publishers, be their guest. But if you want to *be my guest*,' he went on, returning to his own voice, while waving at the waiter to bring the bill, 'learn some fucking manners!'

'I will not be spoken to like that,' said Moorhead vehemently.

'What do you mean you "will not be spoken to like that"? You just were spoken to "like that". Don't they teach you logic in this place?'

Hunter burst out laughing and slapped Moorhead on the back.

'You can always buy the shares back, but then you'd have to sell Little Pisswell Manor, or whatever your Cotswold idyll is called. You wouldn't get the Stamp Duty back and you've taken the roof off, so it's not looking as imposing as when you bought it. Besides, your wife is knee deep in swatches; it's her compensation for decades of humiliating infidelity. So why don't you just make the company profitable, Brains?'

As they hit the pavement outside the Randolph Hotel, Hunter appeared to be in a thoroughly cheerful mood.

'He can add some PTSD to his dumpster of PhDs,' he chuckled. 'Was I too harsh on him, Lucy? Be honest with me.'

'Not at all,' said Lucy, 'he was insufferably condescending.' Lucy had unobtrusively taken a second Xanax while the two men locked antlers over breakfast. She would have given the same answer even if Hunter had plunged a fork into the back of Moorhead's hand.

'Talking of PTSD,' she went on, 'I've been looking at the virtual reality therapy that's being developed at the Psychiatry department, where we're going next, and they've been having very positive results, not just with schizophrenia, which I know you have your doubts about as a profitable market, but also with PTSD, depression, attention deficit, obsessive compulsive disorder, social anxiety, certain kinds of autism ...'

'Sounds great,' said Hunter. 'I don't know a single parent whose kids don't have one or more of those problems – or a single kid who doesn't have parents with one or more of those problems!'

To Lucy's amazement, Hunter was enthralled by the virtual reality demonstration. He watched various paranoid, phobic and anxious volunteers have fake encounters on fake trains with neutral or vaguely amicable avatars, and listened with interest to their reports on the benefits of the simulation. He also tried on a virtual reality headset himself and wandered around in front of a screen in a concrete basement enchanted, as anyone might be, to have his actual surroundings replaced.

'That was a hell of a meeting, Lucy,' said Hunter afterwards. 'Thanks for setting it up. I see a lot of potential there.'

'Awesome,' said Lucy, wondering whether she could make it through the rest of their schedule without passing out. 'I can't believe this is really happening.'

8

There were corrugated-iron shelters dotted around the Howorth estate and one of Francis's jobs was to check them twice a week and record the number of grass snakes, common lizards, toads and slow worms he found hidden under the refugia. While he walked through the scrubland from one shelter to another, he tried to rest in the basic awareness out of which his attention, concentration, observation, judgement, discrimination, emotions and all other secondary states emerged. There was nothing wrong with the states themselves, in fact they were indispensable for navigating life and performing any specific task; it was being engrossed in them that was the problem. Of course, while he was counting the amphibians and reptiles he might find today he would be calculating, but the calculation was only an expression of the basic awareness, a wave on the water, not made of anything different from the rest of the sea, but taking on a particular and transient shape. Just as the American citizen's famous entitlement to the 'pursuit of happiness' was in fact a guarantee of unhappiness, since a person can only pursue something that is missing, so he needed to rest in awareness, like a man lying on the grass, rather than pursue it, like a man getting up from the grass in order to search for somewhere to lie down. Nor did he have to think about awareness, it was the nature of his mind to be aware; to imagine that he was depriving himself of awareness because he stopped contemplating it as a precious object was like imagining that putting on a glove would rob him of his hand. As long as he recognised what he was doing while he was doing it, he could pay attention to where he was stepping, record the absence of any animals under the first shelter, and still be completely reconciled with the content of his own mind. Not that there was anything, strictly speaking, to be reconciled with, just a natural state to recognise; and yet a huge amount of work was needed before that naturalness seemed like anything but a dogma or an abstraction. His particular sensibility continually generated metaphors to remind himself of a natural state that should have come, well, more naturally, but in his case, came with a caravan of similes and arguments. As he walked to the next corrugated cover, he pictured a great sphere of stable and constant awareness surrounding the immediate scene, the world, and the universe, but then he abolished the image, since a sphere must have a centre and an edge, and awareness was limitless and centreless. Did the extravagance of that claim make him a panpsychist? Maybe, but at the moment he had no interest in placing himself on the troubled spectrum of consciousness studies, just in the bare fact that he was resting on the ground of consciousness, rather than impaled on its conceptual summit. He refreshed his attitude by remembering that the relationship of everything to everything else was constantly changing, as an earthworm in the ground beneath him digested another grain of soil, or he moved his hand to lift another cover, and that each reconfiguration was occurring for the first time. As he thought of this continuous arising of novelty out of the bedrock of habit, he immediately pictured heat waves shimmering on a desert road. Still, in the end, there was no need to cancel that image, it didn't matter whether his mind was busy or relatively restful, it was the act of recognition that constituted the resting and generated a spontaneous sense of the weightlessness of the sensations and thoughts and metaphors and arguments, a sense of the 'mirror-like nature of the mind', its ability to reflect everything without the mirror itself being stained or cracked by the reflection. The 'mirror' in that comparison was, of course, another metaphor, but a self-cancelling one: in the 'mirror' of the mind the metaphor of the mirror didn't stick or stay any more than anything else, although it could be gazed at credulously for as long as anyone chose to, like any other object. The point was not to assert beliefs, but to remove the rubble of delusion that constituted almost all beliefs. It was true that he had to start with the confidence that the mind, in its natural state, was clear and had no need to 'believe in' anything at all, since all knowledge was inferred from that clarity. What was unknowable fell away into irrelevance, or into 'noble silence', to put it more traditionally and politely, and what was known, in that clarity, could do without the cheerleaders of belief to kick and spin it into a frenzy of assertion. Lifting the second cover he found two slow worms, legless lizards with tiny eyes often mistaken for snakes. There was also one of the less and less common examples of 'The Common Toad' sitting, with warty imperturbability, under the same refugium. Just as it was almost irresistible to test an infant's grip by gently holding its tiny hand, it was tempting to lift up one of the slow worms from the ground, knowing that it would coil itself around his finger in a series of tight rings, allowing him to form a momentary connection with another way of being and another set of instincts, but he left the slow worms undisturbed; he was connected to them enough already. It was good to see these protected species, which, like so many others, had started appearing at Howorth in growing numbers. They were, of course, other sentient beings, but he felt that his involvement with them was more fundamental than that. Unless consciousness was downloaded from another dimension, an idea that he found disagreeably Platonic, like a scented handkerchief of perfect forms pressed to the sensitive nostrils of a courtier picking his way through the open sewers of the actual world, then it must permeate everything. Space, instead of being a desolate interval between pinpricks of sentience, must be the conscious medium in which these more obvious forms of consciousness were concentrated. If matter was not inherently conscious, then one had to fall back on the official story that the pinpricks of sentience existed in an otherwise inanimate universe thanks to a mind-numbingly long poker game in which the elements of the Periodic Table had been dealt out again and again until one bit of deadness haphazardly acquired the Full House of life, and then only a few million hands later, the Royal Flush of consciousness. This Royal Flush Theory was defended by three rowdy musketeers: Randomness, Complexity and Emergence. Hurrah! They came with all the plumage and the inane bravado of swashbuckling heroes who love nothing better than to get themselves into an impossible position: fighting for reductionism's attempt to subsume the irreducible. Despite all their rooftop antics, the only proposition they really had to offer was that luck multiplied by time transubstantiated matter. It was like claiming that if a child played Lego for long enough her mother might come down one day and find a blue whale emerging from the carpet. After the initial struggle to get her smartphone back from the whale in which enough consciousness had emerged for it to google the location of the nearest beach, and after telling her daughter to please stop playing with that Lego set, a certain perplexity might set in about how matter had rearranged itself so unexpectedly. The authoritative answer would be that it had become complex thanks to Complexity, and that once Complexity passed a critical threshold, consciousness emerged thanks to Emergence, and that it was forbidden to think that consciousness was involved at any earlier stage because Randomness had been placed there to banish superstition. This explanation might not strike the puzzled parent as entirely persuasive. It was, after all, a creation myth with many rivals. The ferocious Yanomami of Amazonia, for instance, believed that the world had been sneezed out by a god who had taken a high dose of the snuff to which the tribe was itself coincidentally addicted, and that his chosen people were leading their violent lives in a jungle of divine mucus. Christians believed in an omnipotent artist, who tossed off his masterpiece in six days, without accepting any editorial guidance, except from his most ardent enemy who suggested, after a wearisome pilot episode of Innocence, that introducing Evil would help to boost the viewing figures. And so on and so forth. Science had swept away these childish stories of sneezing gods and dreaming gods, of divine artists and divine sperm, of golden rain and copulating swans, in order to place some thoroughly sanitised but equally non-explanatory concepts at the inception of its narratives: biology had chemistry's random poker game to thank for its existence, while physics had 'Initial Conditions' presiding tautologically over the microseconds before the Big Bang embarked on the longest story ever told: fourteen billion years of collisions. As a code word for the inscrutability of origins, 'God' at least had the advantage of brevity, rather than rambling on for six syllables, like the equally mysterious 'Initial Conditions'. According to Occam's Razor, the minimalist aesthetic that was supposed to adjudicate over intellectual life for the rest of time, like a fashion editor in a black pencil skirt who simply refuses to retire, decade after decade, despite the screams of protest from an art department longing for a little moment of Baroque excess and a splash of colour, the parsimony of that single syllable should have won the day. How an opaque giant like Complexity was supposed to sit comfortably on Occam's Razor was another question. Presumably, Complexity was sometimes the most parsimonious explanation, although in the case of consciousness, it explained nothing at all; taking parsimony a little too far, even from Occam's austere perspective. Oh no, Francis scolded himself for getting engrossed in the rapid internal murmur of an imaginary debate. He was supposed to be resting in How It Is, rather than generating opinions about How It Began, a subject to which the only coherent response was silence. He didn't have to have an argument, let alone win it, nor did he even have to stop having an argument, if it came to that, he just had to recognise what he was doing while he was doing it. Looking down at the slow worms twisting on the ground, he remembered that they had the strange ability to autotomise: to break off their tail in order to escape a predator. He broke off his own tale, without falling deeper into the trap of self-reproach, lowered the lid carefully back over the refugium, and made a record of what he had seen. As he continued on his walk, the imaginary debate faded away. He hadn't yet told Olivia about the meditative aspect of his life. She would gradually find out as they grew closer. He was in no hurry to explain or justify or be

cross-examined. The drive behind his patchy practice was an obsessive enquiry into whether freedom meant anything at all, not just
freedom 'from' something (hunger, torture, depression) or freedom
'to' do something (debate, vote, protest) but freedom itself, beheading
the Medusa of determinism before it petrified the world. For a true
determinist, events only seemed unpredictable because there wasn't
enough information about them; if all the causes and conditions
leading up to them were known, they would be just as predictable
as oxidisation turning iron rusty or copper green: it was only ignorance that made accidents seem different from decisions, and habits
from spontaneous actions; they were all in fact caught in a continuum
of inevitability, like a ripple of tumbling dominos. There was something superficially impressive about the grinding logic of determinism
in the sense that the present, as Nabokov had said, is 'the top layer
of the past', and since the past is defined by the fact that it cannot
be changed, the present is the necessary product of that irrefutable
model. Nevertheless, it was a model and not an experience. What
did that 'top layer' consist of? Was it a layer of sand waiting to be
trampled into sandstone, or was it the cusp of an unprecedented
wave arising from an essentially impersonal ocean of awareness in
which the neurotic habits of any individual could be drowned, as
long as that person was ready to surrender them? The way the word
'determined' denoted the complete absence of volition, as well as a
special abundance of volition, was what Francis thought of as
Schrodinger's homonym, sitting in a semantic box, not knowing
whether it meant something or its opposite, whether it was dead or
alive, existing in a determined universe it was determined to subvert.
Like the cat in Schrodinger's famous thought experiment, the
homonym was in a thought experiment of its own, and whether it
referred to a world that was inevitable or volitional depended, in
this experiment, on whether the observer was attending to causality
or awareness. Just as physics had offered a legalistic description of
the world on the one hand, including relativity and thermodynamics
and, on the other hand, a probabilistic one generated by quantum
mechanics, and the descriptions could not be integrated, unless they
turned out to be two aspects of something more fundamental, the

argument between free will and determinism could never be resolved while the antagonists insisted on referring to different fields of knowledge. Francis's passion for freedom might have been determined by his conditioning, but wherever it came from, the project had to begin, modestly enough, by training a mind that was able to place its attention where it chose. Oh dear, he had drifted off again into another argument. Where had he been? What did it matter where he had been? His subject wasn't one line of thought or another, it was seeing all the lines of thought for what they were as they crossed his mind. Still, yes, Olivia. She had come to stay again and although she had only left that morning, he already missed her. Their microbiomes, those colonies and clouds of microorganisms that inhabited and surrounded each person's body, were no doubt still mingling 'without obstruction of limb or joint', but unlike Milton's angels, he quite wanted the limbs and joints back, as well as the conversation. On Saturday night, they had continued to discuss the complications of her adoption. It turned out that when Karen had wanted to give Keith away as well as Olivia, Henry had threatened her not only with physical violence but also with exotic metaphysical retributions, about which he was sinisterly well informed, thanks to his fervent, if narrow, grasp of religion, focused almost exclusively on damnation and the tortures of hell. He was particularly preoccupied by the fact that suicide resulted in damnation, and therefore offered no escape. This thought, said Karen, was probably the only thing that kept such a tormented man alive. She wondered every day about going to the police but felt that her claim to have been impregnated by a vicious lunatic was probably too banal to command any attention, without at least a fractured skull to support it. Attitudes to domestic violence were more laissez-faire in those days. Henry was adept at twisting Karen's arm or half stifling her with a pillow without leaving any signs of his attacks. He basked in the confidence of having established that he was capable of anything, reframing his current nastiness, which he alternated with shows of clinging sentimentality, as a form of heroic self-restraint that it would be reckless to push any further. Besides, Karen was desperate to get her teaching qualification and since Henry worked as a night porter in a hospital, she saw very little of him, and at least knew that Keith would not be alone during the day. She inevitably became attached to her son, but at the same time resented and, to her horror, even hated him for being part of the trap she was in. The neighbours complained that he cried all day long, and yet by the time she came home he was listless and sleepy, a state that was eventually explained by the empty bottle of gin she found one evening next to the tin of formula. She was too frightened to confront Henry about it, and in a guilty way grateful for the hours of rest it gave her before Keith woke screaming in the middle of the night. She told Olivia that she bitterly regretted forcing herself to believe the increasingly far-fetched mishaps that Henry described in order to explain Keith's bruises and, when he was eight months old, his broken arm. When she found cigarette burns, individually placed, on Keith's back and legs, she couldn't deceive herself any longer. The next Sunday Henry had planned a day out in Kent with his hard-bitten old mother, a passionate fan of capital punishment, who felt that far from being abolished, the death penalty should have expanded, like a nuclear explosion, beyond treason and murder, through burglary and pick-pocketing, until it finally engulfed and incinerated the little brats who had the cheek to drop sweet papers on the pavements of Ramsgate when she was out with her trolley shopping for teacake. She was the only person Henry was frightened of and Karen knew that he wouldn't dare cancel the trip. She ran the thermometer under the hot tap and claimed that Keith had a temperature and regret-tably would not be able to visit his dear old gran. The moment Henry left, she started packing everything she could fit into the two available suitcases and escaped, in a fever of anxiety, to a women's refuge in Chiswick. The staff at the refuge helped her secure a restraining order against Henry, and she negotiated through lawyers not to press charges if he agreed not to oppose Keith's adoption. The police told Henry that they had detailed evidence, including photographs of Keith's burnt body, and that if he ever bothered Karen in any way, they would be delighted to send the evidence to the Crown Prosecution Service; in fact, they wanted to lock up a bastard like him right now, but were constrained by Karen's refusal to collaborate. It had worked, and Henry had disappeared from Karen's life, as had Keith, who was eighteen months old when she was finally able to hand him over for adoption. She told Olivia that she had never seen him again and didn't even know whether he had been adopted or stayed in an institution, but that she was periodically overcome by an ungovernable sense of sadness when she thought about his early life and was haunted by the idea that her refusal to help prosecute Henry might have put other women and children in danger. Francis had listened to Olivia's story while they were again lying together on the sofa staring at the fire. He felt its horror, but also its remoteness: Olivia had never met Keith *ex utero* and almost certainly never would, and she had come to the decision that an annual visit to Karen was enough to acknowledge her connection with a person whose motives she could now understand and forgive, but for whom there was no need to exaggerate her affection. The immediate point, thought Francis, as he squatted down to lift the cover of the third refugium, was that he and Olivia had gone through the ritual exchange of childhood stories that new lovers make, and it had only drawn them closer. In a brief short circuit between his current action and Olivia's story, he half-expected to find Karen and Keith hiding under the corrugated lid, but instead of human refugees he saw a tangle of young grass snakes, with their distinctive yellow collars, knotted on the ground. They had probably been conceived in the heat of July and born quite recently from their leathery eggs. The grass snake was a protected species as well. Perhaps it would soon be redundant to bother with the words 'protected', 'declining', 'endangered' or 'extinct', since it would apply to every animal that was not a member of a billionaire clan like jellyfish, which seemed set to achieve a monopoly of the oceans, or the rat and cockroach families which flourished in the filth and warmth of great cities, but at least here at Howorth, in this little patch of Sussex, things were on the move, and nature was showing its regenerative power, not just in the return of vulnerable turtle dove, after its annual migration through Southern Europe, in an avian equivalent of the Battle of the Somme, past crowds of exploding shotguns in Greece and Italy, France, Malta and Spain, or the return of the thrilling liquid song of the nightingale, but also in less visible ways, in the density of earthworms underground, no longer sliced or exposed by the plough, or writhing their way through soil fatally drenched in pesticides, but renewing and fertilising the earth on which he was now kneeling with his notebook, admiring the grass snakes. The earth was reviving, but it was also resting after years of exploitation and he was resting too, after years of pursuing happiness, resting on the ground of awareness.

9

Sebastian was dressed in exactly the same outfit he had worn for the consultation last week: jeans, dirty trainers and a green sweater with a large hole in its right elbow, surrounded by thick, unravelling threads of wool. He sat down in the chair, crumpled up his hooded anorak and pressed it to his stomach, perhaps from anxiety that he would put it down in the wrong place, Martin felt, but also to comfort himself by not entirely letting go of the outer layer of protection he had brought with him.

'I'm on my meds,' said Sebastian listlessly, 'so I'm feeling topped and tailed. I might try lying down on the couch. That's what they do in films, isn't it? It might feel more real, I suppose.'

Martin restrained himself from asking whether 'real' or 'reel' or 'unreal' or 'unravel' might be the right word in this case, but more immediately he wanted to restrain Sebastian from lying down on the couch.

'Well, at our first meeting,' he said, 'we sat facing each other, as we are now, and perhaps we should go on doing that for some time, while we get to know each other, and face up to things together.'

'I might try the couch,' said Sebastian, as if he hadn't heard.

'Of course, you're welcome to, but the couch is really there to help people "free associate", and you have no problem free associating.'

'I did when I was in the hospital.'

'No, not in that sense. It's a term we use for letting the mind make unexpected connections, but you make them spontaneously all the time.'

'When do we start?'

'We started when you came into the room,' said Martin, 'and you told me that your meds make you feel "topped and tailed".'

'Now I feel you're spying on me.'

'Well, in a way I suppose I am, but only because we're working on the same team, like codebreakers, trying to uncover the same secrets, so that you don't have to suffer so much.'

'Like Bletchley Park.'

'Yes.'

'We're building a Turing machine, so less boats get sunk.'

'Exactly.'

'Nobody has ever wanted to be on the same team as me. At least not since my episodes began.'

'Well, I want us to be on the same team,' said Martin.

'I don't believe you,' said Sebastian, but then he looked as if he wanted to cry. He eventually compromised by staring vacantly at the carpet.

There was a long silence.

'My mother always used to ask me to top and tail the beans for Sunday lunch. Now I'm topped and tailed because of the Clozapine; but also because of the reason I take it. They're inseparable. Siamese twins. David Bowie's brother had schizophrenia, but David Bowie was a superstar. It's Russian roulette. If you're a has-been, at least you've been something. I've never been anything. In the centre, there's only drowning cats attacking each other in a sack someone is holding just high enough for one of them to survive by climbing on top of the rest.'

Martin let the connections come to rest, without any comment, like an ornithologist trying to stay still as he sees a flock of migrating birds settle on the water nearby. He mustn't frighten them away, he mustn't ask who was holding the sack, especially since Sebastian didn't yet know.

'So, would you like to tell me about your first episode?' he asked.

'Okay,' said Sebastian.

He moved over to the couch, and lay down, still holding his scrunched-up anorak tightly against the middle of his body. Although he would have preferred him to have remained seated, Martin decided not to derail the story.

'The first time it happened I'd been smoking skunk with Simon. We've been friends since primary school, although I only see him a couple of times a year now. It's like charity visits, because he wants to seem loyal, but he doesn't enjoy seeing me any more. In those days, people used to say we were "inseparable", which is the sort of stupid thing people say. Anyway, we went to the Portobello Road, and I started to hear everybody's thoughts, like running through all the radio stations very fast and getting bursts of words exploding in my head. I said to Simon, "It should be called the *Portal* Bello Road, because it's a portal into another dimension," and Simon laughed, because he thought I was just being stoned and taking the piss. Sorry,' Sebastian interrupted himself, 'this is too intense. I feel like I'm having a flashback. I think I want to sit down again. I don't feel safe on the couch, because I can't see what you're doing. You might stab me with a pen, stab me in the eye, or stab me in the back.'

'I'm not going to do that,' said Martin.

'Yeah, I *sort of* believe that,' said Sebastian, rocking back and forth on the edge of the couch, pressing the rolled-up anorak against himself. 'In a way, I know it's a fantasy, because I'm on my meds, but the feeling is just too strong. Sometimes things are more powerful when you know they're not true, because you have to imagine them so hard, if you see what I mean.'

'Absolutely,' said Martin. 'I think that's very well put.'

'Now you're buttering me up. Topped and tailed and buttered up. A dish fit for a king. My mum would be proud.'

Sebastian moved back to the chair. He looked at Martin with a strange mixture of suspicion and yearning.

'So, I said to Simon,' he resumed, '"No, don't you get it? Everyone thinks it's the cameras and the smoke detectors and the people on television that are watching you ..." "Well, the frigging cameras are watching you, aren't they?" said Simon. And I said, "Yeah, but it's the mirrors that are really watching you! When you look into a mirror, it sucks you in so you can look at yourself and then you get trapped behind it." Simon got angry and said I was a paranoid wanker and I was doing his head in and he left me on my own.'

Sebastian suddenly grew furious.

'How do you think that made me feel, Dr Emotions? You're supposed to be the fucking expert. I was abandoned in the middle of a crowd, in the middle of my first episode by my so-called best friend, so I felt *abandoned*, didn't I? Fuckwit.'

'We don't know how you feel until you tell us,' said Martin calmly. 'You might have felt sad, or frightened, or angry, or indifferent, or relieved.'

'I did feel relieved, that's right,' said Sebastian, suddenly eager to agree. 'I felt that if he couldn't understand, I was better off without him. He was holding me back when I was seeing something really important, really deep.'

'About the mirror?' asked Martin.

'Yeah, I realised that the whole sky was a mirror, the ultimate mirror, like a silver dish cover, keeping us warm until Death makes a meal of us. I knew I was the last one who wasn't under its control, and so I concentrated and sent a blue beam from my forehead into the sky to shatter it, but the mirror sent a yellow beam down from the sky to push the blue beam back into my head and make it melt down. I used all my concentration and after a massive struggle, I managed to shatter the sky and it rained down bits of mirror all over London. It was the most beautiful thing I'd ever seen and I could feel that all the mirrors in the city had gone black, and that I'd set everybody free.'

'You must have felt very powerful,' said Martin.

'Yeah,' said Sebastian, 'it was the best feeling I've ever had, but I was terrified at the same time. I knew the sky was going to go mental and try to take revenge on me. That was when the two policemen came up to arrest me, saying that I was causing a public disturbance, because I'd been screaming at the sky when we were fighting and throwing bits of clothing at it and I was almost naked, although I hadn't noticed. I tried to run away, but they caught me and twisted my arm and forced me into a car and took me back to the station and all the time I was screaming through the window, trying to warn people because I could see the bits of sky floating back up and rebuilding the dome. That's when I was sectioned for the first time. They tried to give me pills in the hospital, but the pills were yellow, so I knew where they came from and I refused to take them. In the end, they started giving me injections once a fortnight and said I was all right to go home and live with my parents. They call it "care in the community", but seeing as I hate being there and my parents hate having me there, it doesn't seem like a very good description.'

'What would be a good description?' asked Martin.

'"A cat in a hat" would be a better description, because at least it rhymes,' said Sebastian.

'Or a cat in a sack,' said Martin.

Sebastian darted a look at him. 'I see what you're doing,' he said, 'I see what you're doing, but it's all just dead words, isn't it, like "schizophrenia"? The doctors say that I have "schizophrenia", but that's just a word. It doesn't mean they understand anything. They say it's genetic, or caused by a chemical imbalance, or it's because of the skunk, or the speed, but they don't know what it is, what it really is …'

Sebastian seemed gridlocked from trying to use words to affirm the impotence of language.

'All we care about here,' said Martin, 'is what it feels like for you, what it is, as an experience, and I promise you that the better we understand that the less you will suffer.'

'It's hard to stay on my meds because they make me fat and sleepy,' said Sebastian, 'and that first time was the most important day of my life, the most alive, but when I go off the meds now it's not like the first time any more. It's more chaotic and frightening each time, but that might be because the Clozapine has weakened my powers. Pin me to a bed, pin me to a wall, pin me to a pin. I call it the Wizard of Ozapine, because when you get there, it's all fake, like the Wizard of Oz, it's just a trick. It doesn't cure you at all, it just tricks you and makes everything fake.'

'Well, if you agree, we're going to find out what's true,' said Martin.

'That could be the biggest trick of all,' said Sebastian, like a child creating an infinite regress by saying, 'Why?' to every answer. 'People who talk to me about the truth are always trying to prove that I'm "delusional", so "the truth" is their trick for stealing my truth: I know that I shattered the sky.'

'What is true can't also be fake,' said Martin, 'that would be an untenable position and that kind of logic generates the word "delusional", but here we are less interested in that kind of logic, we're interested in a symbolic truth, where those contradictions might be reconciled. It's true that at that particular moment you felt you had to shatter the sky to save yourself and the rest of humanity, and it's also true that there is an emotional history that led to that symbolic act. We're not here to talk you out of your "delusions", we're here to understand your symbolic language, your own network of images. Your mind is not like a great lazy river that everyone can see from the aeroplane window, meandering its way through the plain, it's like a mountain stream that goes underground and then bursts out of the hillside in what seem like haphazard places, but that doesn't mean we can't follow its course and find out why it goes underground and why it reappears.'

'A mountain stream,' said Sebastian, seemingly pleased. 'So, can I stay here?'

'We're coming to an end of the session now, but I think we've made a very fruitful start.'

'So, you're just going to throw me on the street? You and Simon,' said Sebastian, becoming agitated and aggrieved. ' "You're a mountain stream, now just fuck off." '

'I'm not throwing you on the street,' said Martin firmly. 'It's because we've had a fruitful session that you want it to go on, and it will go on, at the same time next week.'

'Next week?' said Sebastian, in despair. 'So, I'm just left with all these thoughts until next week?'

Martin made a rapid decision.

'Listen, Sebastian, I know how urgent this feels to you and I want to help as much as I can. I normally practise from another office and, as it happens, one of my long-term patients has just completed her analysis and I now have an opening on Friday mornings at eleven forty. If you'd be interested, I would like to offer you that session. We would also have a second session a week so that you come regularly to the same office both times.'

'So, you still had a card up your sleeve,' said Sebastian, 'one more ciggie hidden away that you weren't going to share with me.'

'It's an opportunity that only arose this week and it only occurred to me just now that you might like to have that session. It would be free of charge, like here. You can think about it if you like.'

'I'll take it,' said Sebastian. 'I don't want to think about it.'

'Good,' said Martin, getting up and smiling. 'I'll see you on Friday then, at eleven forty. This is the address.'

He went to his desk, took out a card and gave it to Sebastian.

Sebastian said goodbye and then paused at the door with his back still turned.

'I think you're a kind man,' he mumbled, and then left abruptly, without looking round and without closing the door.

10

Now that her book was done, Olivia had the feeling of being on holiday for a while, a period in which she could choose between various research projects without any particular pressure or urgency. She was lying on the bed in her old room in Belsize Park, with a copy of *Brainwashed* face down on the bedspread beside her. She was already halfway through but had decided to take a break. It had been a long time since she had felt the extravagance of having nothing in particular to do, gazing at the familiar configuration of trees and roofs and windows that she had looked at throughout her life, season after season and year after year. Today, the last autumn leaves were clinging to the damp branches and the lights were already on in many of the windows opposite.

The house felt peaceful. Partly, no doubt, because it was in a quiet street and had no party wall on one side; also, perhaps, because it was a place where troubled people came to find some peace by talking to one or other of her parents; but mostly, from her perspective, because it was a perfect family house. Ever since she could remember anything, she could remember being there, and when her parents died, she would no longer be there, since neither she nor Charlie could keep it. It was a family house for the precise family that the four of them constituted, giving it a complete continuity and a realistic impermanence. It had neither the financial nor the sentimental burdens of being ancestral, nor the restlessness of being part of an ascent or a separation or a decline. It had the additional stability of hardly ever changing. Until something definitively broke, neither Martin nor Lizzie could ever quite face having things done up. It was a place for work and hospitality, but mostly it was a home for the family she had almost been born into – making Olivia suspect that she was even more attached to it than any of the others.

Lucy was having an fMRI today to find out if her tumour was operable. When Olivia had spoken to her on the phone yesterday, there had been a pace and compulsiveness to her description of what she was going through that made Olivia sense the traumatic grip of the experience. She had never heard Lucy sound so frightened. It was hardly surprising, but the effect was strong enough to constitute a new layer of personality, entirely devoted to managing fear. Olivia had embarked on reading *Brainwashed,* at Ash's recommendation, partly to give more authority to whatever reassurance she could offer Lucy, but also because she had been intrigued by neuroscience for some time, not least because its flamboyant imagery seemed to have usurped DNA's double helix as the popular emblem of the irresistible power of hard science to penetrate nature's secrets. And yet, there were crucial differences between the status of these two scientific icons: whereas the actual structure of DNA consisted of two helices running in opposite directions and laterally bonded by base pairs, no brain surgeon, without a high dose of psilocybin, had yet opened a skull and been treated to the multicoloured light show fabricated by neuroimaging, and so often reproduced on magazine covers, and deployed in the slide shows that accompanied lectures on every subject from oncology to impulse shopping. Pop Art brains made talks about violence or advertising, unconscious processing or political preferences, Alzheimer's or sexual arousal, look thoroughly scientific. The pictures had become so ubiquitous that students might soon demand them at a Jane Austen lecture, just as they might feel entitled to ketchup, mustard and mayonnaise at a hot dog stand. What part of the brain lights up when the reader first encounters

Mr Darcy and his odious pride? Can literary criticism afford to ignore what is happening to the reader's amygdala when Elizabeth Bennet rejects his first proposal? It is a truth universally acknowledged that any topic in search of a reputation for seriousness must be in want of neuroimaging.

But what was the real status of those vibrant snapshots? Apart from valuable information about its fixed anatomy, much of the excitement that came from making the brain visible had led to exaggerated inferences about what was going on in the mind, and indeed about what was going on in the brain beyond a certain level of complexity. Dynamically, they measured the blood-oxygen-level-dependent response (BOLD). The scans represented local activation based on statistical differences in BOLD signals. That was it; and the level of resolution of these computational artefacts depended on voxels – the 3-D equivalent of pixels. A voxel was minuscule from a human perspective, but from a neuron's point of view, it was a vast forest in which to remain undetected, nowhere near the level at which synapses, dendrites, axons and electro-chemical activity could be represented, let alone proved to be the cause of complex psychological states. In Lucy's situation, it was clearly beneficial to see the location and size of a tumour. Images of the brain revealed something about the brain, that much was clear, but to what extent they could reveal anything about the mind and the personality was much less clear. Not only was the brain not the mind, but an image of the brain was not the brain.

At the same time as her concern about neuroimaging had been stirred up by the way it had suddenly crashed into Lucy's life, Olivia was also hearing about it from her father, who had remained obsessed with the inadequacy of the *Very Short Introduction* to schizophrenia that he had been reading from on the day that Lucy told the Carrs about her tumour.

'It's full of claims about brain scans,' he complained, 'showing that the areas "associated" with hallucination light up when people are hallucinating or concluding that patients with schizophrenia "tend" to have a hippocampus and an amygdala that is "slightly" smaller than normal. People who believe this sort of high-tech phrenology are truly mad, but unlike the patients whose brains they scan, they don't seem to want to recover. There may be some justified scepticism about women suffering from Penis Envy, but Physics Envy is all too real: trying to build a machine big enough to remove psychological experience from mental illness. It's absurd!'

'The genetic correlations with schizophrenia are not convincing either,' said Olivia.

'It's open season when it comes to correlations,' said Martin. 'There's a parasite carried by cats, *Toxoplasma gondii*, which is more prevalent in people with bipolar disorder and schizophrenia than in control groups. Some people even think that Blake may have written "The Tyger" under the influence of his cat's toxoplasma.'

'Really?' said Olivia. 'It's amazing there isn't more visionary poetry, given the number of people who own cats.'

'Maybe we should write a joint paper about the role of cats and genes and scans and psychotherapy in the diagnosis and treatment of schizophrenia,' said Martin. 'I could write up some case studies and you could look into the genetics and neuroimaging.'

'Hang on,' said Olivia. 'I'm on holiday. Anyway, I'm not qualified to make the neuroimaging case. You could ask Ash, Lucy's friend; he's a neuroscientist as well as a medical doctor.'

'Excellent,' said Martin. 'A project! Schizophrenics are a hundred times more likely to kill themselves than ordinary people. If genes were the culprits, why has the scythe of natural selection not eliminated something so disabling?'

'Well, the true believers have an answer for that: the reason why there are so many feeble and widely dispersed correlations is that the big culprits have been eliminated by our hero Natural Selection.'

'So, in that story,' said Martin, 'schizophrenia used to be a much more genetic disease than it is now, but although it's becoming more common, it remains genetic – amazing, truly amazing.'

Although Olivia had parted from her father protesting that she wouldn't take on a project just yet, she was in fact tempted by the idea of working collaboratively after the long haul of writing alone. She thought about where she might start from. There was only a short passage mentioning schizophrenia in her book, but it showed that there were one hundred and twenty-eight genes in one hundred and eight loci associated with 'enduring psychosis', and most of the variants were also associated with bipolar disorder, attention deficit and autism. In the extreme case of 22q11.2 deletion syndrome there were one hundred and eighty clinical associations, of which schizophrenia was only one. When this immense scattering of tiny, ambiguous effects was swept together, the resulting pile of dust still only amounted to a meagre genetic difference between schizophrenia patients and control groups. Nevertheless, she wasn't going to commit to a joint paper today, despite her father's enthusiasm.

As she was going to see Lucy in the flat that Hunter had lent her, Olivia made only token preparations for going out. What she needed above all was a strong cup of coffee to ward off the listlessness and creeping headache and faint despair that seized control of her decaffeinated body after four or five hours. Perhaps she should have a scheduled withdrawal in Willow Cottage, with Francis bringing her black and then green and then white tea, while she thrashed and sweated and mumbled, strapped to the bed in a locked room.

When she came through from the kitchen to the living room carrying a gigantic mug, she found Martin sitting in the comfortable old armchair with crushed springs, where she had been intending to install herself. He was dressed in one of his three mid-grey work suits, a V-necked sweater and a woollen tie. It was a psychological rather than a sartorial outfit, designed to reassure his patients that he was indeed a professional man of a certain age, who dressed respectably without having the slightest interest in expressing himself through his clothes. He was interested in what the patient had to tell him, not in telling them anything about himself. Knowing the range of his wardrobe, Olivia was always impressed by the consummate neutrality of these outfits. She imagined that spies must be taught to dress in a similar way, so that nobody could remember them.

'Hi, Dad,' she said, settling down on the sofa opposite him.

'How are you, darling?' said Martin.

'Oh, I've just been lolling about,' said Olivia, 'and I'm off to see Lucy in a moment.'

'Dear Lucy,' said Martin. 'How is she bearing up?'

'I'll know more after dinner,' said Olivia. 'She's being very brave, but there's no need to be very brave unless you're very frightened, which of course she is.'

'Of course,' said Martin. 'There's a limit to the benefits of stoicism. I'm sure it'll be a great help to her seeing you.'

'I hope so,' said Olivia, taking her first gulp of coffee. 'On the upside, she seems to be on better terms with her boss.'

'Oh good,' said Martin, pausing briefly. 'I've been thinking about our joint paper.'

'I'm on holiday!' Olivia interrupted him.

'We could write it at a holiday pace,' said Martin. 'I still have to see my patients and I would have to research and write up case studies.'

'Ah, yes, the anecdotal end of science,' Olivia teased him.

'Well,' said Martin, 'what is a theory, after all, except an incredibly stable anecdote? And what is a fact, except an incredibly stable theory?'

'Luckily, I'm about to leave for dinner,' she said, laughing, 'and I don't have to answer that question.'

She got up and kissed her father on the forehead.

'Goodnight, darling,' he said. 'Give my love to Lucy.'

'I will.'

11

By the time he arrived back in California, Hunter was experiencing peripheral hallucinations, not a full-blown usurpation of the visual field, but the constant flicker of mistaken identities on the edge of his vision. The shadows of camels and axe murderers thrown up by the headlights on the hillsides and the rocks, as Raoul drove him back from Carmel to *Apocalypse Now*, were less disturbing than the improbable mouse that had just scurried across the empty seat beside him and disappeared when he turned to confront it. He had been to New York, Oxford, London, Assisi, Paris, London and New York again and was now, just ten days later, back on the West Coast. He had powered on because there were so many meetings, decisions, time zones and acquisitions, and so much pressure to be charming or ball-breaking, as the occasion required, that sleep had been sent to the back of the line again and again. Bullying his body with prescription medication made each collapse more brutal than the last. On the flight from New York, he felt as if a mafia enforcer had thrown him out of a helicopter into a rat-infested landfill site, among shards of broken china and twisted metal, cushioned only by illegal hospital waste and bulging diapers. It was a feeling he was prepared to do almost anything to change. He definitely had a problem accepting any form of disappointment, and he had made the stupid decision to pop another pill. Now he was paying the price, not only with hallucinations of scuttling mice, but also with the hordes of barbarian thoughts pouring through the undefended gates of his editorial intelligence and vandalising even the most basic concepts until they looked unintelligible and menacing.

Driving along Route One was reminding him of the sense of crisis about motion he had first felt when he was fourteen, sitting in the back of his father's car, returning to London on a Sunday afternoon. He had been half-listening to his ridiculous, embarrassing parents as they analysed the social currents of their deadly weekend in a draughty English house, with most of its rooms closed and the rest packed with the pompous caricatures who had stood between him and a cool weekend cruising around Camden Lock with his school friends from Westminster. British motorways in those days were usually down to one lane, making it marginally quicker to walk back to London, but on this occasion, due to some miscalculation at the Ministry of Transport, all three lanes were fully operational, and the family car was hurtling through the rain well above the speed limit. Like someone concentrating on a single instrument in the orchestra, Hunter tuned out from his parents' tedious post-mortem and focused on the sticky sound of the tyres clinging to the wet road. In the midst of this self-imposed soundtrack, he found himself suddenly overwhelmed by the paradox that his body was immobile in the back seat and at the same time rushing along at ninety miles an hour. What was really going on? He moved his hand away from the direction of travel and wondered whether he was slowing down its journey but decided that it didn't have a journey separate from the rest of his body or, more precisely, separate from itself. Everything was at rest relative to itself: his body, the car, the Earth, the Sun; they only achieved motion from their relation to something else: his body to the car, the car to the Earth, the Earth to the Sun, and, of course, the other way around and in relation to all other objects. His body, isolated from any other reference point, was simply always where it was, whether he was diving off a cliff, sitting on a plane or dead. On the one hand, everything was moving: waves undulating, blood circulating, particles thrown or pulled by one force or another, planets spinning, stars erupting, the Andromeda galaxy racing towards the Milky Way at a quarter of a million miles an hour; but on the other hand, everything was at rest relative to itself, just being where it was. The two rival pictures seemed to be throttling him, with both their thumbs pressing on his windpipe.

'Stop the car!' he shouted.

'Excuse me, Mr Sterling, you need to stop here?' asked Raoul.

'No, no, sorry Raoul, I was just remembering a story.'

'No problem, Mr Sterling,' said Raoul, relieved not to have to stop on the cliff edge of a hairpin bend.

After a lot of protests from his parents and a lot of screaming from him, his father had drawn over to the side of the road, letting Hunter lurch outside and pace along the hard shoulder, with the traffic rushing by dangerously close, trying to see if he could make any difference to his confusion by penetrating space with his own motive force, but although he eventually calmed down and got back resentfully into the car, he knew that it was futile and that there was something unresolved lurking at the root of his panic, something he simply tried to ignore from then on. Hunter could feel it again right now; the memory was so vivid that it had managed to replicate that old British motorway angst from thirty-four years ago. If anything, it had gotten worse. He had learnt more about science since then, especially from Saul and his other advisers during the two years they had been collaborating on *Digitas* acquisitions, but there was still no way of escaping his root confusion; in fact it had grown worse as he became more knowledgeable. The tension could only be resolved if he could conceptualise absolute motion, motion relative to nothing else. That, however, could only exist in absolute space, a vacuum containing an immaterial grid of mathematical coordinates. And how would *that* be measured, except by the very thing he was trying to measure in the first place: the motion of a solitary particle, not subject to any forces – since gravity, for instance, would require another massive object – from one coordinate to another, along a grid that itself could only be measured by motion, since it needed to stretch in at least two directions in order to exist? Jesus, he really needed some rest.

This latest trip may have been a mind-fuck, but it had been a business bonanza. Saul had beaten the competition by securing the new ceramic armour patented by a brilliant French inventor. It was not only stronger and lighter than other ceramic armours, with a unique visor which was a transparent version of the same material, but the suit also drew inspiration from snakeskin to create a set of overlapping scales that provided total flexibility. A filter system ensured protection against chemical and biological weapons. Once you were inside that armour, the only thing you could die from was a heart attack, a stroke, an aneurysm, a pre-existing condition or a systems failure.

Assisi had been fantastic as well. Poverty, chastity and obedience were not Hunter's special areas of interest; in fact, chastity was the last thing he had on his mind, especially when it came to Lucy, who he was increasingly fascinated by. In any case, despite his contempt for these three phoney virtues, he could see that Catholics, a captive market of 1.2 billion consumers, really got off on the Assisi pilgrimage deal. St Francis had been Italy's patron saint since 1939, a tough year to start a tough job, but he was also a global icon of authenticity and exceptionalism, a Catholic who wanted to be a Christian; not a politician, a murderer, a paedophile or an art collector, but a Christian. Powerful message. As to the Blessed Fra Domenico, himself a Franciscan contemplative, living in a hut in the woods near St Francis's old hermitage, he was a logistical pain in the ass, who had taken a vow to remain on a silent retreat, forcing Saul's team to get a scanner, a generator and a whole bunch of special equipment down leafy slopes, outcrops of rock and rutted paths, to his fucking hut in the woods. If anybody ever doubted that humility was the ultimate arrogance, they should drop in on the Blessed Fra Domenico, but when they finally scanned him, he turned out to be an El Dorado of data that was going to take *Brainwaves* to another level. 'BFD', as the team took to calling him, had been on retreat for thirty years and had a quotation from St Anthony of Padua over the door of his hut which turned out to mean, 'Contemplation is more precious than all works, and nothing else desirable can compare to it.' Father Guido, the kindly Abbot in charge of the contemplative division of the Franciscan Order, had eventually been persuaded that he would be doing God's work by agreeing to get BFD into the test tube to submit to an hour's scanning, allowing the faithful to witness the cerebral stigmata of such a prodigious ascetic discipline. What blew everybody's minds when they saw the scans was that BFD's language-processing centres were off the charts. The dual pathways connecting the auditory cortex to the frontal lobes were like the Yangtze and the Ganges in full flood.

'Holy shit,' said Saul, 'look at that middle temporal gyrus!'

Some people might think that thirty years of silence would generate such a harrowing sense of loneliness that the poor man talked to himself the whole time, or that the transition from the simple pallet bed of his sanctuary to the thudding and throbbing cacophony of the scanner had induced a panic attack and BFD was screaming silently in order not to break his vow, but Father Guido, pointing to the beatific smile on the friar's face as he slid into the inferno of claustrophobic technology, had another explanation, which was definitely the one they were going to put on the *Capo Santo* version of Happy Helmets, aimed at the Catholic market: 'It is very simple,' said the bespectacled Abbot, in his rustic Italian accent, 'ordinary people speak to each other for five or maybe ten hours a day about a variety of mundane concerns, but Domenico, who has devoted his entire life to prayer, speaks for twenty-four hours a day to God about the most profound questions of the universe. He even prays while he sleeps! Here is the scientific proof of a truly miraculous level of spiritual attainment!'

'Incredible,' said Saul, 'just incredible; that dopamine pathway must be humming. Go, Baby, go! His nucleus accumbens is giving him an Olympic Gold every few seconds. If we could replicate the trans-cranial stimulation loop between these different areas,' he said, sweeping his excited hand over the entire polychrome image on the screen, and into the woods beyond, 'we are going to have some very happy customers!'

Saul had also been excited by Hunter's proposed acquisition of the Oxford virtual reality app. He totally got that it would provide a narrative arc for the next-level *Brainwaves* consumer, who didn't just want the bliss, but some spiritual and intellectual entertainment along the way, labouring through the jeering streets wearing the crown of thorns; sitting under the spreading Bodhi Tree in Bodhgaya; joining the throbbing orange mass following the juggernauts that dragged a marigold-strewn statue of the elephant-headed Ganesh; vultures circling above Zoroastrian towers of silence, and all the rest of it, *The Varieties of Religious Experience* niche within the Happy Helmets range.

Thank god, he was almost home. Hunter could see the lights and the outline of the house against the crest of the hill and felt immense relief at the prospect of dissolving into sleep in his own bed, after the luxurious but shattering vagabondage of the last ten days. His apartments in New York and London didn't feel like home; *Apocalypse Now* was home. Once he arrived, he hurried away from his solicitous staff to the inner den, the ultimate sanctuary: a red lacquered sitting room with no windows, adjacent to his suite of private rooms, which occupied half the Pacific side of the first floor. He washed down his sleeping pills with some bourbon. After pouring himself another shot, he placed his glass on the low brushed-steel table in front of him, sank back into the soft turquoise leather of an art deco sofa, puffed out his cheeks theatrically, to signal to himself that he had made it, even if he hadn't shaken off his sense of encroaching insanity. He was intending to have a word with Jade while the sedatives took effect, but instead found himself drawn into the brilliant surface of the golden screen in front of him, an exquisite sixteenth-century Japanese painting of a gnarled pine branch on a ledge of rock, its swirling bark and dark needles reaching into a gold-leaf canyon of indeterminate depth. Hanging opposite this masterpiece by Tōhaku was a video screen of exactly the same size, on which an artist had made an animated version of Hokusai's famous wave, programmed to curl and crash, in slow motion, over the course of fifty minutes. When Hunter was in California, he could stretch out comfortably on the second sofa of the pair, opposite the one he was now on, and turn on the Hokusai video by remote control, so that it completed its cycle at exactly the moment that his daily conference call with his two New York psychotherapists came to an end.

Despite the intense silence and the therapeutic associations of this deeply enclosed, studied and controlled space, not to mention what should have been the calming effects of the bourbon, his mind was still racing, and still disintegrating under the pressure of cumulative sleep-privation. If only Lucy were waiting for him next door, curled up naked in his bed, perhaps he would have found some peace. As well as feeling strongly attracted to her, and being impressed from the start by her agile and forceful mind, since their confusingly sincere dinner on his return visit to London the other day, when his combative personality had fallen away, without any forethought, and she had opened up to him, without making too much of it, about her fucked-up background, he found himself wanting to look after her as well. Her particular combination of strength and fragility had elicited a sense of tenderness he hadn't even known he could feel. More strength might have aroused his competitiveness and more fragility would have bored him. He normally delegated his somewhat vague feelings of compassion to his chequebook, but this new feeling seemed to have taken up a stubborn residence in his heart and somehow, by making room for the idea that he might look after her, he had created the longing for her to look after him right now – while he was at his most fragile. Why wasn't she here? He was going to die if he didn't have her – although, to be fair, he was going to die even if he did have her.

The brutal fact was that she was not next door, at the moment, and although he was in an allegedly safe setting, his mind seemed hell-bent on making him feel even more threatened than ever by a primitive terror of his surroundings. Added to the incomprehensibility of motion that had afflicted him in the car, now that he was at rest, he was being persecuted by the incomprehensibility of space. When an object, like the steel table in front of him, occupied a space, did the space get annihilated by the solidity of the mass? Or was it just denser space? Or was it a dented space, in the way that all massive objects dent the fabric of space-time. The more massive they are the deeper the hole they make, ultimately a black hole, sucking everything into itself. But the mass was itself mainly made up of space, everybody knew *that*. On the scale where the nucleus of the atom was the size of a marble, the electron was the width of a human hair two miles away from the marble, but matter must be irreducibly dense, at least in the nucleus itself, and so what happened to space in that place? If matter deleted space by moving into it, did the space get reborn when matter moved out again? Was space popping in and out of existence, as matter occupied it and then set it free? He tapped Saul's name on the screen of his phone, but the call went straight to voicemail.

'Hi, Saul, I know it's late, but I'm worried about some things I need you to clear up for me. Like, you know the way we think the house is the walls and the roof,' said Hunter, 'but we live in the space contained by the walls and roof – I have a Rachel Whiteread: she solidifies the empty space and deletes the containers, she plays with all that – and in this Tōhaku, in front of me in the den, the branch is like the nearby wall of a house and those cloudy mountaintops in the distance are the broken parapets that mark the outer edge, and in between them is the empty space that is the true subject of the painting. But, without getting into art, just staying with the physics, and without getting into the quantum vacuum that's fizzing with potential, or the mind-fuck of non-locality, or not being certain where the particle is located, or leptons and the whole subatomic thing, or neutrinos shooting through the Earth, totally unimpressed by the fields or charges or density, blah-blah-blah-blah-blah, forgetting all of *that*, and sticking with *this*,' said Hunter, leaning forward and holding the phone next to his fist as he thumped the steel table, 'can you tell me exactly what the relationship is between matter and space? Is this a fucking solid object, Saul? Call me back! Give me a clear answer, because if physics doesn't have clarity about the most basic concepts that it deploys, maybe I should … I mean, okay, so under ordinary conditions we can treat a tightly bound lattice of atoms as solid, as having extension and impenetrability: steel can crash into space, but not the other way around, right? So, what I want to know, what I *need* to know, is this: when they put this steel table into this room, what happened to the space that used to be *in the space* that the steel table is now in. I mean ...' Hunter broke off abruptly.

'Saul? Saul? My muscles are cramping. This is something that sometimes happens. Saul? Fuck. Saul?'

Hunter felt a tightening in his arms and shoulders and chest muscles. That last pill on the plane might have been a symptom of his immaturity, but now that he was about to die, he really-really got it and was truly-truly sorry and promised that, if he was allowed to survive, he would never do it again. Fuck, this was not part of the plan. Raoul was used to finding plenty of empty bottles and a whole lot of incriminating drug paraphernalia, and he was paid enough to keep quiet about it, but a corpse would definitely test his discretion and loyalty beyond breaking point. As he fell sideways in the direction of his jacket, Hunter started to imagine the disastrous newspaper coverage: *Apocalypse at Apocalypse Now. Trusted family butler, Raoul Dominguez, commented, 'Señor Sterling, may he rest in peace, was a truly great man, but I tell you, when it came to narcotics, the guy was like a pig in a trough.'*

Hunter forced the rigid muscles to inch his right arm towards his jacket. His hand, which intermittently convulsed into an agonising, clutching claw, finally insinuated itself into the breast pocket. He could feel his chest growing more constricted and a pain climbing up his left arm and he knew that he was about to be cut down by a well-deserved heart attack. With a final gesture of defiance, he worked the pill box out of the pocket and managed to press the little button on its side. The lid sprung open and he tipped the contents on to the sofa. Scattered among the multicoloured pills were the two round pink pills he needed, maximum strength beta blockers that might bring his muscles and his hypertension under control. Normally, one would be enough to handle a hostile cross-examination for crimes against humanity on primetime television, but this was an emergency and so he pushed both into his mouth and ground them up with his teeth to accelerate the effect. He then lay motionless, making frantic deals with fate to negotiate his survival. He must get Jade to clear his schedule and book him into his favourite room at Nuova Vita Ranch. No more pills and powders – at least no more stimulants; natural sleep was a rumour he refused to believe in – and when he got out, gallons of herbal tea and fresh vegetable juice, with only a little alcohol on special occasions.

Half an hour later, half-reassured that he was not going to die immediately, he sat up and finished his second shot of bourbon. He wished Saul had picked up. He had questions about matter and space that he needed answered by someone who knew what he was talking about. For instance, thought Hunter, even now unable to crush his undermining speculations completely, there wasn't supposed to be any space before the Big Bang, so what had that super-hot singularity expanded *into*? It made space as it expanded, it made space with matter in motion, it came into existence by having an edge that was not in the same place as its origin: by being relative. Of course! He could ring Lucy. She might be able to help, and it was deep into the working day in the UK, and anyhow it would be great to have an excuse to talk to lovely Lucy.

Her phone, like Saul's, went straight to voicemail. 'Fuck!' he shouted, ending the call, not sure whether he had shouted 'Fuck' before or after ending it. Whatever. He was going to give a huge Christmas bonus to someone who could tell him what space and matter and motion were in themselves, their intrinsic nature and not just their mathematical relationships to each other, but now perhaps the time had come to get a little rest, to lay some coins on the eyelids of the nearly dead, to invest in a long and dreamless sleep, to weave his frayed nerves back into cables strong enough to carry the surging current, the sheer juice of being Hunter Sterling. With a show of belated puritanism, he poured himself a glass of his own carbon-filtered water – according to his nutritionist, most mineral water was pure poison. With the downers he had taken, he knew that he could achieve his ideal, which was to wake up late tomorrow afternoon, fully refreshed and ready for the next set of challenges with which he packed his life, like a man loading more and more brushwood on to a camp fire to keep the hyenas of boredom and triviality at bay. His fear of a heart attack, psychosis and the other discouraging footnotes to his gargantuan lifestyle was trivial compared to his horror at the idea of doing anything ordinary.

Experience had taught him that eighteen hours of heavily drugged sleep could deforest his memory overnight, and he wanted to focus one more time on what it was, or more economically, on what it *wasn't,* that had disturbed him about the world view that had shot past the window of his mental bullet train over the last few hours of reflection, and perhaps record a memo for Jade to type up tomorrow.

He must get to his bed, though, before he passed out. After swaying down the corridor, Hunter made it into his bedroom, locking the outer door and then closing a further soundproof door behind him. He pressed the button to bring down the steel shutters and, clumsily peeling off his clothes, fell on to the bed and insinuated himself under the covers. He must try to connect with Jade before it was too late.

'Jade?' said Hunter, trying to keep his eyes open while he croaked into the phone next to him on the pillow.

'Hey, Hunter!'

'Did I wake you?'

'No, it's seven o'clock in the morning. I'm already up working with the legal team in Paris. That acquisition you made is amazing, Hunter. You're amazing.'

'You think so?'

'Everybody thinks so,' said Jade.

Hunter's eyelids closed and he felt himself swooning into unconsciousness, but he made one last effort.

'You've gotta take a memo ...' he gasped, forcing his eyes open. 'Space ... matter, what is it? Space ... and also motion – and fields: are they halfway between space and matter? I mean ...'

'Hunter?'

'Is anything solid?' whispered Hunter.

'Hunter, I've taken some notes,' said Jade, 'and they sound really interesting to me, but you have to get some rest now. You've been working so hard.'

'At rest,' said Hunter, 'or in motion … and, Jade, book me into Nuova Vita … and block out the first week in May for a *Digitas* party at *Plein Soleil*.'

'Great, that'll flow beautifully into Cannes,' said Jade. 'Hunter? Hello? Hunter, don't forget to switch off your phone!'

'Oh, yeah, thanks,' sighed Hunter, just managing to shut it down in time.

12

Olivia was chopping the vegetables for the soup that Francis was going to make for lunch. They had fallen into a rhythm of collaboration as she grew more familiar with the house, no longer searching for the sieve or the peppercorns, or wondering where to fetch the logs when the basket was empty. It was hard to keep her concentration as she diced the carrots; she kept thinking about the weekend she had spent in London helping Lucy through her 'needle biopsy'. Lucy was now asleep on the sofa next door, trying to recover from the operation in a twilight of painkillers and anaesthetic. Olivia was haunted by yesterday's drive from the hospital and the memory of Lucy trying to protect herself from the rapid-fire seizures induced by the sunlight darting into the car. At one point, they had been forced to draw over to a shady spot to give her a break. For the rest of the drive, Lucy kept her hands pressed tightly over her eyes to block out the shafts of light. When she arrived at the cottage, Francis had embraced her for rather longer than Olivia would have liked, and then she had gone straight to bed, engulfed by seizure-saturated exhaustion.

Preparations for the surgery had started on Friday afternoon. Olivia joined Lucy in a gloomy hospital room overlooking a brick wall. Its only decoration was an artistic black and white photograph of a lamp-post in the square outside, hung there, presumably, as compensation for not having one of the rooms across the corridor which enjoyed a view of the lamp-post itself.

'They're just going to drill a little hole in my skull and take a sample with a needle,' said Lucy, unpacking her pyjamas and a soft down pillow she had brought from home. 'There's a less than one per cent chance of death from this procedure, and I have huge confidence in Mr McEwan's skill with the drill. Also—'

Lucy's deluge of anxiety was interrupted by a knock on the door. A friendly Filipino nurse came in to manacle a plastic identity tag to Lucy's wrist and ask her to wash her hair before the doctor came to shave her.

'Shave me?'

'Yes, the doctor will explain,' he said, handing Lucy a bottle of bright red Hibiscrub.

Soon enough, a young doctor came in carrying a Ziploc bag. She spent much of the first few minutes managing her own mane of glossy brown hair, tossing it from side to side and pushing thick cables of unruly abundance out of her eyes and behind her ears, but eventually she extracted a disposable Bic razor from the bag and started shaving six patches on Lucy's skull, each about the size of a two-pound coin. As she did her work, she threw thin strands of Lucy's bright blonde hair into a yellow metal bin covered with warnings about how to dispose appropriately of toxic waste and sharp objects. She then placed a small, sticky, white plastic doughnut on each shaved patch as well as across Lucy's forehead and temples, explaining that they were needed to make the pre-op MRI more precise and to generate a 3D model of the tumour. That model would help Mr McEwan's computer-guided needle to take the best sample with the least risk. Using a black permanent marker, she then drew a circle around the position of all the fiducials, as they turned out to be called, with a black dot at its hollow centre, in case any of them fell off in the turbulent hours ahead.

After the doctor left the room, Lucy stood in front of the mirror, in her striped silk pyjamas, and started to cry. 'It's not that I look ugly,' she said, 'although I do. It's just that I left home looking like a healthy woman in her mid-thirties, with no obvious problems; and now I look like a cancer patient.'

Olivia went over to comfort Lucy, who was already wiping away her tears, but she was interrupted by another doctor who swung open the door, knocking on it as it started to close behind her. She wore black slacks and a sleeveless sweater. A big lumpy bag hanging from one of her shoulders forced her into a posture that cried out for medical intervention.

'Hi. I'm Lucy,' she said. 'No, sorry! I mean, *you're* Lucy; I'm Victoria,' she laughed, as if this kind of confusion was just one of the unavoidable hazards of working in a neurological hospital. 'I'm part of Mr McEwan's team. We'll be performing the surgery on you tomorrow.'

'I'm Lucy,' said Lucy lucidly. 'Pleased to meet you.'

'You will have several options to discuss tomorrow with Mr McEwan,' Lucy-Victoria began.

'Will I?' asked Lucy. 'What do you mean exactly?'

'Mr McEwan will explain everything to you tomorrow. But we might want to open up a bigger piece of your skull to give us more options.'

Lucy-Victoria made a gesture reminiscent of an obsequious extra in a costume drama doffing his cap at a passing coach.

'More options? For what?' said Lucy, 'I thought I was having a needle biopsy.'

Another doctor, a young man in scrubs, swung into the room and said that he was also part of the team.

'Well,' Lucy-Victoria persisted, 'we might want to test some functional areas. It's good to map the brain, you know.'

'Also, it might mean that we can take more samples of the tumour; some may be higher grade than others,' said the newcomer.

'But isn't that associated with a much higher risk?' asked Lucy. 'Mr McEwan has been emphatic about what a sensitive area he has to navigate in order to get to the tumour.'

'As I said, Mr McEwan will be able to go through all the details with you in the morning.'

'You mean right before I'm being wheeled into surgery? Will I still be able to be awake during the procedure?'

'Yes. You will have all the options available to you.'

'Actually, the Awake Team isn't available on Saturdays,' said the other doctor.

'You're absolutely right,' said Lucy-Victoria, 'thank you for reminding me. But, apart from that, all other options are available.'

And with that enormous and disconcerting promise, the two team members left the room, eager to get home through the thickening Friday traffic.

'Jesus,' said Lucy, staring at Olivia incredulously.

Olivia shook her head sympathetically. 'I'm sure McEwan will clarify everything tomorrow.'

She hurried towards the consolations of gossip.

'I meant to tell you that Charlie has got permission to see you,' said Olivia, 'so that should cheer you up.'

Olivia knew from her brother that it had not been easy for him to make the visit, despite its blatantly compassionate nature. Lucy occupied a place of special jealousy in his girlfriend Lesley's pantheon of rivals. She suspected that Lucy was 'the real love of Charlie's life' and that she was just 'good wife material' – Lesley was one of those people who thought that originality consisted of a fluent and knowing use of cliché, vigorously imprisoned with inverted commas to make sure it couldn't escape the further boredom of being vaguely ironic. Although she was right about Charlie's nostalgia for Lucy, Olivia fervently hoped that she was wrong about being 'good wife material' for her brother.

'Oh, great,' said Lucy, reaching for her bag and beginning to rummage for the woollen cap she had been intending to keep for after the operation.

There was a knock on the door. Olivia and Lucy braced themselves for the trauma of another medical briefing, but it turned out to be Charlie, bearing a bottle of the same champagne he had drunk with Lucy on their first anniversary when they were still undergraduates. It was a romantic, or at least a sentimental gesture, which touched Lucy, who hadn't seen him in a long time, and wanted to be reassured that the palace coup being mounted by her brain had done nothing to reduce his passionate admiration for her mind and body, and that he would stand beside her in defending them. She had pulled her woollen cap down to her eyebrows and over her ears and looked as if she was about to set off for a walk on a frosty morning. Charlie extracted some flimsy plastic cups from a dispenser by the sink and poured the champagne.

'I associate these cups with urine samples,' he said. 'It's good to see them playing a more primary role.'

'Upstream,' said Lucy.

'Exactly,' said Charlie.

'You missed your vocation as a sommelier,' said Olivia, 'sweet-talking people into enjoying their wine even more than they would anyway.'

Lucy tried to wrap up the rough, sharp edges of the day with layers of description, as anyone would, but only succeeded in provoking an animated discussion, typical of the Carr family, about the psychopathy of surgeons; the most audacious and godlike healers, who were also the only group of people encouraged to slice open human bodies, saw off limbs, cut out flesh, remove organs and excise brain tissue, operating at the edge of paralysis, stroke and haemorrhage. It was a profession that seemed to fuse compassion and brutality, without having to reveal which was the dominant impulse, as long as both were accompanied by a high degree of precision.

'Can I point out that I'm not finding it comforting to have my surgeon compared to a serial killer?' said Lucy, and because they were all tipsy and anxious and tense, they burst out laughing, and for a moment it was like it had so often been, twelve or fifteen years ago, when the three of them had sat in the King's Arms, laughing about a ridiculous tutorial or a disastrous night out.

When Olivia finally stopped preparing lunch, she went upstairs to have a shower, but found Francis already in the bathroom, shaving, shirtless, half his face covered in foam, the other already done.

'How come I've managed to chop eight different kinds of vegetables and you've only managed to shave half your face?' she asked, kissing him on the shoulder.

'The early days were just designed to rope you in,' said Francis. 'Next weekend I'll still be in bed when you come up from the kitchen.'

'That'll be nice,' said Olivia, peeling off her sweater.

Lucy lay on the sofa, curled up and still, like a wounded animal, staring at the fire in Francis's grate, or more precisely, at the mound of ash on which it smouldered. She couldn't think of a time when she wouldn't have sprung up and loaded more wood on to the fire-gouged logs decaying radiantly in front of her, but in her current state, it was absurd to imagine doing anything so strenuous and affirmative. Fire, like cancer, destroyed its host and by doing so, led to its own extinction. Couldn't she come to a deal with her tumour that allowed them both to keep going, like coming to an 'accommodation' with a blackmailer? The tumour had found accommodation in her brain without asking her, but now it was time to negotiate. The few people she had told about her medical difficulties had all at some point generalised about death, volunteering that they might be run over later that afternoon, but it was not as if she had renounced the opportunity to have a fatal accident by getting cancer. Everybody had a question mark hanging over their head; she had an additional one lodged inside it.

Whatever combination of psychological qualities lay behind Mr McEwan's calling, Lucy had grown to like him. He had popped in to say that the biopsy had gone 'perfectly'. She didn't labour the point that she could hardly walk but did mention that her stitches were throbbing painfully. This, it turned out, was 'perfectly normal', due to the tightness of the skin on the skull, which meant that the flaps made by the incision around the drill hole had to be sewn back robustly with the strongest thread.

Today she had no anecdotes to wrap around her miseries, just splashes of discrete memory: circulation socks, operation gown, baggy hospital knickers; when she asked the anaesthetist if anaesthetic was dangerous, he countered by asking her if she had ever crossed the road. Yes, there was no denying it, she had crossed the road. 'Well, that's more dangerous!' he said triumphantly, getting up, tripping over the neighbouring chair, and almost falling over, without any comment or discernible sense of irony. Perhaps he wanted to show that almost everything was more dangerous than anaesthetic and she was lucky to be having a break from a hazardous world. Due to a 'traffic jam' around the pre-op room, she had to be put to sleep in the operating theatre itself. Looking around, she saw a dark green piece of medical equipment that reminded her of a butcher's block.

'Is that where you are going to put me after I've gone to sleep?'

'Yes,' said the nurse. 'It's really important that your head doesn't move, even a millimetre, during the procedure. The margins are tiny – so we have to clamp your head using that equipment.'

Horrified by that thought as she went under; waking up shaking with cold, her teeth chattering; holding back tears of gratitude as nurses rushed over with heated blankets. The pause between deciding to make sure and then making sure she could still move her arms and legs.

It was as if she had woken from fifty years of sleep rather than two hours of surgery and had been mysteriously catapulted into decrepitude, with wrists and ankles that might snap, a body that might bruise and a skull that might crack with only the flimsiest pretext. On the morning of her departure, she took a shower, although she was not allowed to wash her hair for a week and had to wear a cap. In the shower, the bottle of gel slipped from her hand and triggered a seizure as it thumped and clattered around the floor. She tried to stay calm and not to pull the red emergency cord, but afterwards, when she mentioned the incident to the registrar, he said it was 'perfectly normal' for her seizure-threshold to go down after surgery. On the terrifying drive to Howorth, his prediction was fulfilled, although it was the most imperfectly normal drive of her life.

After waking up today, she had hobbled over to the window and drawn open the curtains, immediately shielding her eyes from the brilliance of an immaculate winter's day of frosted fields and ice-coated puddles gleaming under a cloudless sky; bright and still and promising, like a silver flute lying on a page of music. She stood there for a while, dull and damaged, and frightened of the light, with her right leg feeling twice as heavy as the other one.

When she lowered herself apprehensively down the steep staircase, without any sensation in her right foot, she either banged it down emphatically or hesitated above the step, unsure how far away it was. Her pallid cheerfulness over breakfast was compromised by an obsessive exploration of the thick bandage on her head. Unable to see the wound, she could only pat and stroke it again and again with the tips of her fingers, mapping its soreness and its size. Underneath the thick stitches was the hole that Mr McEwan had drilled. Before the operation, he told her that he still planned to do a needle biopsy, but that he would like to make the hole larger to give him more angles of approach. Since the tumour was wrapped in so much functional tissue, he wanted to be able to try alternative routes to 'the hot spot' he needed to sample, without having to drill additional holes.

Lucy opened her eyes wearily, recognised the fireplace, and realised that she had half drifted off again.

'Oh, hi,' she said.

'Hi, darling,' said Olivia. 'I didn't want to disturb you.'

'Oh, I'm just drifting in and out.'

'Is there anything I can get you?'

'A new brain,' said Lucy.

'Let me just check if we've got one in the freezer,' said Olivia.

Before Lucy had time to abandon, continue or complete their brain sketch, the thrum of an approaching helicopter became audible. Its whirring engine and chopping blades grew louder until, slow and deafening and low, it thundered over the roof of Francis's cottage and receded on the other side.

'What the hell?' said Olivia, running to the cottage door to see what was going on.

Lucy felt the familiar tensing and tingling of a seizure grabbing at her leg.

'Hi, Lucy,' said Francis, hurrying through the room. 'I've just got to check this out. I'll be back in a moment. Nobody is allowed to land a helicopter here.'

Lucy decided to wait for the seizure to pass without mentioning it to anyone. She could still hear the helicopter hovering somewhere nearby. Then its blades started slowing down and, with a final high whirr, came to a halt. The disturbing impact of the seizures was not diminished by their familiarity: whatever triggered them, they always triggered the thought that she was declining rapidly. When this episode passed, she felt yet more depleted and curled up still more tightly on the sofa, with a cushion between her knees and her eyes closed. She didn't react to the opening of the cottage door; she would find out soon enough why a helicopter had throbbed and sliced the air over the cottage roof and sent its Doppler sound waves through her volatile body.

'Hey, Lucy, how's it going?'

Lucy's eyes clicked open. What on earth was Hunter doing here? She made an effort to sit up.

'Oh, hi, Hunter,' she managed to say, leaning up on one elbow, the base camp for her assault on the summit of an upright position. 'What a surprise. How on earth did you find me?'

'I did some detective work when I saw you were on sick leave and came down as fast as I could. It seems my helicopter upset some Stone Age ponies, which I'm very contrite about, but I had to see how you were doing.'

Finally sitting upright, Lucy saw Francis staggering through to the kitchen with a hamper. She could tell that he was trying to calm down from his fury at Hunter's cavalier arrival.

'I've brought us a few things,' said Hunter. 'Some lunch, which I've given to your host ...'

'Francis,' said Lucy.

Hunter came and sat beside her on the sofa and took one of her hands in his.

'We're going to look after you,' he said, 'and you're going to get better.'

'Thank you,' she murmured, feeling the conviction in his words. He seemed more relaxed and refreshed than she'd ever seen him before.

Olivia came in from the kitchen.

'Well, Hunter, that's definitely the biggest tin of caviar I've ever seen,' she said, raising an eyebrow. 'Thanks so much. We've put the vegetable soup back in the fridge and warmed the blinis. The vodka has stayed extremely cold in that special pouch of yours, although I don't know how many takers you're going to have for vodka shots on a Monday morning.'

'We'll definitely have to toast Lucy's health,' said Hunter.

'That's true,' said Olivia, 'but Lucy can't drink for the moment, Francis is going to meet some bird-ringers this afternoon, and I'm trying to do some research for a paper I'm writing, so we can't get *blind* drunk.'

'Not on one bottle,' said Hunter with a burst of laughter, 'that's for sure.'

As they all sat at Francis's kitchen table, loading blinis with toppling mounds of sour cream and caviar, Hunter somehow persuaded them that Lucy's health was not the only reason to knock back a shot of vodka. His acquisition of the remaining shares of *YouGenetics* provoked another toast and, when he found out about Olivia's old antagonism with Bill Moorhead, he insisted that they must raise a glass 'To the downfall of pompous men and false friends!'

'So, what are you writing your paper on, Olivia?' asked Hunter.

'Oh, I'm working on a paper about schizophrenia, with my father, Martin Carr. He's a psychoanalyst. I'm looking into the genetics, while he's writing up some case studies. And we're also trying to get a neuroscientist on board.'

'What's the lowdown?' said Hunter.

'Well,' said Olivia, 'briefly, there's an impressive list of environmental stresses correlated with schizophrenia: war, bullying, the early death of a parent, physical and sexual abuse, migration, deracination, racism, and so on. They're strongly associated with schizophrenia on their own, or possibly in combination with a multitude of marginally implicated genes, but there's no evidence that the genes on their own can cause schizophrenia. Also, even if genetic expressions are switched on or off by stresses, the results would still shed only a hazy light on the question of inheritability since many of the mutations in schizophrenics are "de novo", occurring for the first time in that person and, therefore, by definition, not inherited.'

'What about twin studies?' said Hunter. 'Aren't they the gold standard for a lot of this genetic analysis?'

'They're often treated that way,' said Olivia, 'but lots of clinical psychologists, like my brother Charlie, question the Equal Environment Assumption on which they rest. They attribute outcomes to purely genetic causes by ignoring favouritism, scapegoating, imposed narratives and, in the case of identical twins, the effects of often being dressed in the same clothes, being in the same class at school, having the same friends, being mistaken for each other and experiencing "ego fusion". Genetic enthusiasts try to get around these social and psychological facts by saying that the genes of identical twins "create" confounding non-genetic influences, as if two infant twins, lying next to each other in the same pram, cast out a powerful genetic force field that compels their mother to dress them identically, while the rest of the world turns to stone. The mother herself is not, in this persuasive scenario, subject to any environmental, financial, social or psychological forces, or indeed genetic influences of her own, but is just controlled by her monozygotic twins' genetic "creativity". It's the kind of circular argument, assuming what it set out to prove, that appears again and again in twin studies, like a wagon formation protecting a beleaguered dogma.'

'You know,' said Hunter, with an appreciative smile, 'now that I've bought all of *YouGenetics*, you're making me think that we should rename it. It's up to you, Lucy. Give it some thought over the next few weeks.'

'I already know,' said Lucy. '*EpiFutures*.'

'To *EpiFutures*!' said Hunter, knocking back another shot. 'I love it. And Francis, I am so sorry about disrupting your experiments and disturbing the denizens of the forest. I had no idea this was a nature reserve. I'm going to send the pilot home before he needs to turn on all the lights and I'll get a car sent down.'

Hunter took out his phone.

'I'm afraid there's no signal here,' said Francis, 'but we can go up and tell the pilot and, if you want to find out about the wilding project, you can come for a walk with me.'

'That sounds great,' said Hunter.

Francis lent Hunter a pair of heavy boots to replace his suede loafers, took his notebook from the high shelf by the front door and the two men set off. Olivia led Lucy back to the sofa. When they could no longer hear Hunter's booming enthusiasm, let alone Francis's quiet answers, the two friends burst out laughing, sprawled next to each other on the cushions.

'What was *that*?' said Olivia, clasping Lucy's forearm and turning around to look at her. 'He's a bit mad! But much kinder than I'd imagined.'

'I really didn't expect him to be so supportive,' said Lucy.

'He's obviously in love with you.'

'God, I hope not. I need an affair with Hunter like ...'

'A hole in the head?'

'God, no,' said Lucy, 'not nearly as much as a hole in the head.'

Later she climbed slowly to her room and collapsed on the bed. She always had to read something, however briefly, before going to sleep and so she switched on the bedside light and picked up the novel she had been hurtling through until she checked into the hospital. Since then, she seemed stuck on the same page and again today, before she could turn that heavy page, the book slipped from her hands as she tumbled into sleep.

When she woke, she saw the light of her lamp smeared across the glassy blackness of the window. She had no idea whether it was late afternoon or the middle of the night. Opening her bedroom door, she heard a brief interchange from downstairs and embarked again on the slow descent to the sitting room, guessing that it must still be quite early and that she would wake in the middle of the night if she rested any longer. She found Olivia on the sofa with her laptop on her raised knees, and Francis reading at the other end, his legs entangled with hers.

'Has Hunter left?' she asked, sitting down in the armchair nearest the fire.

'Yes, about an hour ago,' said Olivia, closing her computer. 'He said to say goodbye and sent his love and said you should take as much paid leave as you need.'

'Well, that's amazing for me, but I'm sorry he burst in on you like that.'

'He's welcome to bring lunch every day,' said Francis, 'by bicycle. Normally, I'm against fast food, but I thought Hunter's hamper was an excellent solution for "people on the move".'

'Was he fun to take round?' asked Lucy.

'He was,' said Francis. 'He really seemed to get it. We talked about soil a lot. I told him what Roosevelt said: "The Nation that destroys its soil destroys itself." He loved that. And then we were away with Darwin and earthworms and artificial fertilisers and declining nutritional values in foods. I also told him the annual global cost of soil degradation: 10.3 trillion dollars a year.'

'Your idea of heaven,' said Olivia, 'terrifying people with soil stats.'

'It's true,' grinned Francis, 'it was pretty great. I think he had a little eco awakening. Howorth has a strange effect on people. Walking around a place that isn't being exploited gives them a holiday from wondering how to exploit everything themselves.'

'Capitalism and nature need couples counselling,' said Olivia.

'Yes,' said Lucy, again exploring the edges of the dent hidden under the bandage on her head, 'there's a price to pay for out-of-control growth. Anyhow,' she said, moving on quickly, 'it sounds as if it was worthwhile all round. He certainly took a lot of pressure off me.'

'Oh, and we're all invited to his house in the South of France in May,' said Olivia.

'We are?' said Lucy, astonished.

'Yes, *Le Plein Soleil*,' said Olivia. '*Oh, les beaux jours!*'

PART TWO

13

Instead of the damp bricks and skeletal branches that until recently had dominated the view through the glass doors of his consulting room, Martin could see salt-white hawthorn and the dark pink cherry blossom screening the walls, a trellis disappearing behind a tangle of honeysuckle shoots and, beyond that, the thick foliage of his neighbour's chestnut tree, melding separate gardens into a single flourishing scene. Many of his patients commented on the beautiful view, if only as the starting point for a contrast to their inner state, or as a source of envy compared to what they were doomed to contemplate at home. Those with properties that 'enjoyed' or 'commanded' a magnificent view, without their owners being able to enjoy or command anything much themselves, were not likely to be consoled by Martin's little pool of greenery when they had already been let down by Hampstead Heath or Westminster Bridge. Others hardly seemed to notice, but Sebastian was the only current patient who was almost certain to attack the burgeoning life of the garden, just as he attacked everything else. He was going through a period (if it was a period, if they were going to get to the other side of it) of psychotic transference, in which Martin was an amalgamated bad object: the person on whom Sebastian could project his deepest disturbance, paranoia and despair. This apparent deterioration was a cause for optimism: it showed that Martin's consulting room was a safe place for Sebastian to bring more and more troubling material which, until now, had always driven people away from him and deepened his loneliness and terror. They had built up to three times a week – Wednesday, Thursday and Friday – in Martin's home and not in the more institutional clinic where they had started out.

Today, Sebastian was late again, but Martin suspected that he would turn up eventually. Pure absence was too stark to express his current turmoil and, even if being late was the beginning of the attack, he would probably need to attack Martin in more detail. He had missed sessions before, but then a routine kicked in: Martin rang the halfway house where Sebastian lived and told the staff that he hadn't turned up; he was either informed that Sebastian refused to come or, when he returned from his wanderings, told that he was back safely. If he didn't come in person, the projection of his sense of abandonment, privation and unreliability found no real home, whereas when he did turn up, it found a resting place of sorts. Not that Sebastian wanted to have his symptoms removed, any more than he wanted an amputation, but he was tempted by being able to express them in a more targeted way: punching the doctor who was proposing to cut off his arm. Nobody came to such a painful and distorted state of mind unless clarity was the more terrifying alternative. Even the most collaborative and well-informed neurotic patient had some resistance, but in those cases the price of abandoning an archaic defence was a wave of anxiety, or the renunciation of a cherished self-image; for the schizophrenic patient, it felt as if the price of abandoning psychosis would be annihilation. Sebastian had tried undermining the therapy again and again. In the early days, he would come in, after taking extra anti-psychotics, claiming to be cured. Now, six months later, he came in to act out.

The session had already started and so Martin sat in his usual chair, holding his patient in mind, giving him the security of a dependable concern, even when there was no obvious way for Sebastian to appreciate it. If he did show up, Sebastian would find his therapist imperturbably keeping their session going. To Sebastian, at some level, Martin's dependability was like discovering that a torturer was still waiting for him in his prison cell, and yet, at another level, one of the things infiltrating Sebastian's mind was the regular rhythm, the rocking cradle of their three weekly sessions. Just because there was an eruption of unconscious material constantly bursting into Sebastian's consciousness didn't mean that he was able to understand its meaning; his mind was more like the 'darkness visible' of Milton's hell. Sebastian had encrypted his secrets, using a system he had taken the further precaution of not knowing how to decipher. That way, if he were tortured, he could honestly say that he had no idea what the secret was. Patience was paramount; if too many delusions were removed too rapidly, he might feel too threatened to continue the work and Martin might lose him. How delusional he was being was sometimes hard to tell. When Sebastian had come in claiming that Satan had followed him from the bus stop, Martin treated the news at face value, saying how worrying that must have felt, and asking if this had ever happened before, but he was clear in his own mind that he was dealing with a fantasy. Outside the most extreme cases, though, it was important to keep an open mind, however strongly his experience pulled him towards one interpretation or another. Quite apart from the issue of data protection, and the reluctance or inefficiency that made it hard to get medical notes and detailed biographies, Martin was a psycho-analyst who preferred not to read prejudicial material about his patients, but to deal immediately and directly with the facts, in so far as they could be established, and the symbolic language that emerged from the sessions themselves. Sebastian had been referred to him at the clinic simply as Sebastian Tanner, a man of thirty-four, who had first been admitted to psychiatric hospital fifteen years before, with a diagnosis of schizophrenia, and had suffered from recurring episodes ever since.

When the basement doorbell finally rang, Martin buzzed Sebastian in and opened the inner door to his consulting room to welcome his patient. Sebastian often stopped in the bathroom to delay his arrival and only emerged with a few minutes of the session left, but on this occasion, he stormed down the corridor, swept past Martin and marched straight up to the garden door.

'You fucking lied to me!' he said. 'The cow jumped over the moon long before Armstrong landed on it. One giant – stepping on mankind.'

'Really?' said Martin. 'How did the cow do that?'

'Armstrong probably gave it a huge kick, unless it had a rocket up its arse. Wernher von Braun, Wernher von Braun / What goes up must come down! Animal-tested. The Russians sent a dog, but Armstrong sent a cow. Being a Nazi isn't rocket science, you just have to invade everything.'

Sebastian opened the door, went into the garden, took out a cigarette and paced up and down, singing inaudibly while Martin sat in his chair waiting. There were only twenty-three minutes of the session left and there was always the worry that it would be difficult to persuade Sebastian to leave before the next patient arrived. Martin tried to relax and do his work. If Sebastian didn't come in of his own accord, he would invite him to come in a few minutes before the session ended. Until then, he would wait and work with whatever evidence he had. Every interpretation was a threat to Sebastian's defences. There was only so much that Martin could hazard about Wernher and Armstrong and the moon, but he could persist in treating them as meaningful communications.

Before long, Sebastian threw his cigarette on the grass, ground it underfoot, and came hurtling back into the room.

'"You say Sigi/ I say Ciggie,"' he sang at the top of his voice, '"I say Ziggie/ you say Sigi. Sigi/Ciggie/ Ziggie/Sigi/ Let's call the whole thing off!" Seriously, seriously, let's call the whole thing off. Please. Seriously. Please, let's call the whole thing off.'

Sebastian hid behind the armchair he was meant to be sitting in and continued to whisper 'seriously' again and again.

Martin could only see the edge of his arm. He let him whisper to himself for a while, and then said, 'I take what you have to tell me very seriously, Sebastian,' in a soothing and conciliatory voice, not much louder than Sebastian's whisper. Sebastian reappeared around the edge of the armchair, not far from the ground.

'I wasn't always called Sebastian,' he said, like a child telling a secret.

'Really?' said Martin. 'What did you used to be called?'

'They won't tell me. They said I had to get used to my new name when they adopted me. I was only two. Two for the price of one. If they had told me my real name, my real parents might find me again, but they were Nazis who would stop at nothing.'

'Like Wernher von Braun?' asked Martin.

'Raining down rockets, V1s and V2s on innocent men, women and children. Ripping people apart.'

Sebastian made a high-pitched whistling noise, but instead of ending with an explosion, it went on and on. An adoption fantasy (if it was a fantasy; he must of course keep an open mind, but it almost certainly was) represented a kind of progress. So many patients, at all levels of disorder, played with the idea of adoption, to escape their fate or to embellish the rejection of their families. Martin had treated borderline patients with convincing and elaborate adoption stories which turned out to be fake, but in the case of a schizophrenic patient, the story was even more likely to be the displacement of forbidden, life-threatening feelings of terror towards a real source of harm.

'My granny,' said Sebastian, 'during the war' (high-pitched whistle) 'was sitting on the floor of her bedroom, playing with her favourite doll' (high-pitched whistle) 'when a bomb came through the roof and snatched her doll away and went down' (high-pitched whistle) 'through all the other floors of the house and lodged in the basement.'

The whistling stopped.

'Did the lodger explode?' asked Martin.

'No, of course it didn't explode! Did it sound like it exploded?' shouted Sebastian.

'No, it didn't, that's why I asked,' said Martin sympathetically.

Sebastian stood up and walked out furiously from behind the armchair.

'She spent the whole of her miserable life sitting on an unexploded bomb. Can you imagine what that feels like, you heartless bastard?'

Sebastian rampaged around the room, tearing books from the shelves and flinging them to the floor. Oh, no, thought Martin, not this again. Perhaps he was getting too old to take on psychotic patients.

'Is this what would have happened if the bomb *had* exploded?' asked Martin.

'This?' shouted Sebastian. 'A few books on the floor? Are you fucking joking? We're talking about innocent men, women and children being ripped apart. The smell of burning human flesh. We're talking about my granny, when she was just a little girl, having her life ruined for ever.'

Sebastian sank to the floor, lay on the carpet and started to run, lying down, making his body turn in agitated circles.

'You can't even tell the difference between what's alive and dead!' he screamed. 'You're nothing but a monster.'

Martin stayed silent for a while, aware that they only had five minutes left.

'So, your new parents called you Sebastian to help protect you,' said Martin.

'You'd have to ask William Tell,' said Sebastian.

'Well, maybe he'll come to our next session and tell us his side of the story,' said Martin.

'Time's running out, time's running out,' said Sebastian, spinning more frantically than ever around the floor. Then, he suddenly stopped, got up and knelt with his hands clasped behind his back, tilting his head and twisting his body in a perfect impersonation of a Renaissance painting of St Sebastian tied to a post with his body full of arrows.

'What kind of monster would force his son to stand there with an apple on his head, in front of everybody, waiting for a cigarette to go through his body?'

'Well, that's a very important question which we can take up on Wednesday,' said Martin, inured to the endlessly repeated phenomenon of the most important material emerging at the end of a session.

'Can I stay here?' asked Sebastian desperately.

'I'm afraid, as we've discussed—'

'Hang on, hang on,' said Sebastian, switching his tone abruptly. 'If my name was changed, who's to say that yours wasn't?'

'My name has always been Martin Carr,' said Martin firmly. 'And we'll resume—'

'Put a sock in it, Wernher. For all I know, you're my father. You're the fucking Nazi!' said Sebastian, walking out with the belligerence of a man determined to avoid rejection.

Martin sat motionless in his chair as Sebastian slammed the basement door behind him (if it was behind him). He listened carefully to detect any signs of his patient not having genuinely left. He heard nothing. Could it really be true? Adopted at two, covered in cigarette burns. And he had said it was his birthday last month. It was too much of a coincidence, but a coincidence was always too much, otherwise it would just be an incident. With their passion for synchronicity, this sort of thing must happen to Jungians all the time, but Martin was not at all thrilled to find himself wondering if his maddest patient was also his daughter's twin. It might still very well be a fantasy, but he couldn't help being reminded of some of the turbulent family discussions Olivia had provoked during her adolescence, when she was trying to process her own story and had found out that adopting parents often had detailed access to the socio-economic and health backgrounds of the children's birth families. Describing candidates from the most troubled families, the author of one article had written, 'One might ask, "Who would adopt such a child?"' Olivia had confronted Lizzie about how much she had been told about her biological parents' history and background.

'We knew that it was an accidental pregnancy,' said her mother, 'and we knew about your father's criminal record.'

'Was that appealing to you?' asked Olivia, half-joking.

'I wouldn't put it that strongly,' said her mother, smiling at Olivia. 'We just wanted to look after you.'

'I suppose,' said Olivia, who had emerged too recently from looking up 'Adoption' in the index of dozens of books from her parents' shelves.

'Was I an experiment?' she asked.

'Don't be so silly,' Lizzie said, kissing Olivia on the forehead, 'you were a child who needed help.'

Mr and Mrs Tanner must have known about Sebastian's background, if indeed he was adopted. It seemed to have involved considerable physical abuse, similar to the torment that Karen had described to Olivia when she first told her about Keith. If the Tanners were adoptive parents, they must have been naively or morbidly or courageously drawn to such an extreme situation, but whatever their level of motivation and awareness, they had not been competent to deal with the highly traumatised child they adopted. Martin felt that in some way, by being so difficult, Sebastian might have become an unconscious punishment for the sterility of one or both of the parents. Perhaps they had adopted a traumatised child because of the trauma of spending years trying unsuccessfully to have a child of their own. Instead of making up for their failure, Sebastian summarised it. They were not necessarily bad people, in fact they must have been ambitiously good people, to have adopted a child of nearly two from such a troubled background, and then celebrated his martyrdom by renaming him. If he was Karen's son and if she had been telling Olivia the truth when she said she had put him up for adoption at eighteen months, Sebastian must also have been kept in a holding pen of social services for nearly six months.

What was he doing? This was all speculation, and yet he found himself so disturbed by the possibility that he had been unknowingly treating his daughter's brother that he was tempted to break his own rules and ring the halfway house, or the adoption agency, or one of the psychiatric hospitals Sebastian had been admitted to, and see if he could find out the facts of the case. He gazed at the phone on his desk for a while and then drew back. He couldn't abandon Sebastian, whatever family he had been born into, and he had a professional obligation not to disclose his suspicions to Olivia, so there was no immediate conflict, but he would certainly have to think about the ethical ramifications when he had time, and disentangle whatever counter-transference might have been triggered by the subject of adoption. For now, though, he had to clear his mind and prepare for his next patient.

14

'Lord have mercy upon us, Lord have mercy upon us,' muttered Father Guido, his small eyes tightly shut and his knuckles white from the tension of gripping the armrests. The Cardinal had insisted that he fly directly from Rome to Nice, despite Father Guido's admission that he had never flown before and had a mortal dread of travelling by plane.

'Think of it as a just punishment for your incompetence, and a test of your faith,' said Cardinal Lagerfeld. 'This is the most flagrant case of mystical espionage that has ever come to my attention.'

The Curia's *Congregation for the Doctrine of the Faith*'s Intellectual Property department had declared that the scanning of the Blessed Fra Domenico's brain by atheistic foreign capitalists, motivated entirely by greed, was 'an act of diabolical piracy'.

'He is one of our own,' said Cardinal Lagerfeld, pacing his magnificent apartment in the Vatican City, 'nursed at the bosom of Mother Church since he was a child.' He paused next to a small but exquisite Madonna and Child by Raphael, as if to emphasise the magnitude and depth of Father Guido's betrayal. 'And you have allowed him to be raped – the word is not too strong: it is not strong enough – by worshippers of Mammon and the machine.'

It was undoubtedly the most humiliating dressing-down of Father Guido's life, delivered by the Vatican's most ferocious enforcer. The Cardinal gave Father Guido a contract, drawn up by *The Pontifical Council for Legislative Texts*, securing fifty per cent of the revenue from the sales of *Brainwaves' Capo Santo* helmet, payable into an account newly opened at *The Institute for the Works of Religion*. Father Guido's mission was to fly to Nice immediately and persuade Hunter Sterling to sign the contract.

'If he signs,' the Cardinal explained in a more emollient tone, 'he will benefit from a harmonious, collaborative promotional campaign. We will recommend our product from every pulpit, make it available in every cathedral gift shop, and have it endorsed by the highest authorities of *The Prefecture for the Economic Affairs of the Holy See* and possibly,' Lagerfeld paused tantalisingly, 'by His Holiness Himself.'

'That would be wonderful,' said Father Guido, smiling incredulously.

'But,' said the Cardinal, returning to his more familiar tone as a servant of *God's Vindictive Side*, 'if he fails to sign, we will tie up this predator in red tape for decades to come in every country in the world. Not only do we have two thousand years of experience with red tape,' he added, standing beneath a sumptuous tapestry depicting the decapitation of Holofernes, 'but ours is drenched in the blood of Christ.'

In Father Guido's modest opinion, there was something distasteful about this remark, but who was he to question the authority of Cardinal Lagerfeld, even if he was the sort of monster who would force an ageing Abbot to confront one of his lifelong terrors? On the way to the airport, Father Guido telephoned his secretary, Brother Manfredi, to tell him that he had left the Vatican, 'with my tail between my legs'.

'Do not reproach yourself, Father,' Brother Manfredi replied. 'We are simple Franciscans and do not understand the politics of *The City*. You were motivated by the purest ideals: to give ordinary people the chance to enter into the highest union of which the human mind is capable.'

'Where are you now?' asked Father Guido, clutching at any alternative as he saw the control tower of Leonardo da Vinci airport looming through the taxi window.

'In the vegetable garden, Father.'

'Ah,' said Guido, close to tears, 'what I wouldn't give to be with you there now, Manfredi, in the vegetable garden in Assisi.'

Since then he had been praying uninterruptedly: 'Lord have mercy upon us, Lord have mercy upon us.'

When his plane finally touched down on the runway at Nice, which seemed to have arisen miraculously from the sea at the very last moment, like the finger of God, saving the passengers from drowning in the brilliant waters of the *Baie des Anges*, Father Guido suddenly realised that due to the administrative demands of his office and his earlier years of managing the immense flow of tourists visiting the many holy sites of Assisi, he had not prayed so long and so fervently since his zealous youth in the seminary. Walking down a corridor pierced by dazzling Mediterranean light, Father Guido understood that far from being a monster, Cardinal Lagerfeld was a great spiritual teacher who had sent him on this outward and worldly journey in order to take him on an inward journey for the sake of his immortal soul. He wept quietly with gratitude, with recognition, with humility and with awe as he followed the increasingly blurred signs for the exit.

John MacDonald had been invited by Saul Prokosh to fly down from Edinburgh to the South of France for a weekend at *Plein Soleil*, the home of the legendary Hunter Sterling. John was hoping that he would finally get the investment he needed. He had called his company *Not As We Know It*. It was a *Star Trek* allusion – 'It's life, Jim, but not as we know it' – which Saul was encouraging him to leave behind. He was fond of the old name, but if the price was right, they could call it *Fifty Shades of Grey* for all he cared. John had a dream: the creation of inorganic life with no carbon in the mix. Instead of a digital computer that reduced the world to binary information and brought it under the imperium of mathematics, he would make an analogue computer, using matter rather than numbers to inform its simulations. Its rhythms and processes would imitate biology, while freeing the concept of life from the tyranny of carbon. He would synthesise compounds from any of the non-carbon elements to model all the features of life jealously guarded by biology: cellular containment, movement, growth and reproduction. If chemistry could not yet explain life, then the definition of life must be expanded to include the processes that chemistry could describe and demonstrate experimentally.

'*Passeport, s'il vous plaît, monsieur.*'

'*Ah, excusez-moi,*' said John, handing over his passport to the policeman in the glass cubicle.

Bill Moorhead stood by the luggage carousel, keeping an eye out for his cases, but also regretting the sky-blue linen suit he had bought himself as a rejuvenating present, only to find that on its first outing it was already more creased and wrinkled than its owner's handsome but weather-beaten face. Caroline seemed to have gone completely mad. After thirty years of tolerant, sophisticated and civilised marriage, he had suddenly received a letter from a firm of solicitors banging on about the infidelity, anguish and years of humiliation she had suffered. 'Frailty, thy name is woman.' Could the timing have anything to do with the sale of the second half of *YouGenetics*? Opportunistic bitch. She knew that all his life he had wanted to retire in just the kind of house that a knighted Oxford professor (or at least one with entrepreneurial gusto) should be able to live in. When Little Soddington Manor had come on to the market, a failed hotel that needed to be carefully restored to its natural place as the big house on the edge of a charming Cotswold village, he had snapped it up. It included the land on which the village cricket ground and its black and white pavilion enjoyed their immemorial slumber, waiting silently through most of the year for the crack of bat and ball, the roar of catch and wicket; three large fields let out to local farmers for grazing and, of course, the magnificent garden; the copse at the foot of the garden and the little river that paid its respects to the manor house before gossiping its way through the village, beneath two picturesque stone bridges that only allowed the passage of one car at a time. By demanding half his capital, Caroline knew that she was sabotaging a lifelong dream. Well, it wasn't going to be that easy to prise Little Soddington from his grip. He still had his consultancy at *YouGenetics*, his Fellow's rooms and rights in college and, in a bold move that he must keep under the radar until the divorce was finalised, he had strongly indicated his preparedness to accept, for a very handsome sum indeed, an offer made by the University of Riyadh to spend five years as a Distinguished Visiting Professor. Why not break the back of the British winter in the Saudi capital, and then return for the crack of bat and ball, the long summer evenings and bibulous weekends with splendid old friends in his splendid new house?

Bad luck, Caroline, thought Moorhead, as he dragged his clattering suitcase towards the unattended Customs, he may be bloodied but he was unbowed.

Jade was waiting for Hunter's special guests to arrive at the private jet section of Nice airport, accompanied by two young men from the *Plein Soleil* team, easily identified by their short-sleeved khaki sports shirts emblazoned with a red solar logo. She didn't usually come to the airport, but Hunter had asked her to take care of Lucy and her friends from England. Jade had watched many women come and go through Hunter's life; they were the variables; she was the constant. She was always charming to Hunter's latest crush, friendly without being familiar, sisterly without being presumptuous, and if she thought he had truly finished with one of them (she was always right), ruthless without being rude. To those who might be recycled, or remained occasional lovers connected with a particular city, she was meticulously polite, but showed, in the total rigidity of Hunter's schedule, the futility of any hopes they might have of ever being on equal or open terms with such a prodigious human being as her boss. Jade had slept with Hunter, but had made no demands and showed no expectations, no sentimentality and no jealousy. Slowly,

slowly, though, she would reel him in, and turn out to be the only indispensable woman in his life.

'Lucy! Hi, I'm Jade. I feel like we know each other already, after all the emails. It's such a pleasure. Welcome to France. You must be Olivia and Francis. A pleasure to meet you, too. Hunter has sent his own car, so let's get you on the road before the other guests find out that they're not travelling in a convertible Bentley. We don't want to start the weekend with a riot! Gilles is right outside. Don't worry about your luggage; we'll take care of it.'

Jade lowered her sunglasses and led the way to the car, her black hair shining, her white T-shirt, mysteriously burnt open at exactly the right places to reveal glimpses of her perfect body, her tight black jeans, carefully frayed at the ankles, and her vintage cream sneakers, making her impossible to lose sight of.

'Ah, Gilles, voici les invités speciaux de Monsieur Sterling.'

'Enchanté,' said Gilles, opening the back door for Lucy, while Olivia went around to the other side and Francis settled into the front passenger seat.

'See you guys back at Soleil,' said Jade. 'Enjoy the ride!'

'So, your ceramic guy is flying himself down,' said Hunter, scanning the guest list, under a canopy of wisteria that shaded his private terrace. The air was motionless and, beyond the edge of his vast lawn, a rearing speedboat slowly unzipped the silky surface of the bay.

'That's right,' said Saul, 'he's not the guy with the air ticket, or the guy with the private jet, he's the guy with the pilot's licence and his own prop plane.'

'I know that guy,' said Hunter. 'So, is it family money or did he invent something before the armour? What kind of a name is Marcel Qing, anyway? Are they Chinese?'

'It's a strange story,' said Saul. 'Marcel is ultra-French. He went to all the right schools, the Lycée Henri-IV, the École normale, wears black corduroy suits and round tortoiseshell glasses and complicated scarves – all of that – but his grandfather was the young Chinese cook to a French family in Shanghai. They fled when the Japs invaded Manchuria in 'thirty-three and took Marcel's grandfather with them: they couldn't face life without his *General's Chicken*. He worked with them for five years in Paris, but then his employer sacked his mistress one day and she knew the thing that would piss him off the most would be to lose his cook, so she financed the grandfather's first restaurant. By the time he died in the eighties, he had five great restaurants scattered around Paris. Out of respect for the old man, Marcel's father waited until he was dead, then he froze Master Qing's ancient, secret recipe for *General's Chicken* and turned it into a supermarket staple.'

'So, there's no way he's selling more than forty-nine per cent.'

'It'll depend on the manufacturing costs,' said Saul. 'He's determined to prove to his father that he can make his own fortune in something more glamorous than frozen foods, but he may not have enough to build the factory and go into full production.'

'Okay, got it. And what about John MacDonald? Can we buy him out and, if we can, do we want to?'

'He's at the other end of the spectrum,' said Saul. 'We could probably buy his company for the price of an abandoned crofter's cottage. The trouble is that we're a long way from any application, but the IP on fake life could be huge. On the other hand, if it turns out to be the model for life itself, we'll be in Genome territory, where Clinton stopped Craig Venter from getting patents on genes and genetic structures: three hundred million down the drain. The government says it's pro-business, but when it comes to the secrets of life, capitalism is left begging on the sidewalk outside the party.'

'Especially when it gets daily results from a three-billion-dollar, publicly funded research programme while only publishing its own results once a year,' said Hunter. 'It's confusing to let people patent someone else's work. Besides, socialism in America was never intended for some schmuck to shadow the most conspicuous global science project of all time; it has to be ideologically purified by only being given to its most ferocious opponents in the Pentagon or on Wall Street. If someone wants to start an illegal war or get bailed out after bringing the world's economic system to its knees, then, by golly, if the beneficiaries are already rich and powerful, we can show the world what a welfare state really means.' Hunter glanced at his phone, throbbing on the broad arm of his deckchair. 'Guest alert, Gilles has just turned on to the Cap. He's got *Los Tres Amigos* in the car. Anyhow, as long as MacDonald has got something better for us than a crystal garden, and less "public domain" than the secret of life, we can buy him out.'

'You don't like crystal gardens?' said Saul. 'They're my happiest childhood memories.'

'I hope your therapist is qualified to deal with that level of trauma,' said Hunter.

'Are you sure it was a good idea to invite Bill Moorhead now that he's completely sold out of *YouGenetics*?' asked Saul.

'A good idea? It's a great idea. It'll be like watching a bullfight, with two beautiful female matadors torturing a pompous old bull.'

'I guess it's good to be closing the matador gender gap,' said Saul, 'and it's more humane than watching gladiators hacking each other to death.'

'I hope not,' said Hunter, with one of his big laughs. 'If Lucy doesn't finish him off, we can count on Kraftwerk freaking the hell out of him, when he's used to rocking atheistically to Thomas Tallis in the college chapel.'

'Kraftwerk,' said Saul, 'cool. Robotics Central.'

'Tomorrow night. Don't tell any of the guests. Only you and Jade know.'

'They must be expensive.'

'Not as expensive as Elton John, the local talent.'

'OMG,' said Saul, 'you got Elton John?'

'Are you kidding?' said Hunter. '"Candle in the Wind" – get a torch!'

Olivia was having that feeling, rare since adolescence, that her life had turned into a film. She was reclining next to her best friend in the bulging seat of a night-blue convertible, as it flitted past the hedges and driveways of Cap d'Antibes. They were on their way to a house named (irrelevantly, she hoped) after a murderous thriller, also shot on the Mediterranean coast. The Cap was looking especially photogenic in early May, before the convoys of tourists and the flotillas of sewage and jellyfish, supported by The Airborne Melanomas, moved in to secure the hedonistic headland for the summer.

She had only been given this glamorous part in the back of Hunter's car thanks to his impetuous visit to Howorth last December. That day had set off a cascade of changes in all their lives, especially for Lucy. Hunter had carved out an enclave of gentleness for her (and for himself) in his at times overbearing personality and by the end of January they were going out together. He seemed to be undaunted, perhaps even inspired, by the insolence of her illness: a hostile take-over to outmanoeuvre, a tax for which there must be a loophole. Lucy had been frustrated by waiting so long for her biopsy results and by the time she finally got her appointment, Hunter was ready to rip apart Mr McEwan for British inefficiency. He calmed down when they were told that the first indications from the lab had been that her tumour was a glioblastoma, the worst type, but that further testing had established that it was in fact a grade-two astrocytoma.

Lucy asked McEwan if she should avoid any particular activity, given her propensity for seizures.

'My only advice is not to drink a case of champagne and go swimming at night in shark-infested waters,' he replied.

'I'm going to give that up as well,' said Hunter, 'to show support.'

Since there was no surgical option without a high risk of paralysing the right side of her body, McEwan wrapped up the surprisingly cheerful meeting by saying that he would refer Lucy to his colleague Dr Gray, an oncologist specialising in low-grade brain tumours. Hunter was due back in America and so Olivia and Francis accompanied Lucy to the Gray consultation. To reduce misunderstanding and catastrophic speculation, Lucy had put a ban on internet research with the result that much of the meeting was jarringly harsh for her compared to the tone of her consultation with Mr McEwan.

Olivia had overruled the ban, without telling Lucy, and that was part of the reason the meeting had made her so angry.

Dr Gray's job, it turned out, was to tell Lucy that, sooner or later, her tumour would convert and become more aggressive, but that it should be monitored with regular scans for the time being, since attacking it while it was relatively dormant would be ineffective. When Lucy asked if she could do anything to improve her chances, Dr Gray said there was nothing except chemotherapy and radiation, and possibly surgery at a later stage. He was a short, friendly man in a shirt and tie, wearing a black velvet kippah.

'So, I can just order fish and chips, a bottle of rum and some deep-fried ice cream?'

'Eh, well, there just isn't enough evidence that diet plays a significant role.'

'Really?' said Lucy with resolute scepticism.

When he told Lucy that the median survival of someone with a grade-two astrocytoma was about five years from the time of diagnosis, she was completely shocked and looked at Olivia and Francis in anguished disbelief. Olivia didn't know whether to intervene. From her own research she knew that Dr Gray was quoting an old study from the nineties with the shortest survival rate. She had seen a more nuanced and more recent one in which women of Lucy's age lived twice as long.

'Amongst all the patients you've treated over the years,' asked Francis, seeing that Lucy was too stunned to speak, 'is there any common factor in those who have done well?'

'No. None whatsoever,' said Dr Gray. 'I have one patient who was diagnosed twenty years ago and is still doing extremely well. His wife prays for him every day. Then again, I have another patient who doesn't have any religious beliefs at all, and he has also been around for about two decades after being diagnosed.'

Dr Gray seemed relieved by this self-cancelling evidence from beyond the tight perimeter of the world he had portrayed, a world of four objects, containing only a statistic, a scalpel, a poison and a gamma ray. Did he believe it himself? Was he going home to processed food drenched in pesticides? Did he really believe that a sense of purpose, a lower level of anxiety and a capacity for love played no part in 'outcomes'? His second long-living patient may not have had any religious beliefs, but did he walk the Pennine Way each year to defy his diagnosis, or had he been determined to leave his family with as much security as possible, like Anthony Burgess, who rushed out his first novel after his diagnosis of a fatal cancer, and then continued to rush out novels for decades to come? The world was full of schizoid accommodations: adulterers who loved their spouses, atheists who prayed while they rushed their child to Accident and Emergency, concentration camp officers who went home to relish Proust or marvel at Relativity; not to mention someone like Bill Moorhead, who had been happy to spend much of his career declaring that ninety-eight per cent of the human genome was 'Junk DNA', while mocking any shaping power in nature other than natural selection, the ruthless executioner of waste and redundancy. Was Dr Gray another example of this human genius for incoherence and fragmentation, or was he constrained by a hospital culture of legalistic pessimism, so determined not to give out false hope that it was in danger of offering false despair? Perhaps his kippah and his patient's praying wife were unofficial salutes to the role played by beliefs in the unfolding of results; or perhaps he was a deeply compassionate man, protecting the vast majority of his patients, who might not have a powerful sense of purpose, who could not afford organic chia seeds, who were not surrounded by love, and whose relationship to their illness was a close contest between the high anxiety of living and the unreliably higher anxiety of dying. Whatever the reasoning, Olivia felt that it amounted to putting a curse on Lucy. Dr Gray seemed to be a decent man, telling them candidly about the meagre evidence he was allowed to take seriously, but still, she had been determined to help Lucy rebel against his World of Four Objects from the moment they walked out of the building in which they had been assured of its scientific validity.

'Nous voici!' said Gilles, turning off the main road, down a lane marked by a rough wooden arrow with the words Le Plein Soleil written on it in faded red paint. The signpost was more of a veil than a guide, almost certain to be missed by someone who didn't already know it was there. It was a faint allusion to something that turned out, after a few bends in the lane, to be intimidatingly solid: great arched wooden portals, reinforced with black iron studs and flanked by two lodges embedded in a high wall of massive grey stones. No one without a medieval siege engine could hope to catch a glimpse of what lay behind the bristling spikes that crested the wall. Despite their antique appearance, the gates were already gliding open as the car approached. Beyond them, a serpentine drive twisted down, through a sloping lawn, dotted with oleander bushes, just breaking out in pink flowers, and umbrella pines with clumps of needles so rounded and brightened by fresh growth that they looked like bonsai clouds hanging in a cloudless sky. As the car grew closer to the sea, a large ochre house with dark green shutters came into view.

'Coo-wee,' said Lucy.

'My thoughts exactly,' said Olivia.

The car turned into a parking area, clearly designed to be invisible from the house.

'How did she get here before us?' said Lucy, seeing Jade sitting on the bonnet of a black Porsche, texting.

'Hi!' said Jade, putting away her phone just when it would have been rude to continue using it.

'You must have driven fast,' said Olivia.

'Well, Hunter told me to welcome you, so I thought, "I can't just welcome them at the airport, I have to welcome them at *Soleil*." Also,' she said, in a confessional whisper, 'I love to race this car. You can take the girl out of LA, but you can't take LA out of the girl.'

'Really?' said Olivia. 'The only time I went there, it seemed to be one huge traffic jam.'

'Not if you know the short cuts.'

'I bet you're an expert on those,' said Olivia.

'*The* expert,' said Jade, opening the door for Francis.

It was already Saturday afternoon and Father Guido was pacing his bedroom, rehearsing ways to raise the subject of profit sharing with

Signor Sterling's *Brainwaves* and praying that an opportune moment would present itself before the end of the day. It had seemed too precipitous, not to say ill-mannered, to slam the contract down on the dinner table the very evening of his arrival. Cardinal Lagerfeld, however, took a different view of the matter, as he had made clear when he rang Father Guido at quarter to six in the morning to ask him if he had locked down the deal.

'I have only just arrived, Your Eminence,' stammered Father Guido, patting the bedside table in search of his glasses.

'My patience is not infinite,' the Cardinal warned him.

'I can see that,' said Father Guido, as the digits on his clock came into sharper focus, 'but you must understand that the house is crowded with guests, many of whom are working with Signor Sterling on scientific projects of great complexity. Besides, I had to share the journey from the airport with two British intellectuals, one of whom turned out to be a famous enemy of the faith, Sir William Moorhead, the author of *Why the Sublime is Ridiculous*. It was extremely taxing on my nerves—'

'That man!' interrupted the Cardinal. 'If only the *Index Librorum Prohibitorum* had not been suspended, *The Sacred Congregation of the Index* would certainly have placed his odious work at the top of any contemporary list, but alas, the epidemic of lies which is ravaging the minds of the faithful has proliferated beyond our control. Gone are the days when we could have ordered Sir William Moorhead to be burnt at the stake in the Campo de' Fiori, after "imprisoning his tongue".'

'Indeed, they have,' said Father Guido, without the nostalgia that clung to the Cardinal's vocal cords like pleading children. 'And I must tell you,' he continued, determined to complete the tale of his traumatic transfer from the airport, 'the other passenger in the car told me that he is trying to create life in a test tube, or on a computer of some kind, I'm not quite sure, without using carbon, which I suppose is good for the environment, but still, it seemed to me that there was something sacrilegious in his attitude, or, at the very least, extremely arrogant.'

'Where will it end?' sighed the Cardinal. 'Even in profane literature, we are warned again and again against Man's hubris, whether in mythology, with the stories of Icarus and Prometheus, or in the well-known tales of the Terrible Doctors: Faustus and Frankenstein, with their blasphemous lust for unconstrained power and forbidden knowledge.'

'You are wonderfully learned, Your Eminence,' said Father Guido, trying to appease the volcanic irascibility of his superior.

'Surely, you are familiar with these works,' said the Cardinal, demonstrating the suppleness of his disapproval.

'My parents urged me to shun works of fiction and only read the words of God, and of course of distinguished theologians such as yourself.'

'Very commendable,' said Lagerfeld. 'It must be wonderful to come from such simple stock. I can scarcely imagine how much less demanding my life would have been if I had not felt obliged to master the great achievements of human civilisation, of philosophy and literature, of art and science, of theology and engineering.'

'Well, it can still feel demanding, even for those of us who have not been endowed with such a majestic intellect,' said Father Guido, feeling that he really knew what he was talking about.

'I dare say, I dare say,' muttered Lagerfeld. 'So, Father Guido, it is your sacred duty to retrieve the knowledge with which God has endowed Fra Domenico from this *noeud de vipères* in which you have allowed it to fall. Do not let me down! Ring me before Morning Mass tomorrow and give me something to celebrate.'

'Surely, the sacrifice of Our Lord—'

'Impertinent idiot! Do not lecture *me* on the meaning of the Mass,' shouted Lagerfeld. 'I was intending to shelter you from the full consequences of your crime, but you leave me no choice but to tell you, in the very strictest secrecy, that the *Vatican Laboratories* have been working on a virtual reality project, codenamed *Crown of Thorns*, not dissimilar to *Brainwaves*. We were intending to engage the young, who are addicted to these virtual worlds, with our *Via Dolorosa* package, following the traditional fourteen Stations of the

Cross, and then, after a debate which took place at the very highest levels, and with the blessing of His Holiness Himself, exceptionally, we decided to include in our *Crown of Thorns Platinum Package*, the *Via Lucis*, the highly controversial fifteenth *Station*, the Resurrection itself, not accepted as one of the *Stations* in some conservative circles. It was our intention to scan Fra Domenico's brain in order to give the faithful the full experience of Our Lord's Resurrection and perhaps even beyond *that*, to His ecstatic reunion with His Father in Heaven.'

'What have I done?' said Father Guido, giddy with remorse.

'You have done immeasurable harm,' said Lagerfeld, unable to resist tearing out another fingernail before offering his victim a cigarette. 'However, you can show your remorse not only by getting the contract signed, but also by finding out exactly how these so-called *Brainwaves* work. The *Vatican Laboratories* have run across certain technical difficulties. They have successfully scanned members of the clergy meditating on each of the *Stations* – except the fifteenth, thanks to you. Imagine the shock, and yet the deep fulfilment, of His condemnation to death; the tenderness and sorrow of His meeting with His Holy Mother; the humiliation of the Falls, taking on the Fall of Adam on our behalf; the relief and the mutual compassion shown by allowing Simon to share the weight of the Cross – I suppose your parents at least allowed you to learn the names of the *Stations*. I take a particular interest in the *eleventh Station* ...'

'The Crucifixion,' said Guido.

'Ah, bravo, Father Guido,' said Lagerfeld, 'you've heard of the Crucifixion! Well, as an expert, I am sure you know that some of our more enthusiastic brethren, in Mexico and the Philippines, for instance, have themselves crucified at Easter. I had my doubts about the literalism of this approach to *The Passion*. It is the redemptive power of Our Lord's suffering that requires faith, after all; our own suffering is painfully self-evident. So, I decided to go and see for myself, and I can tell you that it is truly inspiring to see these young men stripped of their clothes, humiliated and nailed to a cross, in the great tradition of *The Imitation of Christ*. I took a particular interest in a sincere young man called Ignacio Gomez, who had himself crucified year after year, from the age of fourteen, when I first met him, without any impairment to his hands or feet.'

'A miracle,' said Father Guido.

'That will be determined by the *Congregation for the Causes of Saints*,' said the Cardinal, 'not by a gullible fool like you, who allows himself to be bamboozled by an American businessman.'

Not for the first time, Father Guido found himself conflicted between his profound commitment to Obedience and his growing feeling that the Cardinal was a fiend, who took pleasure in hurting others.

'Your penitential path is clear,' said Lagerfeld. 'Not only must you persuade Signor Sterling to sign the contract, but you must confiscate the personal computer of Signor Prokosh and bring it to the *Holy See* tomorrow evening so that our technicians can understand the algorithm *Brainwaves* has been using.'

'But, Your Eminence, that would be theft,' said Father Guido.

'Theft is not theft when it returns property to its rightful owner,' said the Cardinal.

'I am not a philosopher, like Your Eminence, but surely Signor Prokosh's computer *is* his personal property.'

'Not when it contains a scan of Fra Domenico's brain,' said Lagerfeld, 'handed to him by a servant of the Church.'

'But—'

'Need I remind you that not only am I a Cardinal and you are an Abbot,' said Lagerfeld, 'but that you are a Franciscan and I am a Jesuit? It is therefore not only impertinent to argue with me, it is futile.'

And with that, the conversation ended, leaving Father Guido exhausted but too shaken to go back to sleep. He lay in bed feeling challenged from every direction. In addition to a thoroughly irreligious loathing for the Cardinal, he was also experiencing, in direct conflict with his vows, a voluptuous entanglement with his surroundings. His bed, for instance, felt as if it belonged in a Baroque painting of angel-laden clouds. It made his simple pallet in the monastery seem like a bed of nails on which an ostentatious yogi might show off his indifference to circumstance. And yet there was more to it than that: the house was beautiful; not the trophy of a vulgar pluto-crat, but quite simply marvellous. La Signorina Jade had explained to him that the whole property was decorated with works by artists who had lived at one time or other within a hundred kilometres of Antibes.

'We're art locavores,' she had said, an opaque expression that Father Guido had countered with a polite smile.

They had been standing in front of a paper cut-out by Monsieur Henri Matisse that managed to celebrate, with three simple colours, the joy of sun and sea and leaf. A delicately calibrated Calder mobile in the garden, of equally primitive colouring, responded to a light breeze, which, after the torpid afternoon, nudged it into a gentle rotation in the early evening, so that the shifting relationships between its elements made it seem alive. A large painting of a white bird by Monsieur Georges Braque, like an intersected C, flew across a blue-grey sky in the hall; and his own bedroom was a little museum of oil paintings by Paul Signac, an artist whom La Signorina Jade told him had spent his summers in the famous port of St-Tropez in the early part of the last century. All around him, bright blue, orange, pink and pale green water, trees, boats and bays glistened on the walls. He was reminded that his own faith was far more directly rooted in a love of nature than in the encrypted allegories, disturbing martyrdoms and favourite stories that crowded the monumental if somewhat monotonous art collection accumulated by the Church over the centuries.

When he finally recovered sufficiently from the Cardinal's dawn raid to get out of bed and prepare himself for the day, Guido drew open his curtains and saw La Signorina Nadia from the *Plein Soleil* Wellness Team, who had kindly, if somewhat outrageously, offered to book him in for a massage soon after his arrival, leading a yoga class beneath his window. Half a dozen guests were on all fours on the lawn arching their backs in the air and, the next moment, hollowing their backs in a posture from which part of him naturally wanted to avert his gaze, but then found himself looking at fondly, overcome by a sense of sadness that he had been taught to mortify his body rather than enjoy it, to fix his mind on the next life rather than this one. Perhaps he was in error, but it seemed to him that there was something basically healthy about these young people, who were not rushing to be crucified, like the Cardinal's young protégé, or to have a breast sliced off or have themselves lashed to a burning wheel or strapped to a post and shot full of arrows.

At lunch, Father Guido, instead of placing a restraining hand over the top of his glass, as he usually did, allowed it to be filled with a swirl of deep red wine. He found himself seated next to a charming Frenchman who turned out to be an expert on ceramics.

'My family was originally from Xi'an,' Monsieur Marcel explained, 'where the great Terracotta Army was discovered. I think that ancestral connection is what inspired me, ultimately, to develop my ceramic armour. You are in the business of protecting souls, *mon père*, and I am in the business of protecting bodies.'

He raised his glass and clicked it lightly against Father Guido's.

'To the protection of the vulnerable,' said Marcel.

'Yes,' said Father Guido, 'an excellent toast. And an excellent wine,' he added, after taking a mouthful.

'It is *Unico*,' said Marcel, 'the greatest wine to come out of Spain. The pottery is also by a Spaniard, Pablo Picasso.'

'Picasso,' said Father Guido, looking around at the owl-jugs bulging on the table, and at the bullfight taking place within the arena of his own plate and, as the food was served, the dancing figures and the heavy-uddered goats and serene women's faces and the men's profiles, like the heads on ancient Greek coins, that gradually emerged from beneath the platters of green beans, pomegranate, feta, rare beef and grilled fish. Was he falling into Epicureanism? Was it sinful to feel such delight, surrounded by these exuberant ceramics, in this magnificent garden, with the sea glittering through the drifting Calder and the best wine he had ever tasted flowing into his glass, as if he were a guest at the Wedding Feast at Cana? Although he was not at Mass, he suddenly felt that all wine was sacred; in fact, that if anything was sacred, everything must be. Was he falling into the Error of Pantheism? He didn't care! If he was, he had been driven to it by Lagerfeld, a Cardinal who had ordered a special Cruciform MRI machine to be made so that he could watch pictures of poor Ignatio's brain lighting up as nails were driven into his hands and feet; a bully who had ordered him to steal another man's property.

Marcel explained that Picasso's Communist leanings had inspired him to mass produce pottery at Vallauris, a nearby town, in order to make ownership of his work more accessible to ordinary people.

'Communism is practical Christianity,' said Marcel.

'I suppose it is,' said Father Guido, who was by now on board for more or less any heresy. 'To Communism!' He clicked glasses with Marcel again and drank another gulp of the splendid Spanish wine.

Marcel showed him photographs of his ceramic armour and told him that the design had been inspired by snake scales.

Father Guido found himself wondering why the poor serpent had been selected to carry the burden of emblematic evil. Were snakes not also God's creatures?

'To serpents!' he said. And that was the last toast he could remember making.

When he woke, Father Guido was thoroughly confused. He had so seldom left the monastery it was fundamentally bewildering for him to imagine himself anywhere else. It was already night, and yet a pulsing green light suffused the air outside his windows and an eerie, amplified voice was counting slowly in German: '*Fünf ... Sechs ... Sieben ... Acht.*'

For a moment, he imagined that Cardinal Lagerfeld was speaking to him in a dream, counting the seconds before a detonation, or some other terrible punishment that would be unleashed on him and his fellow guests. And then he remembered: he was in the South of France, staying with Signor Sterling. With that recognition came a wince of shame. He had obscure but intermittently piercing memories of the afternoon, like blades gleaming in the fog. Had the lovely Signorina Nadia really persuaded him, after his crushingly delicious lunch, that it was his turn to come to the spa area for a massage? He could feel his heart tightening at the uncertain recollection of a candlelit ceremony; the knots of tension that she had kneaded with her powerful hands, and the warm tears spilling from his eyes, down his nose and dropping through the hole in the massage table on to the petals of a lotus that floated in the pewter bowl below. After he was fully dressed again, she had given him advice on his posture, easing back his burdened shoulders and delicately touching his lower spine and the crown of his head, making him feel taller and taller, although in truth he was not a tall man. Somehow, in that moment, he had felt his deepest aspirations turn into sensations, as if his body was part of a cord that ran from the core of the Earth into infinite space, lifting his mind effortlessly towards heaven.

The rest was blank. He must have passed out after returning to his bedroom. Now he was still fully clothed and was clearly missing some important scientific lecture organised by his host. Where were his manners? He must join the others with all possible haste. He hurried out of his bedroom and down the broad, curving staircase that led to the hall. He felt guilty and dehydrated, but luckily there were two waiters standing at the foot of the stairs, one with a tray of champagne, which Father Guido had no intention of drinking, and one with glasses of icy lemonade. He smiled at the waiter and took a tumbler of the cold yellow liquid, drinking it eagerly.

'I'm sorry, I was so thirsty,' he said, placing the empty glass back on the tray.

'Would you like another?' asked the waiter.

'Well, you are so kind. It is very refreshing. Thank you,' said Father Guido, taking another glass and wandering towards the double staircase that led into the garden from a terrace on the far side of the hall. As he approached the branching steps, the music grew louder and a screen gradually appeared, perhaps a hundred metres from the house, seething and twisting with lurid green numbers. Four figures silhouetted against the giant screen, in black costumes ribbed with strips of light, stood behind sharply delineated consoles on which they made delicate adjustments to invisible instruments. Father Guido walked down the steps in a trance, unable to work out whether he was attending a concert or some sort of science presentation about the robot future that Signor Sterling and his associates were planning to unleash on to the public. Suddenly, COMPUTERWORLD appeared on the screen. That must be the name of the product. Next, a series of huge words appeared, while at the same time being spoken by a portentous, half-human, half-synthesised voice: INTERPOL/ DEUTSCHE BANK/ FBI / SCOTLAND YARD/ CIA/ KGB/ CONTROL DATA/ MEMORY/ COMMUNICATION/ TIME/ MEDICINE/ ENTERTAINMENT. It was clearly a product with a list of powerful clients and a wide range of applications, but what really moved Father Guido were the vibrant irregular patterns of colour that started to dance around the screen, sometimes in sync with the underlying beat of the music, and sometimes with the long breaths and plangent echoes that shimmered and stretched over the frenetic bass. Father Guido drained his second glass of lemonade and looked on with amazement. He was reminded of the ever-changing combinations of tumbling stained-glass fragments in the rotating kaleidoscope his mother had given him for his sixth birthday.

'Infernal racket,' shouted a familiar voice in Father Guido's ear. It was Sir William Moorhead. 'I suppose we can at least agree on that!'

'It reminds me of stained glass,' said the enchanted Abbot, 'but modernised, of course, for young people.'

'These Krauts have been pretending to be robots for at least half a century. It's retro-futurism rather than modernity,' said Moorhead witheringly. 'I think you'll find Soviet poster art, medical monitors and musical visualisation have had a rather larger influence on their work than the rose window in Amiens Cathedral.'

Father Guido could not really understand what Moorhead was complaining about, but he recognised the tone of a man who was used to proving that he was right about everything. Although His Eminence wanted to anathematise Moorhead, Father Guido couldn't help feeling that these two dogmatic, ill-tempered men were really spiritual twins. The truth was that, at this moment, he didn't care what either of them thought; he simply felt too well, too delighted to be part of this jubilant occasion. He only ever watched television at Easter for the Pope's blessing – and also, caving into pressure from the younger friars, when Italy played in the World Cup Final of 2006. Now he could not help gazing in wonder at the film of a white spaceship approaching the snowy ground outside a large institutional building. When it landed, the music also came to an end, with some applause, whistles and whoops from the audience. The stage went dark but soon, out of the pregnant darkness, a new melody emerged. There was a roar of recognition from the guests as the stage lit up again.

Suddenly, La Signorina Jade appeared before the two old men in a short red dress, her black hair stacked up and pierced with a beautiful ivory chopstick, chased with red and black pictograms. 'Come on, guys! This is a classic, we've got to dance.' She joined the musicians in singing the opening words of the song.

She's a model and she's looking good
I'd like to take her home – that's understood

'No possible definition of dancing …' Moorhead began, but Father Guido did not hear the rest of the paragraph, since Jade had clasped his hand and was dragging him towards the stage. When they reached the outer edge of the crowd, Jade let go of Guido's hand and threw herself into a frenzied dance, thrashing her body from side to side, undulating her arms, and then, still swaying, more slowly now, she bowed towards Father Guido and, as her head drew closer, unpinned the grenade of her hair and lashed it from side to side only millimetres from his somewhat prominent waist. Just when the poor Abbot thought he might faint, she arched backwards, making the same writhing motion, but this time with her own waist thrust forward until the longest strands of her hair were touching the grass behind her.

Madonna, thought Father Guido, moving his elbows nervously back and forth and trying to make his old knees move at the same time. Then, in an abrupt change of style, Jade jumped neatly beside him and started to do a perfect impersonation of an old-fashioned cyborg, as if to make Father Guido's rather awkward and rigid dancing style seem like the perfect complement to the music.

'Go Guido!' shouted Jade. 'The mensch-maschine merger! Yay!' She mirrored the old Abbot, walking on the spot with exaggerated jerkiness; shadowing his movements, while gradually encouraging him to increase their complexity. When the song stopped, she leant over and kissed him on the cheek.

'Thanks, Father, I loved that. You're quite the dancer,' she said, bumping her hip against his and then swaying down among the pines and palms and people, artfully reassembling and skewering her hair as she disappeared from view.

Guido was stunned. His heart was pounding and his face trickling with sweat. He felt that perhaps he was in love. What a confusing weekend it was proving to be.

'Another margarita, sir?' asked a waiter.

'Oh, yes, thank you, I am quite hot from dancing,' Father Guido confessed, picking up another glass of the excellent lemonade.

'Un-fucking-believable, hey?' said Signor John MacDonald, the young Scotsman he had shared a ride with from the airport. 'Kraftwerk! Un-fucking-believable. I am properly impressed, properly fucking impressed. What's also totally blowing my mind, at a totally different level, is that some of their visuals look *amazingly* similar to the simulations I'm getting with my Inorganic Life Modelling Program.'

'Perhaps it is a sign pointing to a deeper pattern,' said Father Guido, trying to sound supportive, without having the least idea of what the young Scotsman was talking about.

'That's right! That's what I've ended up thinking,' said John. 'If I were even more paranoid than I am – which would make me really *fucking* paranoid, I can tell you – I might think that Kraftwerk had been hacking *my* Computer World – do you know what I mean? But, as it is, I've taken so much E, I'm much more into the "great-minds-think-alike-slash-two-aspects-of-a-higher-unity" type of space – basically, what you were saying. Would you like some, by the way?' he asked, holding up a rhomboid orange pill. 'It's a religious experience.'

'Believe me,' said Father Guido, 'I have them all the time.'

'Really?' said John. 'That's great to hear. I didn't know you were allowed to. I'm a bit hazy on the vows.' He gave Father Guido an unexpected hug. 'I know you've got your own supplies, but this is *really* good stuff,' he said, dropping the orange pill into Guido's lemonade and giving him a wink.

'But I do not have a headache,' said Father Guido.

John seemed to find this remark inexplicably funny and only recovered from his fit of laughter when the music changed again.

'Fuck!' he shouted, clutching his head in disbelief. 'It's "Radioactivity". I love this song.' He squeezed Father Guido on the shoulder, gave him another embrace and set off into the crowd with his arms outstretched.

A slow synthesised *basso profundo* exhalation of the word *Radioactivity* throbbed through the air. On the screen, a finger tapped out a Morse code, establishing a feverish pulse beneath the deep and resonant syllables. Soon, huge individual words flashed on to the screen, simultaneously pronounced by the robotic voice: CHERNOBYL. HARRISBURG. SELLAFIELD. HIROSHIMA. A red and yellow radioactivity hazard sign receded down a red and yellow tunnel. STOP RADIOACTIVITY.

Father Guido drifted further down the gentle slope towards the stage, sipping his drink appreciatively. Everyone was so friendly. He was in love with La Signorina Jade, and also, if the truth be told, far from indifferent to the lovely Signorina Nadia, with her special healing gifts. The young Scotsman had been unusually affectionate and although the aspirin he had insisted on giving him was completely unnecessary, it was a generous gesture that Guido couldn't help admiring. As he drew closer to the stage, Guido was arrested by the sight of two young women dancing together. One, he recognised as Signor Sterling's lovely blonde girlfriend; the other he had not been introduced to yet, but the two of them were clearly close friends, singing along to the lyrics, while interpreting them with dance.

Stop Radioactivity
Is in the air for you and me.

They both looked up and around with stylised alarm, pointed at each other and then reached out for mutual protection.

Discovered by Madame Curie.

They sang these words while holding each other's shoulders. The line seemed to give them both special pleasure, but they soon suppressed their smiles, separated, widened their eyes and clasped their cheeks as they continued:

Chain reaction
Mutation
Contaminated population.

'Hi, Father G,' said Saul Prokosh, approaching Guido from behind and wrapping an arm around his shoulder. 'Don't you love them?'

'Yes, I do,' said Guido, 'truly I love all of them.'

'Is this the best party you've ever been to?'

'It is, it is,' said Guido, feeling a pang of disloyalty towards Brother Manfredi, whose birthday party in the vegetable garden last year had been the talk of the monastery for weeks.

'Signor Saul, I wanted to discuss a delicate matter with you ...'

'You want the number of my proctologist in LA?'

'I'm sorry,' said Father Guido, 'I do not understand.'

'Just kidding,' said Saul. 'Say it how it is, Guido; tell me what's on your mind.'

'I have been asked by the *Curia*,' Father Guido launched in blindly, 'to approach you about a share of the profits from the scan of Fra Domenico's brain.'

'Well now, technically, that's our data,' said Saul, 'because of a certain form you signed before we did the scan, and without which we would *not* have done the scan, but we're hoping for a big endorsement from His Holiness – we don't want you guys saying we stole one of your relics, right? – so we could certainly look into profit sharing on that basis. I'll get our legal team on to it on Monday, but I can tell you we'd be totally open to a collaborative approach.'

'Oh, wonderful! God be praised!' cried Father Guido. 'It is a great weight off my mind.'

'Don't sweat it,' said Saul. 'Just keep on enjoying the party.'

'Yes!' said Father Guido. 'Thank you. I am enjoying this party more than I can say.'

On the screen, there were now vertical blocks of brilliant colour. The synthesisers were playing a gentle meandering melody.

Neon lights
Shimmering neon lights

This city's made of light

Father Guido felt the radiance of each colour filling his body. Stained-glass windows had been designed to make cathedrals into images of Paradise, but here he was, in the open air, flooded with light, in the cathedral of nature: the whole world was Paradise, these musicians were angels masquerading as robots to camouflage themselves in the contemporary world; his heart, in fact every cell in his body, was a rose window through which the light of eternity was streaming, but also *from* which it was streaming at the same time. It seemed to be everywhere, not just beamed down like a spotlight from a remote location beyond the sky.

'This is the city of light,' he whispered to himself. 'This is what I was looking for through the kaleidoscope.'

So much lawn, thought Francis, and so much night lighting, disorienting the moths and bats. Although it was still quite early and none of the other guests were yet in circulation, most of the signs of last night's party had already been dismantled and removed. He had promised Hunter that he would take a look around *Le Plein Soleil* and see what could be done to increase the biodiversity of the property. Ploughing up the lawn would be a good start. A field of mixed grasses, with mowed paths winding through it, would be filled at this time of year with wildflowers and poppies. Hunter had nine acres, an astonishing amount of land in the circumstances, but a relatively small amount in the context of wilding. The larger drama of this part of the Mediterranean landscape was its dryness and the abandoned, unmanaged scrub covering the hills and mountains a few miles back from the monstrously popular coast. It was a brittle zone, a fire hazard made more incendiary by the lack of animals, wild or domestic, to control the accumulation of leaf litter, pinecones and dead wood that made fires so violent and hot that nothing could survive their passage. The average amount of dead wood was three times higher than a hundred years ago, and after each fire, the rain washed away more topsoil making a poorer environment for the regeneration of pines and oaks.

On the smaller scale of *Le Plein Soleil* a lot could be done by taking simple measures. The property was divided and contained by walls that could be turned into dry-stone walls by removing the cement fillings, leaving nooks for lizards and salamanders and lichens. Hunter could join the Mediterranean 'amphibian ark' by creating a shady pond for frogs to breed in. A third of amphibians in the region were endangered, and worldwide the whole class of Amphibia was under threat from chytridiomycosis, a deadly set of fungal diseases with no known cure. To prevent the pond from becoming a stagnant nursery for mosquitoes, there could be fish that ate mosquito larvae while the tadpoles grazed the algae growing on the walls, and lily pads for the frogs to sit on when they were grown up, and a gentle flow of water that would eventually run into an orchard, irrigating trees to provide unsprayed fruit for Hunter's household, as well as food and flowers for bees and wasps and caterpillars and birds. Amphibians were especially sensitive to chemicals in water and so he would suggest large storage tanks, hidden along the top of the slope, perhaps behind a new olive plantation, for collecting the winter rainwater and then releasing it slowly through the arid summer months. At the far end of the orchard there could be a few log hives and tree hives, not to harvest honey but for pollination and support for the beleaguered bee. Lavender, which would attract butterflies as well as bees, could replace the fertilised, heavily irrigated beds of gaudy, flimsy flowers. Maybe he could persuade Hunter to plant a small oak grove. Oaks supported over three hundred other species, many more than the palms and pines that currently dominated the property. Yes, an oak grove, perhaps beyond the orchard, among the wild beehives and a new herb garden of rosemary and thyme and basil and sage, and lemon verbena.

In the last tapering triangle of Hunter's land, there was a white-washed hexagonal pavilion, its arched windows edged with pale orange marble and an open doorway overlooking the sea. From the pavilion, two paths curved through the rock garden to the edge of the water, where a flight of steps led down to a private harbour, tucked out of view from the house. There was nothing growing on or immediately around the pavilion at the moment, which could easily have an orange-flowered trumpet vine encircling it, or ever-green ivy with dark berries to feed the birds in late winter and early spring; or honeysuckle, favoured by the amazing hummingbird hawk-moth. Two or three lime trees with their soporific blossom might replace some of the rock garden and mark the far end of the property with shade and a place to rest.

As he was staring at the pavilion, imagining the appearance and impact of various climbing plants, Francis saw Father Guido on its threshold, still gazing at the sea in the early morning light. He eventually stepped out, seeming rather dazed and lost in thought.

'Good morning,' Francis called, across the rock garden.

'Ah, *buongiorno*,' said Father Guido. 'It is very beautiful. Everything is very beautiful, you agree?'

'I agree,' said Francis, walking over to the pavilion, smiling. 'You're up early.'

'I have not been to bed,' said Father Guido. 'I have felt too exhilarated by the party and the kindness of the guests and the power of the concert, and then, when I was determined to go indoors, I was enchanted by the rising sun. I have been sitting here.' Father Guido indicated the cushioned bench inside the pavilion.

'May I?' said Francis.

'Of course,' said Father Guido, seeming delighted to have an excuse to go back to his favourite spot. 'Let's sit down and look through this archway. For some reason it is even more beautiful, when it is ...' Father Guido searched for the English word.

'Framed?' suggested Francis.

'Exactly. Like a picture,' said Father Guido. 'Nothing is added to the view, except the edges, and so it becomes a picture!'

'Yes,' said Francis.

'So, you are the one who is up early,' said Father Guido.

'That's right,' said Francis. 'I'm a naturalist, and Hunter asked me to have a look around and think of some ways to help more plants and animals make a home here.'

'Oh, that is excellent,' said Father Guido. 'I am a Franciscan and we love all forms of life, all aspects of creation.'

'Perhaps you can help me come up with some ideas,' said Francis. 'Saul tells me you have some lovely woods and gardens around your monastery.'

'Ah, yes, it is lovely,' said Father Guido. 'I have always lived in Perugia, which is very fortunate, but you know, everything has grown quieter there since I was a boy. The birds are quieter in the spring, the cicadas are quieter in the summer. When we were children, we used to go into the woods to watch the fireflies; now many of the woods are dark. My mother used to warn me to watch out for the *cinghiale*, how you say?'

'Wild boar.'

'Yes! Now I would be so happy to see more of them. The country has grown ...'

'Thin?' suggested Francis.

'Yes, thin. Instead of an orchestra, we have a harpsichord, an old harpsichord, so to speak, with many dead keys.'

'Ninety-three per cent of the biomass of all the birds and mammals on this planet is made up of human beings and their domesticated animals,' said Francis, 'only seven per cent is wild.'

'Can this be true?' said Father Guido.

'Yes, that's how much wildlife is crushed under existing conditions.'

'Incredible!' said Guido, removing his glasses and wiping his eyes with his sleeves. 'Forgive me, I am very emotional today. We must help.'

'Everyone can help,' said Francis: 'plant a window box with seeds rather than with plants propagated with pesticides, reintroduce bison to the Carpathian Mountains, give the sea a rest, stop drowning dolphins and turtles in fishing nets, put out a birdfeeder; and between now and lunchtime, you and I can help by coming up with some ideas about how to revitalise this little park. The distribution of species is not fixed, it changes constantly with local immigrations and extinctions. Unless we insist on extinction, the natural cycles of a place are like a kaleidoscope, with pieces falling in and falling out.'

'Ah, *sì*!' said Father Guido. 'Yes, yes, I have had this vision also, last night, it is ...' He took Francis's hand, but seemed unable to say anything, wonder and incomprehension taking turns in his old and innocent face. 'Forgive me, I have not the words.'

15

'Hi, darling, let me put on my headphones,' said Lucy. '"Stop radio-activity",' she chanted, 'or, at least move it a little further from my brain.'

She was lying in a hammock on Hunter's private terrace, watching a bumblebee crawl into a wisteria bell and clamber out encrusted in pollen. The other guests had gone, except for Saul, who was leaving later that day. She and Hunter would then have a few days alone; alone, that is, apart from the unavoidable Jade – she sometimes expected to find her in Hunter's bed, with her radiant teeth, asking if there was anything she could do to help – and, of course, the *Plein Soleil* 'team', which numbered somewhere between ten and twenty, it was hard to tell, since each day new people greeted her from behind a rose bush or stood politely aside on the staircase, carrying fresh linen or bottles of mineral water.

'So, how are you?' she asked, when she had the phone far enough away from her to talk comfortably.

'I've got some big news,' said Olivia, 'or, at least, some growing news.'

'Oh my god, you are pregnant,' said Lucy, who had already talked with Olivia over the weekend about her emphatically late period.

'Yup.'

'Wow,' said Lucy, hedging between congratulations and compassion.

'We're both a bit stunned.'

'Are you still unsure what to do?'

'It's just that ...'

'Have the baby,' said Lucy impulsively. She realised, as she said
it, how much she was longing for a set of multiplying cells she could
be wholeheartedly enthusiastic about, and how much her vote was
driven by a wave of sadness about no longer being able to have a
child herself, given her uncertain prognosis. 'As long as I can be a
godmother,' she added. She was going to have to compromise, given
that she wasn't going to be a mother or, for that matter, a god. She
watched another bumblebee launch itself, weighted with cargo, into
the air. It seemed to be her own atmosphere she was trying to lighten,
as much as Olivia's.

'Obviously you'd be *the* godmother,' said Olivia.

'Francis is great, you're great ...' Lucy felt herself getting lost in
a complex, hollow mixture of regret and relief. Three years back,
Nathan had talked fervently about having a child, wanting to tie
down their relationship with the steel cables of parenthood. She had
prevaricated, perhaps already knowing that she didn't ultimately
want to stay with him.

'Francis *is* great,' said Olivia, 'but we haven't been together for
that long, and he doesn't make a fortune counting nightingales and
living in a tied cottage. Nor do I. And I'm attached to my independence – or at least used to it. Attached to being non-attached; it feels
like there could be a problem lurking there.'

Lucy didn't answer immediately. She was thinking about how
divided she had always been about having a baby: wanting to give
it what she hadn't had, while fearing she would pass on the worst
of what she did have. Recently, she had been thinking more and more
about the stresses of her childhood in relation to her illness. It was
one of the penalties of her holistic approach, not to allocate blame,
but to wonder about the psychosomatic chain, if there was one.

'Is the adoption thing coming up for you?' she asked. 'I mean,
Karen didn't want to have a child when she was pregnant with you.'

'Sure,' said Olivia, 'but I didn't meet her until I was twenty-six, so she doesn't play a huge part in my thinking.'

'Hmm,' said Lucy, agreeing in a way that implied that it couldn't be quite so simple, but hurrying on to a more affirmative note. 'I can so easily picture Francis walking around Howorth with a baby strapped to his chest.'

'So can I,' said Olivia.

'And also,' said Lucy, in a more practical tone, 'Hunter has become wild about wilding and is planning to give Francis all sorts of gigs, including wilding his ranch in California, which is huge compared to this place.'

'I know, that's exciting,' said Olivia, 'and Francis is already halfway through his report on *Plein Soleil*, but we can't rely entirely on Hunter to pay for the costs of bringing up a child.'

There was a sharp edge to Olivia's tone that made Lucy feel that she was more of a charity case than she would have liked. She was running *EpiFutures*, but she was also following her doctor's instructions not to push herself too hard. In her experience, what 'too hard' meant in the corporate world was the point at which insanity became counterproductive. At *Strategy*, there had been a semi-satirical competitiveness about late hours and work-annihilated weekends from which she knew she was now exempt but also knew that she was now excluded.

'That's another thing that worries us about having a baby,' Olivia went on, 'there are seven billion of us already de-wilding the planet.'

'True,' said Lucy, 'but there's a drastic shortage of *sane* human beings, and you and Francis would definitely provide the world with one of those. How does he feel, other than co-stunned?'

'Open,' said Olivia. 'Hang on, here he is, I'll ask him.'

Lucy could make out some muffled response from Francis. She took the opportunity to swallow the medicinal mushrooms she had ready on the ledge beside the hammock: chaga, maitake, lion's mane, reishi, coriolus.

'He says he's apprehensively excited by the pregnancy,' said Olivia, 'but stoically resigned to ending it, if that's my decision.'

'In other words, he's being perfect as usual,' said Lucy.

'Perhaps too perfect,' said Olivia, 'I think he may be a cyborg.'

'You could be the mother of the first cyborg-sapiens child,' said an awestruck Lucy, 'and the child shall be called The Chosen One.'

'That's made me feel much better about my decision. There's nothing like starting a new race and a world religion to take the pressure off,' said Olivia. 'Hang on, Francis is trying to give me a long list of his all too human failings.'

'A classic cyborg move,' said Lucy.

'Absolutely classic,' said Olivia. 'I think I'm going to have to adjust his settings – switch off Human Camouflage to get my perfect companion back.'

'For God's sake hurry,' said Lucy, 'before Human Camouflage achieves a black box recursive learning autonomy, making it more human than any human being, until it ends up destroying us on the logical but unintended grounds of our sub-optimal humanity.'

'That's exactly what I was worried about,' said Olivia.

'I'd better leave you to deal with that emergency,' said Lucy.

'I'll call tomorrow to check up on you,' said Olivia. 'I feel I've taken all the airtime today.'

'Well, not quite,' said Lucy, 'and, anyway it's a huge moment in the history of the species.'

'Thanks for putting it in perspective,' said Olivia, 'it's so easy to lose sight of the big picture.'

After they had said goodbye, Lucy switched her phone to silent. She wondered how helpful she had really been to Olivia. These playful riffs had always been a feature of their friendship, especially when there was something going on that was too charged to be worked out logically or conclusively. She saw now that the news of Olivia's pregnancy had released an undertow of grief about the fact that she could no longer, in her own eyes, responsibly have a child. She had defended herself against that grief with a muddled fantasy about having a child with Nathan, as if the missed opportunity to be a single parent with a menacing diagnosis, bringing up a young child with a man who now hated her, were something to regret.

Apart from anything else, if she had a small child she might well not be lying in Hunter's private hammock; although six months ago it was the last place she would have imagined herself being under any circumstances. When she had first met him, he had been far too charming to be lovable and when she started working for him, she often found him positively obnoxious. It was only over their dinner in November, on his second visit to London, when he had chosen to be open rather than impressive, that he became impressive for the first time. She could see that his manic lifestyle was scheduled by chronic loneliness and by the suspicion that any surrender to true feeling would act as Kryptonite to his superpowers. He was obviously attracted to her, but his relative authenticity was still too new for her to be able to trust him with her diagnosis. After that dinner she had thought about him more often, with a vague erotic curiosity, but she still chose to register her biopsy as 'sick leave'. It was only when he turned up unexpectedly at Howorth that things changed more convincingly. His charm was replaced by kindness. His professional audacity turned out to be an extension of his emotional courage, rather than a substitute for it, as she had first suspected. He enveloped her in a protection that not only made her feel safe, but left her free to feel unsafe: when she was overcome by terror and despair (which she sometimes still was) he would meet her in whatever black site she had been abducted to by her fears.

In any case, she must try to do better next time she spoke to Olivia. For the moment, though, she wanted to rest and stare at the sea, albeit a little guiltily, and daydream for a while. First, she had to force down the remains of the Chinese herbs she was taking twice a day. She had prepared the bitter brew instead of breakfast, but Olivia's call had interrupted her halfway through consuming it. In the World of Four Objects into which her diagnosis had marched her, like a bored prison guard pointing out the amenities of a cell – statistic, poison, scalpel, radiation – there was no room for Chinese herbs, or a low-sugar and low-carb diet that starved the tumour without starving the patient, or medicinal mushrooms, or enhanced mental health. There was 'no evidence' that any complementary approach worked because the presumption that it did not work prevented funding for the expensive, controlled, large sample, double-blind, replicable experiments that would constitute 'evidence'.

Nobody could be more grateful than Lucy that chemotherapy and surgery and radiation were available if her tumour became active enough to warrant their deployment, but she remained sceptical that there were no other actions to take, no other factors in play. How could her general fitness, the strength of her immune system, her will to live and her levels of stress make no difference? She wanted to create an environment that was as inimical to her cancer as possible and as favourable to the strength she would need in order to live with it. She hoped to add many years to the 'long right-hand tail' of the prognostic graph and felt that it was unscientific to assume that only blind luck and three types of aggression could carry her there.

While proper scientists defended true methodology by pouring boiling oil and dropping rocks on the besieging hordes of pseudo-scientists, with their diets and their herbs, their acupuncture needles and their Ayurvedic spices, their meditation practices and yoga positions, it turned out that some parts of the citadel they were defending were rotten by their own 'double blind' standards. A 'replication crisis' was rippling through one discipline after another. Carl Sagan's remark that extraordinary claims required extraordinary proofs, so often quoted by Bill Moorhead, didn't mean that orthodox claims needed no proof at all, and yet many of those claims, which had taken on the complacency of unexamined assumptions, had recently been held up to the ordinary test of being replicable, and failed. The crisis itself had now been given the imprimatur of serious science by appearing in *Nature* and all other leading scientific journals. There was no need to storm the melting citadel; in fact, it aroused Lucy's pity. She didn't want to replace dogmatism with an equally obstinate iconoclasm, she just wanted those parts of the impressive stone walls that had been borrowed from the prop department to be sent back to the warehouse where they belonged with the other fake boulders and soft battlements; with the debris of broken theories, of phrenological busts and treatises on phlogiston, and giant pre-Copernican maps of the cosmos painted with lapis lazuli and gold.

'Hi, baby,' said Hunter, stepping on to the terrace, carrying two glasses. 'Emile just made this juice for us. It's got kale and beetroot and flax oil – I can't remember all the ingredients, but it's a super-food cluster-fuck that means we're going to have to face up to our immortality.'

'"The woods decay, the woods decay and fall … Me only cruel immortality consumes,"' Lucy quoted wearily.

'Hang on, I'm having one too. This is an immortality pact.'

'Farewell, cruel death!' said Lucy, taking the drink with a smile.

'So, what's happened in the agonising hour of separation since I last saw you?' asked Hunter.

'Well, Olivia told me she was pregnant.'

'No kidding,' said Hunter.

'Funny you should use that phrase,' said Lucy in an astute German accent.

'Okay, so they're kidding,' said Hunter, 'but are they serious? It's unplanned – I assume.'

'Yes, but not necessarily unwelcome,' said Lucy, taking a sip of her death-threatening juice. 'They're talking it through in the next few days.'

Hunter leant over and gave Lucy a kiss on her beetroot-stained lips.

'Apart from that, are you feeling well?' he asked.

'I feel great,' said Lucy. 'After talking to Olivia, I just lay here daydreaming and thinking about complementary medicine and why it works.'

'Or whether it's a placebo,' said Hunter.

'Placebos work,' said Lucy. 'That's one of the things that interest me: why is a known therapeutic benefit treated as a glitch?'

'Because it's based on deception,' said Hunter.

'What deception?' asked Saul, who had appeared at the terrace gate, photons raining on the sea behind him and the Calder turning very slowly into a new configuration. 'Is it okay if I come in?' he asked. 'I don't want to interrupt but there are a couple of developments on the *Capo Santo* deal that I'd like to run past you before I fly out. We can talk them through on the phone tomorrow, if you prefer.'

'Come on in,' said Hunter.

'Hi, Saul,' said Lucy. 'The "deception" was the placebo effect, and I was asking, where's the deception? If a patient thinks she's going to get better and then does get better, why not call it persuasion, or self-healing? The deception is built into the experimental method, it's not inherent to the effect.'

'Right,' said Saul, 'the deception is in making sugar pills look identical to the pharmaceutical pills they are being tested against; the psychogenic effect is real.'

'It's hard to see how to harness it, though,' said Hunter. 'It's been treated for so long as a sign of human frailty that it should be relegated to the Daniel Kahneman penal colony for cognitive bias, rotten intuition, groundless prejudice and misleading heuristics. I guess the real test is what happens to the effect if people know they are being given a sugar pill.'

'That's the beauty of it,' said Saul, 'it still works. Ted Kaptchuk is the top placebo guy. He's at Harvard Med and he's shown that what he calls "open label placebo" has a powerful effect. People know they are taking a sugar pill and sixty per cent of them still report significant relief of symptoms.'

'How would you market that?' said Hunter.

'Call it *Open Placebo*,' said Saul, 'and get an endorsement from Harvard Med. The margins would be incredible: close to zero cost for manufacturing the product and at the same time a moral responsibility to augment the patient's sense of receiving something valuable by pricing it up.'

'Could they not be sugar pills?' said Lucy. 'It clashes with my diet, and with everyone's dental health.'

'No problem,' said Saul, 'but it mustn't be something that anyone else is claiming is beneficial, otherwise it'll get lost in the supplement zone.'

'I'm enjoying the supplement zone,' said Lucy. 'Just because something is actually beneficial, like this fabulous juice, doesn't mean that my conviction that it's beneficial can't give it a placebo turbo.'

'Absolutely,' said Saul. 'Ted Kaptchuk's work is all about expanding the definition of placebo beyond a trick pill used in a pharmaceutical trial. He wants to include and quantify the whole therapeutic drama surrounding prescriptions and procedures: the attentive listening, the rituals and the costumes, the diplomas on the wall, the authority of the healer.'

'And being touched,' said Lucy. 'The laying on of hands – not in a faith-healer way, but just as an acknowledgement that my body is in need of attention. I've spent so much time in hospitals looking at computer images of my brain or talking to a doctor who is reading a printout of some test results. I think that's one of the appeals of complementary medicine: the acupuncturist and the herbalist take my pulses and look at my tongue and touch my muscles; they are delivering the massive reassurance of dealing directly with my body and not just with my data.'

'Totally,' said Saul.

'Listen, I must let you have your *Capo Santo* talk,' said Lucy, beginning to sit up in the hammock.

'You don't have to go anywhere,' said Hunter. 'I'm going to lay my hands on you,' he said, gently easing her back into a lying position, 'now I know how much you like that.'

'Why, Doctor, I feel inexplicably well,' said Lucy, as she subsided into the hammock.

'We call it personal haptic gap closure therapy, or PHGCT,' said Hunter sagely.

'I feel so lucky to be involved in this trial,' said Lucy. 'I hope there are some vaguely similar people in vaguely similar circumstances who are not receiving PHGCT as a control.'

'Don't worry, Lucy, this is an experiment structured to the most rigorous standards.'

Lucy smiled at Hunter, who rested his hand fondly for a moment on her tummy before turning to Saul.

'So, where are we with The Inquisition?' he asked.

'They want fifty per cent,' said Saul.

'And I want to be non-executive Pope, with fifty per cent of global revenues,' said Hunter.

'I offered them ten per cent,' said Saul.

'And?' said Hunter.

'Holy indignation,' said Saul.

'Go up to fifteen in exchange for a vigorous advertising campaign, and twenty if they also market the *Equanimity* helmet, which we can rebrand for them without changing the algorithm: *The Peace that Passeth Understanding*, *Blessed Mother of Tranquillity*, whatever works for them.'

'Father Guido told me they were having problems with their *Stations of the Cross* virtual reality program,' said Lucy. 'He became quite confessional over lunch. I think he thought the Espresso Martinis were just iced coffee, but in any case, please don't do anything to get him into trouble; he's such a sweet man.'

'We'll say that the only reason we're considering profit sharing is thanks to his superhuman negotiating skills,' said Hunter.

'With *Avatar*, we've got the technology to help with that,' said Saul.

'No more profit sharing,' said Hunter. 'This techno-religion is going to be huge.'

'How about less profit share and we fix the *Stations*?' asked Saul.

'That could work,' said Hunter.

'The beautiful thing is that whether it's the *Bhagavad Gita*, or Golgotha, or Mara v Buddha under the Bodhi Tree, we can totally nail the journey with a combination of the scans we've already made and the VR from *Avatar* – which, by the way, turns out to be helping with the schizophrenics they designed it for.'

'Yes, I was happy to see that,' said Lucy. 'I mentioned the good results to Martin Carr last week, Olivia's dad, and he thought that exposing patients who are radically confused about what is real to an experience which is designed to seduce even the most robust realist might not be what is making them feel better.'

'Maybe it helps precisely because it's a *known* unreality,' said Saul.

'I ran the same sort of argument past Martin, but he was sceptical that the beneficial effects were taking place at that kind of cognitive level. He's worked for years with paranoid schizophrenics and knows that if one of them, for instance, is terrified of getting on to a crowded train, that taking them into a basement, attaching heavy equipment to their heads and inducing hallucinations of simulated train passengers could easily be experienced by them as a satanic ritual designed to drive them mad.'

'So, why the good results?'

'Because often these patients have been so maltreated and are so frightened that being taken seriously, treated sympathetically, told there is a solution, looked after by experts, encouraged to share their responses, and so on, has a strong salutary effect.'

'Another placebo,' said Hunter.

'Yes,' said Lucy, 'in the widest sense that we were talking about earlier: being cared for by people who know what they are doing. Once that trust is established, then all sorts of other things might come into play: the simulation could act as a way to externalise an inner voice, to place it in a narrative, letting out the evil element and projecting it safely.'

'You've got to nail this *Open Placebo* thing,' said Hunter.

'I'm on it,' said Saul.

'I'm in it,' said Lucy.

'How about the known benefits of an early lunch, before Saul leaves for the airport?'

'Perfect,' said Lucy, swinging out of the hammock with a sense of gratitude at being looked after so well and at the same time with a bruise of sadness about the cloud encircling this peak of kindness and goodwill in her life.

16

For Lizzie, it was a cause for unalloyed celebration when Olivia told them that she and Francis were going to have a baby. She loved Francis, looked forward to having a grandchild, and felt that Olivia's desire to bring a child into the world, despite knowing that she had been an unwanted child at birth, was a deep reparation of her troubled history. For Martin, who had seen Sebastian earlier that day, there were dimensions to the situation, beyond his genuine delight, that he couldn't discuss with anyone around the table, or even fully appreciate himself, in the atmosphere of jubilation that followed Olivia's announcement. She had chosen to have the baby at the Royal Free, just up the road from her parents' house, and had gone on to ask if she and Francis could stay for a while at Belsize Park during the first days of its life. Martin's need to disguise the disorienting suspicion that his most disturbed patient, who came to the house three times a week, might well be his grandchild's uncle had prevented him from thinking clearly about the implications at the time.

Olivia had now set off to Howorth and Martin was able to retreat to the sanctuary of his consulting room fifty minutes before his first patient arrived. Sitting in his worn armchair, staring at the midsummer garden, he couldn't stop thinking about Sebastian's tendency to burst outside in moments of high tension, nor could he shake off the memory of Charlie and Olivia tottering around that same garden as small children or resting there, after being wheeled back and forth across the lawn until they fell asleep in their big old pram – which Lizzie was proud not to have thrown away, all those years ago, despite the children's slightly anxious mockery of her sentimentality (who was she keeping it for?) and the memorable struggle of hoisting it sideways into the loft. The collision of these two images recurred several times while Martin got up to make a cup of coffee, standing at the back of the room by the cupboard where he kept a small fridge, a kettle and some biscuits, hidden from his hungry patients.

At least in January he could keep the garden door locked and, in any case, Olivia's newborn baby was unlikely to go out there during those cold, dark days. Nevertheless, Olivia might naturally wander out on a sunny morning to get some fresh air in that fashionable and elusive enclosure, 'a safe space', only to find that her unknown twin was bellowing psychotically in the basement or crouched behind the curtains in a knot of primal fear. Martin's other patients would lie down, free associating while they gazed at the ceiling, or perhaps closed their eyes, indifferent to the muffled sounds of domesticity that reached his consulting room: the rare, faint ring of the landline or the distant thud of the front door closing, only just audible in a pause. They would probably not notice anyone in the garden, or remark on it if they did, but for Sebastian, who often got up from his chair, or checked over his shoulder, nothing could be more provocative than an infant in its mother's loving arms. At this stage of his treatment, the sound of Olivia's baby crying might make him think he was hearing another delusional voice or being tortured by the sly, knowing soundtrack to his screaming psyche. Even if he were well enough by January to be sure that the baby was in fact a baby, he might not be able to stand the competition of seeing it being loved and looked after.

Martin's growing conviction that Sebastian was Olivia's twin brother came from the strange harmonies between some of the material that he brought with him to the sessions and the stories Karen had told Olivia about her brother's early life. Towards the end of a session that appeared to be a long and rather generic allegory of explosive rage and potential attack – 'where they keep the bombs hidden ... the guns and the bodies riddled with bullet holes ...' – Sebastian revealed that when he was eighteen the Tanners had told him that he was an adopted child, but had refused to tell him anything about his mother, except to say that she was a bad woman who hadn't wanted him, and that she lived in 'the Arsenal area'. They said that if he was mad enough to want to meet her, he must do it on his own. The mysterious weapons depot and the 'Gunners' in Sebastian's free association turned out not to be entirely metaphorical references, but historical and geographical ones as well. Martin knew that Karen lived in Arsenal; he also knew that Sebastian was the same age as Olivia; although his exact birthday still hadn't yet come up, he knew it was in the same month as Olivia's; he knew about the cigarette burns, now transformed into bullet wounds, and he knew that Olivia's twin had been handed over for adoption at the same age as Sebastian. The evidence was hammering at the door, but Martin had still resisted making any official enquiries about Sebastian's identity, preferring to work with the material that Sebastian brought to the sessions, keeping it sealed in the alembic of the psychoanalytic process. Now he wondered if he should just find out the facts of the case. Was Sebastian Olivia's twin or not? And yet, knowing that he would never have tried to find out for Sebastian's benefit, because the official facts would have introduced a foreign vocabulary into the lexicon of symbolic language that they were working to compile together, how could he justify doing that research simply to appease his own curiosity and concern? Part of him also wished he could discuss the matter with Lizzie, but he resisted doing so. She was a psychotherapist, and in theory he was allowed to discuss difficult cases with his colleagues, but she was also his wife and Olivia's mother. Only absolute confidentiality could ensure that Sebastian's insights were not tainted with the distrust and confusion that had afflicted him all his life. Ultimately, Martin could turn to the Ethics Committee; although, as a senior analyst, the Ethics Committee usually turned to him.

How had it come to this? There was an unwelcome Sophoclean intensity in discovering that a potentially hostile stranger turned out to be a close relation; to the possibility of his daughter meeting her mad brother for the first time as her father's patient, or the possibility of his newborn grandchild provoking the anger and the envy of his gravely deluded uncle. A troubling entanglement of family and therapy was part of the foundations of Martin's profession. Anna Freud, who was famously analysed by her father, remained unmarried for the rest of her life; no man could match up to the hero who had helped her to acquire the treasure of self-knowledge and see into the depths of her unconscious mind. The incestuous implications were clear, or at least should have been clear to a man so alert to incestuous implications, and yet who else could Freud have sent his daughter to see and how could he deprive her of the revolutionary benefits of the discovery he was in the course of making? Since those early untrammelled days, more and more boundaries had been put in place to protect the analytic process from the corruption of indiscretion, misuse of authority, counter-transference, inadequate training and all the other difficulties attendant on forming a secure attachment to a therapist in order to turn that successful dependency into a successful independence for the patient. As one of the most careful guardians of those boundaries, Martin was disturbed to think that he might have inadvertently breached them, and yet the origins of all this explosive Arsenal-borne complexity were simple and well-intentioned enough: Martin had arranged to see Sebastian in his home consulting room because he felt he needed more sessions. His room had a separate entrance and usually the only other person at home was Lizzie, working with her own patients at the top of the house, with two entirely private floors in between. Olivia usually came to stay in the evening or at weekends, when the whole house was private. She was also the seasoned daughter of two psychotherapists, although Martin had only started working at home when the children went to primary school and Lizzie had waited until they had left home altogether. When he took Sebastian on as a patient, Francis had just been the rumour of Olivia's new boyfriend, who Lizzie and Martin had yet to meet.

He was also confident that Sebastian was not a source of danger. Schizophrenia's reputation for violence was exaggerated, except in the case of suicide, which about half of the schizophrenic population attempted, with one in twenty succeeding. Martin had worked with psychotic patients throughout his career and was certain that Sebastian was not criminally insane. He hadn't just emerged from Broadmoor Hospital; he was an ambulatory schizophrenic who might have been frightening or repellent to some people, but to Martin, who was not easily frightened, he was a patient with a reasonable chance of recovery, who it would be unreasonable and unkind not to help.

He settled back into his armchair, realising that although he had needed to get up to make a cup of coffee, he didn't especially need to drink it. He had caught himself being a little buffeted by these unexpected developments, but now he was returning to his professional centre of gravity: his basic conviction that it didn't matter what conundrums arose in an analysis, as long as the practitioner was stable and had internalised his own analysis enough to continue reflecting and not to act out under pressure – at least, not more than he had just done by making an unnecessary cup of coffee, moving between the professional armchair in which he saw all his patients and the private cupboard that he never opened when his patients were present. This tiny enactment of his dilemma was forgivable. What would not be forgivable would be to betray either his family or his patient, but both those outcomes could be avoided. Sebastian was only in the house for a hundred and fifty minutes a week, his analysis was progressing well, and Martin only had to tell Lizzie and Olivia the times of his sessions, explaining that he had an especially vulnerable patient who might be confused or perturbed if he saw or heard the baby. The truth was that in practical terms, it was quite manageable; the intensity of his initial response had come from imagining the potential impact of a collision between Sebastian and Olivia. The birth of her child was bound to resurrect Olivia's deepest feelings about her own rejection at birth, but if she met her psychotic twin at the moment that she was standing squarely against the contagion of trauma, then any sense she might have that she could not prevent the shadow of her history from falling on another innocent generation would become that much more daunting.

There was also the fact that, while Martin was not analysing his own daughter, like the founding father of his profession, he was writing a paper with her about different approaches to schizophrenia. It was a subject on which both their professional interests converged, so why shouldn't they collaborate in writing about their findings? This particular entanglement of family and therapy seemed to be taking place at an impeccably academic level of discussion, but the fact that Sebastian was suffering from the complex disease he had urged her to focus on created a secret familial overload that only Martin was aware of. From a certain point of view, it might look as if an adopting father and an adopted daughter were repressing the genetic Caliban of a mad twin for their own convenience and peace of mind. This would of course have been an illusion. They were both aware of the weakness of the evidence for a genetic basis to schizophrenia and the startling contrast between Olivia's mental health and Sebastian's reinforced that view. Still, in the underwater world he had spent the last half-hour exploring, the world of incongruous encounters and potential unravelling, the subject matter of their paper seemed to be wrapping its tentacles around the authors and dragging them into murky depths. It was worth acknowledging these dimensions in order to discount them with more clarity.

PART THREE

17

Olivia was lying in bed, her hands pressed to her bulging belly, feeling the baby kick and turn and enjoying a moment of communion she chose not to share with Francis, although he was lying beside her.

'It is amazing here,' she said instead, as the electric blinds purred up, unveiling the view from their bedroom. On one side, far below, a redwood forest ran down to the edge of the Pacific; on the other, an undulation of autumnal hills flowed south from Hunter's house. In the distance, she could see the sharper creases of the Santa Lucia Mountains, a compressed accordion of chaparral ridgelines. At least a dozen butterflies were resting on the plate-glass window, some with pulsing wings, as if catching their breath before their next flight.

'Those Monarch butterflies have flown down from northern Canada to spend the winter here,' said Francis. 'It takes four generations to make the three-thousand-mile round trip.'

'Each generation must be born knowing the way,' said Olivia.

'Yes, when it comes to navigation, they have bigger minds than any one of us – just more distributed through the generations and the kaleidoscope.'

'Kaleidoscope?' said Olivia.

'It's a collective noun for a group of butterflies.'

'I thought it was swarm.'

'I went with kaleidoscope.'

'Such an aesthete,' said Olivia.

'It's true,' said Francis, staring out of the window, smiling.

The redwoods down in the coastal canyons belonged to a state park that protected *Apocalypse Now* from below. Its flanks were protected by two other large private properties. Altogether the three ranches formed a block of roughly five thousand acres, slightly larger than Howorth but more complicated to integrate. The further thousand acres of the state park had its own policy and its own management, and a bureaucracy that Hunter was better off not provoking, but yesterday he had invited his two other neighbours over to lunch, hoping to persuade them to participate in the wilding project that Francis was devising for him.

Jim Burroughs, the owner of *Titan Ranch*, was a self-mocking Republican with a white moustache, who joked that the only gun-control he could imagine supporting would be a law that made it mandatory for anyone over the age of five to carry a concealed weapon.

'How else are they going to protect themselves in the modern school environment?' he chuckled.

Jim's great-grandfather had bought *Titan Ranch* in 1924 to raise the finest grass-fed cattle in California. Jim claimed that he was planning to celebrate a century of Burroughs ownership by releasing a thousand doves from a patch of woodland on his property, while a hundred friends of his stood nearby, heavily armed. The guests would be protected from each other by flak jackets and pellet-proof visors, since you couldn't rule out a 'Dick Cheney moment' at a circular shoot in the middle of a cocktail party.

'The dove that gets away from that wood alive is certainly going to justify its reputation as the poster bird for universal peace,' said Jim.

'Are the doves going to be armed?' asked Lucy. 'Otherwise, I don't see what they have to justify.'

'Yes,' said Olivia, 'what about *their* Second Amendment rights?'

'We're flying them in from Colombia,' said Jim. 'They don't have any Second Amendment rights.'

'They're just bad *palomas*,' said Hunter, 'rapists and drug doves.'

'That's right,' said Jim, the glass in his hand recoiling several times from his laughing mouth. 'Kidding aside, tree-huggers and hunters need to work together on this one: with no trees to hug, there won't be any animals to hunt. If you and Francis are going to come up with a way to make the land more fertile and the wildlife more abundant, count me in. Science is mostly common sense with a lot of uncommon words snapping at its heels, but as long as you can explain it to me in plain English, I'll sign on the dotted line.'

'Great,' said Francis, 'plain English and common sense coming right up.'

'He's my guy,' said Jim, nodding approvingly at Hunter.

'Golly, Jim, you must have the most awesome mind on the planet if you think that quantum mechanics or genome sequencing or event horizons are "common sense",' said Hope Schwartz, the owner of the other big property bordering on *Apocalypse Now*.

'The fact is, Hope, I *do* have the most awesome mind on the planet,' said Jim, his glass still bouncing against the force field of his irrepressible jocularity.

Jim and Hope were old antagonists in the uncivil war between liberal and conservative values that unfolded even at this high altitude of American society, but the basic solidarity of being rich meant that they could still have lunch together; their antipathy was more like an unattended jousting tournament than a primetime wrestling match, beloved by millions.

With her high cheekbones, her tangled blonde hair and her sun-faded denim jacket, Hope looked to Olivia as if she had surfed to lunch on a Beach Boys album. She was bewildered to discover that Hope was already forty. Her wide-open face could easily have been ten or twelve years younger and her body was sinisterly flexible. She sat through lunch as if she were in a yoga class, arching her back like a stretched bow and folding her legs like shoelaces. For Hope, it was just so much simpler to sit in a double lotus than keep her feet on the ground. She refused most of the food that Raoul brought around, but sometimes took tiny helpings of the healthiest dishes, her slim brown wrists decorated with an alluring turquoise and silver bracelet, as well as an accumulation of red and yellow cotton threads she had promised not to remove until they fell apart of their own accord: tokens of commitment to a surprising number of fragile vows and friendships. When she bought the property next to Hunter's, it had been called, with crushing literalism, *Hilltop Ranch*, but Hope had renamed it *Yab-Yum*, in honour of the Tantric symbol for the union between male compassion and female insight, portraying the highest spiritual state in the most primordial sexual act; an image of copulative fusion that represented the transcendence of duality.

'Oh, Francis has a *Yab-Yum* image in his study, don't you, darling?' said Olivia.

'Yes,' said Francis. 'It's a nineteenth-century Tibetan thangka,' he explained to Hope.

'Beautiful,' said Hope, like a woman glancing approvingly at some new earrings in a mirror. 'Do you have a meditation practice?'

'I practise ineptly,' said Francis, 'when I remember.'

'I've got a dojo at my place,' said Hope, 'that was blessed by His Holiness the Dalai Lama.'

'Gosh,' said Francis. 'Did he just happen to be in the area?'

'He just happened to get a donation from the Schwartz Foundation. My family made a fortune in pretzels and I'm laundering the money with philanthropy. It's a beautiful space; you're welcome to come over and sit there.'

Why don't you just say, 'fuck'? thought Olivia.

'Thank you,' said Francis. 'I do less formal meditation than I used to; I just try to integrate my practice with whatever is going on.'

'That doesn't sound inept to me,' said Hope, flashing him a smile, 'more like the highest path.'

'That's exactly why it's inept,' said Francis. 'I should really go back to counting breaths and realising that I can't even do that.'

To Olivia it seemed like they were communicating in some kind of Buddhist whale song, lost on the uninitiated. Why didn't they just move in together? She felt the weight of her pregnancy with renewed force. Her hormones were all over the place. She wasn't an insanely jealous person by nature, or perhaps she hadn't yet loved anyone enough to awaken her inner Othello.

Today, by contrast, after a good night's sleep, on this immaculate morning, gazing at the butterflies on the thick, silent window, lying next to Francis, feeling the rapture and the intimacy of being pregnant with his child, Olivia was quite shocked by the violence of her emotions at yesterday's lunch.

'I have to go over to see the other ranches later,' said Francis, 'do you want to come along?'

'I think I'll stay here,' said Olivia, defying her possessiveness.

She not only wanted to wash away the guilt of her jealous spasm, but she also felt, as she embarked on her third trimester, that she and Francis were no longer a couple with a pregnancy on their hands, but already a family of three. She had often seen her friends' relationships buckle from the pressure of what was in some ways an archetypal drama, in which the mother and child were bound to be the stars, while the father, like Joseph in The Most Puzzling Story Ever Told, could only play a supporting role. At least she wasn't putting their relationship under the unnecessary strain of claiming to have been impregnated by God without losing her virginity, but whether a mother was about to give birth to Christ or to Oedipus, or to any other child, the father was forced to stand to the side for a while, being a spear-carrier, a confidant and a dutiful provider to the new couple formed by the extinction of the old one. Poor Francis, he should be allowed to go wild in the country.

'Okay,' said Francis, leaning over to kiss her belly while Olivia ran her fingers nostalgically through his hair.

'Hope likes to make fun of me for being a conservative,' said Jim, resting his hand on the roof of Francis's car, 'but the word "conservative" isn't as far from the word "conservation" as she seems to think. I may not know what an "event horizon" is – it sounds to me like a catering company out of Carmel – but I take the stewardship of this land as seriously as anyone and I don't have to quote Chief

Seattle to prove it, although he seems to have been a sensible guy and something of a conservative himself.'

'It's been a revelation seeing what you've done here,' said Francis. 'Thanks for showing me around.'

'You remember how to get to *Hilltop*?' asked Jim. 'I can't bring myself to call it *Yab-Yum*, it's what my granddaughter says when I buy her an ice cream. I don't know when arrested development became a virtue; around the same time as greed and grievance and self-pity, I guess. Resentment used to be something folks wanted to get rid of, now they water it and put it on a windowsill, like a favourite pot plant.'

'Sure,' said Francis, 'but we have to get rid of the causes of resentment at the same time.'

'Good luck with that!' said Jim. 'If you breed a resentment hound, it's going to sniff out resentment, even if you put it in a forest full of truffle and deer.'

'That's true,' said Francis with a smile. 'Anyway, your directions to *Hilltop* were very clear, and I saw the totem pole on the way up.'

'Now that's what I call environmental damage,' said Jim. 'If it had been there in the first place, I would have conserved the hell out of it, but having it *erected* by a woman whose family came over here from Germany to make a fortune in the snack industry doesn't seem to me like a compliment to the folks who used to live here, more like another slap in the face.'

'I can't really judge,' said Francis, in modest defence of Hope's pole. 'I suppose intention plays a key part in it.'

'Her intention was to put the biggest goddam pole she could get her hands on at the entrance to her property,' said Jim with a mischievous chuckle. He tapped the roof of the car twice and called out, 'Send me that proposal,' as he turned to walk back to his house.

'I will,' said Francis, pulling away quietly in Hunter's spare Tesla.

Jim's two-hour tour of his ranch had demonstrated that homespun common sense was not just a requirement he expected from others.

'My grandfather was acquainted with an old forester who was something of a legend up in Washington state,' Jim had told him, as they had driven up to an area he had designated for redwood plantation. 'He managed to make a living off the same stretch of land all his working life and he left the place with more trees on it than when he arrived. "It's really quite simple," he told my grandfather, "I plant more trees than I cut."'

'That should do it,' said Francis.

'Every species grows to excess,' said Jim. 'A blackberry bush doesn't know when to stop growing; it just keeps on spreading. If we harvest the excess, everything is going to stay in balance.'

'True enough,' said Francis.

'Folks like Hope think that conservatives want to frack the ground under our feet, dance on Nature's grave and celebrate the rise of dictatorships, but we're not going to work this thing out if we turn everybody into a cartoon.'

'Maybe that's a cartoon of how she thinks about you.'

'Probably is,' said Jim. 'I have a cartoon in my head about her Tantric conferences.'

'A lot of people have to change their minds before they can change their actions.'

'And a lot of people seem to change their minds about how they're going to change their minds and never get around to taking any action at all,' said Jim, 'and while they're doing that, I'm having the CEO of a big oil company to stay and saying, "You need to switch from being a fossil industry to being an energy business." He may be more inclined to listen to me than some protester chained to the company gates.'

'He may need both,' said Francis, 'as you were saying about the tree-huggers and the hunters—'

'This is the lower edge of the ranch,' Jim interrupted him, 'and we've planted five thousand redwoods that are going to extend the forest from the state park on to *Titan* land.'

'That's *Apocalypse* land over there, isn't it?' said Francis.

'Yup.'

'So, we could extend the forest even further along.'

'That's right,' said Jim. 'Nesting sites for more birds. We've had a pretty successful programme of reintroducing condors to Big Sur.'

'Quail, wild turkey …' Francis speculated. 'And then you could invite some oil men over to shoot.'

'A virtuous circle,' said Jim, 'as long as we don't give them birds that are too hard to hit.'

'In the White House reading *Brainwashed*!' was the answer Olivia received when she texted Lucy to find out where she was in Hunter's multifaceted compound. Olivia sat on the side of the bed and leant over carefully to pull on her shoes. She hadn't been to the White House yet but had been told that it was below the main garden, a few hundred yards down the slope, embedded in a bamboo copse. Like *Apocalypse Now* and *Plein Soleil*, it was inspired by cinema; in this case, by the exquisite white hut with wide windows in *Crouching Tiger, Hidden Dragon*, surrounded by pale green pillars of bamboo. It was there that she and Lucy would meet, like Shu Lien and Li Mu Bai, but not in their case to discuss the wilder shores of self-mastery, honour and disappointed love – at least, not as far as she knew.

As she walked down to the White House along meandering chip-wood paths, Olivia felt exhilarated. She was no longer feeling sick, as she had done at the beginning, nor burdened, as she was bound to later on; the frightening tests were behind her and her energy had come back, along with the sense of being in a thrilling new relationship with a person no one else had yet met. Perhaps she would visit Karen one day with the baby. She hadn't seen Karen for a few years, but if she dropped round with a child who was wanted and well, it might put an old sadness to rest. Or would it extend the sadness into another generation and deepen Karen's sense of failure? Anyway, babies weren't born to redeem or justify other people's lives, they were born to have their own life.

Saul could hardly wait for the driverless car that would take over his repetitious journeys from Caltech to *Apocalypse Now*. Arrival was also less fun than it used to be, now that Hunter had cleaned up his act. Although the birdfeeder was empty, Saul still imagined it dangling brightly from the branch.

Even without a driverless car and the ultimate relief of surrendering his biological intelligence to an artificial one, the journey was now so routine that Saul felt he had achieved a semi-driverless state by burying many of his decisions in the parts of his brain that barely required him to be conscious. He had already droned north to San Luis Obispo and then peeled west and was now weaving his way along Big Sur's legendary coast. The Madonna Inn, that Mecca of kitsch where he sometimes stopped, with its candy-pink allure and confoundingly cosy interior, lay behind him, as did the turning for Hearst Castle, which always provoked him into imagining the same scenes of disgruntled grandiosity and encroaching madness from *Citizen Kane*. He was well on his way to his destination, but no further along in resolving the moral conflict that agitated him constantly, like restless legs syndrome, bobbing up and down in his proleptically guilty mind.

The dagger he saw before him was one that Chrissy could see no reason for him not to plant firmly in Hunter's back. Money had turned his nervously cheerful, basically shy, nerd of a wife into Lady Macbeth, and yet it was Hunter who had made them prosperous, some would say rich. He was paying Saul more as a consultant to *Digitas* than he was being paid as a tenured professor at Caltech. With Chrissy lined up for tenure in the neuroscience department, they had long shot past the half-million-dollar income that had once been their Eldorado of deferred contentment but now seemed crushingly inadequate, what with the frenzied drive to acquire a seafront property, the kids' education, the luxurious new cars, the credit card debts, the state and federal taxes and, perhaps, above all, the corrupting exposure to the habits of the truly rich. Poverty was knocking at the door again, dressed in silk rather than cotton rags, but still insisting that there was not enough, not enough to relax when real enjoyment and security were just around the next bend.

Ah, here was the roadside viewing point that his navigation system, under normal conditions, always told him was twenty-seven minutes from the gates of *Apocalypse*. Yes! Twenty-seven minutes: no rockslides or traffic jams ahead. Although it was a self-inflicted pressure, Saul felt that for his own peace of mind he must attempt to reach a decision before he arrived. At the start of their collaboration, Hunter had set up a tantalising scheme that triggered a one-off, five per cent bonus for Saul when any of the start-ups he had worked on reached a valuation of one hundred million. Saul could picture a future in which packages of five-million-dollar cargo floated down now and again and landed in his bank account over the rest of his career, like supplies parachuted to the besieged Marines at the Battle of Khe Sanh. If *Brainwaves* took off in the way that he expected, the first package should arrive soon after the launch. In that sense, it was a terrible time to make a move for independence, but Chrissy was insisting that this was the moment to break away, now that he was finding so many promising projects; break away and put their marriage once and for all beyond the reach of insufficiency and envy. In theory, if he stuck with Hunter, he might end up with a beautiful seaside home, a few acres of garden, a boat in the harbour, an apartment in New York and three kids at Harvard. Not bad, but would there be enough for the golden retirement that he and Chrissy deserved? Was it enough and was it *fair*? If Happy Helmets went viral, his five million would be the kind of rip-off that would have strangers falling off stools in airport bars while he recounted again and again the story of how he had been cheated of his intellectual property by a wily businessman.

Business ideas kept flowing his way, especially since he was known to be a consultant for *Digitas* and a possible source of venture capital. He was hearing exciting stuff about improved delivery systems for the health benefits of infrared light on mitochondrial cells. And John MacDonald was making some significant breakthroughs with his artificial life modelling that had all sorts of implications for quasi-biological robotics. If only he hadn't introduced him to Hunter at *Plein Soleil*.

As Saul passed the entrance to the state park, the last few hundred yards of his highway journey rushed backwards in the giant screen of his Tesla-X. He slipped into a trance of optimal efficiency, indicating well ahead of the turning, glancing at the screen as he slowed down, and gliding off the highway while commanding his phone to call Raoul. The ringtone thrummed through the car's sound system as it climbed towards the first gate shared by *Apocalypse*, *Yab-Yum* and *Titan*, an almost immediate barrier to discourage the millions of tourists meandering along the coast from attempting to explore the segregated hilltops, or even park on the lower slopes.

'Hello, Mr Saul, I open the gate for you.'

'Thanks, Raoul.'

The gates were swinging open as Saul turned the corner, giving the flavour of a flow state to the end of his humdrum journey. That sense of exhilaration and the relief of arrival and the pleasure of access to an increasingly privileged setting softened Saul's dissatisfied and combative state of mind and by the time he came to the second gate, at the foot of *Apocalypse*, he began to feel that it would be premature to break away from Hunter at this point in their partnership. The first relief package of five million would probably land sometime next spring, enabling him to pay off a chunk of his mortgage and other debts and putting him in a stronger position to strike out on his own at a later date. His contract came up for renewal in just under two years, when he might be able to achieve a relatively frictionless departure. Hunter had certainly mellowed since he had started going out with Lucy, but he was still a ruthless businessman and being the designated target of his legal team was a terrifying prospect. Yes, Saul decided, as he drew into the parking area beneath Hunter's startling house, he would carry on for the moment working for *Digitas*, despite the pressure from Chrissy to grasp the billionaire's crown that he truly deserved.

Bouncing down Jim's drive and then along the track at the lower edge of *Apocalypse*, Francis started to feel that something really exciting could be done with the block of land formed by the three ranches. After a couple of miles, he arrived at *Yab-Yum* and passed under an arch made from sea-worn driftwood, polished by waves and bleached by the sun. The shadow of the totem pole rippled over the car as he started his ascent towards Hope's formerly eponymous hilltop ranch.

The front door was opened by a lightly bearded young man, with his hair in a bun, wearing Turkish trousers and a black ear-stretcher.

'Hi there, you must be Francis! Hope is in the pool. It's just below the deck you can see through those doors,' he said, pointing across the glowing wooden floor of a glass-walled, open-plan living room, scattered with stone and bronze sculptures of various deities from the crowded Hindu pantheon. Islands of sofas and armchairs and low wooden tables rested on brightly coloured rugs patterned with bears and elk and other wild animals. Hanging above the fireplace, on the only plaster wall in the room, was an unframed expanse of blue and white paint, evoking the endless contest between the protean vapours of the sea and the sky: the many-headed foam, the wind-shot or curling wave, the shape-shifting clouds and, towards the top of the canvas, a ragged cylinder of fog rolling in from the far horizon. Maybe the painting worked better on a breezy night, when the windows reflected the interior of the room and the invisible ocean murmured and boomed through an open door, but now, as Francis stepped across the threshold of the upper deck, its appeal to confusion and plasticity was guillotined by the dry precision of the view, the steep hills, the dark sparkle of the water, the cloudless sky.

When he reached the railing of the deck, he glanced down and saw Hope doing a gentle breaststroke along the outer edge of her infinity pool, naked. Francis dithered between the familiar pleasures of the landscape and the guilty pleasure of the more immediate view. At the centre of the pool's mosaic of dark blue tiles was a swirl of orange, pink and silvery-white ceramic koi, and across its surface Hope's slim golden body gliding slowly, her arms reaching out and her legs opening to push the water behind her. He remembered St Augustine's famous prayer, 'Oh, Lord, make me chaste, but not yet', trying unsuccessfully to lift his gaze beyond the pool, towards the tumbling slopes to the placid sea. After one last moment of voyeuristic turmoil, he decided manfully to let Hope know that he had arrived, but before he could say anything she stopped swimming, dipped her head backwards in the water, smoothed her hair away from her face, and looked up at him directly, as if she had known that he was there all along.

'Hey, Francis! Welcome to *Yab-Yum*. Do you want to have a swim? The water here is from the hot springs that run from Tassajara to Esalen, so it's totally natural.'

'I didn't bring my bathing suit,' said Francis lamely.

'I'm shocked,' said Hope, catching her breath. 'I'll avert my eyes.'

She laughed carelessly and arched back into the water until she was lying flat, her arms and legs spread out, as if she were on a yoga mat.

Gosh, okay, I see, thought Francis. Right.

It was not quite the ecological summit he had imagined, but then ecology was really about relationships, about seeing life not in isolated fragments but as parts of a deeply interdependent continuum and so there was, in a sense, something profoundly appropriate, as well as extremely embarrassing, about walking down to the lower deck, peeling off his clothes and wading into the sulphurous pool, in order to discuss how to get the land back to a wild and natural state.

'Yes, it is warm,' Francis commented, as he submerged his body hastily into the slightly steaming water.

'Hmmm,' said Hope, 'it's so relaxing. We have a tank to cool it down, otherwise it's just too hot.'

She swam slowly but resolutely towards him, paused and looked at him fixedly before drifting closer. She reminded him of a lioness stalking through the lion-coloured grass, while he felt like the antelope that suddenly sees the grass break into a run.

'Do you ever see mountain lions around these parts?' he asked, grasping at the local fauna, like a man grasping at a hanging branch as a river sweeps him towards the smooth lip of a waterfall.

'No,' said Hope. 'I would love to see one, but they're so shy and elusive.'

'Probably not that shy,' said Francis, 'from the point of view of a buck with a cougar hanging from its throat.'

'I guess not,' said Hope, stopping again about two feet away from him. 'After the Basin Complex fire, when the deer were driven away, a lion came down from the mountains and ate quite a lot of the local pets.'

'How did you feel about that?'

'I'm on the side of the wild,' said Hope, glancing down through the narrow patch of water that now separated them.

'Looks like you are as well,' she added, resting a hand on Francis's shoulder.

'Well, "inevitable" is probably a better word than "wild",' said Francis, 'to describe my body's response to being in a warm pool with a beautiful naked woman, but sometimes physiology and morality have to be separated.'

'Ouch,' said Hope, 'that sounds painful.'

'It is,' Francis admitted.

'Aren't you into polyamory?'

'Well, if I were, it would be unilateral polyamory and there are other words for that, like "betrayal", which rob it of some of its ideological glamour.'

'It's only betrayal if you've taken monogamous vows,' said Hope. 'Have you done that?'

'Not formally, but implicitly. Anyway, why are we even talking about this? I've only just met you and Olivia is six months pregnant.'

'So, you're deeply emotionally committed to each other,' said Hope, putting another hand on Francis's shoulder, 'that's beautiful and I totally respect it, but I also think you should honour your wild nature and live by what you stand for, not just in the land, but in your life and in your animal and spiritual body.'

'Do you write a blog about this sort of thing?' asked Francis. 'You seem to have all the arguments lined up.'

'Everything is lined up,' said Hope, her breasts lightly touching his chest. She drew back politely, making him wish she hadn't. 'Don't pretend you didn't feel it yesterday?'

'I did.'

'So, why would you not go with that?' said Hope.

'Whatever happened to self-mastery, ethics and the transcendence of desire?'

'Whatever happened to spontaneity and blissful union and Yab-Yum?' Hope replied, her hands sliding towards his neck and playing a soft chord on a set of keys Francis hadn't known existed until then.

'Talking of *Yab-Yum*,' said Francis, in a final effort to escape the apex predator whose fingers were now intertwining around the vertebrae of his neck, 'your ranch, I mean, rather than the symbol of ultimate union with the true nature of mind – I had a good talk with Jim on the way here. He's planting redwoods along the lower edge of *Titan*. If you and Hunter agree, we could make a lovely new redwood grove.'

'I would love a redwood plantation along the lower edge of my property,' said Hope, hooking one leg around Francis's hip while bending the other leg, like a dancer about to spring, 'it would make such a rich habitat and welcome refuge for all the wildlife.'

'Yes. Yes, I suppose it would,' said Francis, as he heard the creak of the branch and felt the power of the current pulling him towards the falls.

Lucy had put down her book after reading a passage scored by Olivia: 'The anterior cingulate cortex is one of the most promiscuously excitable structures in the brain, participating in the perception of pain, emotional engagement, depression, motivation, error prediction, conflict monitoring, decision making and more.'

She knew that Olivia had given her *Brainwashed* to help her undermine the hypnotic power of neuroimaging, on which Lucy had found herself, as her scans came around, understandably but morbidly fixated. In a sense Olivia's efforts were misguided. There was no doubt that MRIs could detect structural abnormalities in the brain and there was no chance, alas, that Dr Gray was going to ring her to say that her brain tumour turned out to be a smudge on the lens. At a more subtle level, though, Olivia was right that she must stay rooted in her own sense of well-being and not allow the limited authority of neuroimaging to disembody her. The Keppra had her seizures under control, her mobility was unimpaired, she was not in pain and her mind was lucid. These facts should impress her at least as much as her quarterly glimpses of an iridescent image on a computer screen. The further trouble with a brain tumour was that the dominant physicalist doctrine made it seem to be a mind tumour. How could you get your brain off your mind when your mind was purportedly in your brain? Equanimity or acceptance, or humour, or detachment, or profundity might give you a chance to get another tumour off your mind for a while, but a brain tumour was much more prepositionally intimate: it needed to be taken out of, not merely off, your mind. Under the physicalist dispensation, that could only be done with a surgeon's knife.

Hunter had told her this morning about the way Saul used to get obsessed with the 'explanatory gap' between experience and experiment, between science in its current form and subjectivity in its perennial form. To them, it had been a talking point, but to Lucy it had never seemed more urgent or more real. A physicalist, like Moorhead, who was content to reduce consciousness to cerebral activity, created the problem of why there was any consciousness at all, why the brain bothered to generate this distracting display of mind when it was doing all the real work on its own. This so-called 'zombie problem', which might keep zombies awake at night, didn't worry Lucy any more than the problem of why her television went to the trouble of generating the news. It was simply a false description. Who was it who had said, 'Consciousness must be a strange kind of illusion if you have to be conscious to have it'? Consciousness was primary and everything else we knew, including data about cerebral activity, derived from it.

'Hi, Luce,' said Olivia, stepping into the White House. 'Wow, this place is so like the movie.'

'Yeah, Hunter got the same people to do it. Didn't you bring Francis?'

'No, he's off seeing that Tantric slut, whoops, I mean incredible human being, Hope Schwartz, as well as Jim "Titan" Burroughs.'

'Maybe you should run this past your dad,' said Lucy cautiously, 'but I think I'm detecting a hint of jealousy.'

'Me? Jealous? What on earth makes you think that?'

'Maybe my amygdala is too large,' said Lucy.

'That would explain it,' said Olivia. 'Or too small.'

'The smaller the better, I suppose,' said Lucy, 'given that it's a site for fear – oh, and happiness, anger and sexual arousal.'

'And it has the most receptors of any part of the brain for testosterone,' said Olivia.

'Testosterone! The aggression hormone,' said Lucy, horrified.

'But also, aggression in the defence of status,' said Olivia, picking up Lucy's book and running her thumb through its familiar pages. 'If someone acquires status from fighting to save the humpback whale, testosterone could be correlated with compassion. Maybe you haven't got to that bit yet ... Hang on, I think I can hear a car. Perhaps it's Francis.'

Olivia walked down the curving path to the edge of the bamboo.

'Oh, no, it's Saul,' she said, disappointed. 'And he's spotted me. Where *is* Francis?'

'Planting trees,' said Lucy soothingly.

'As long as he's not planting wild oats,' said Olivia, resting her hands on her bulging belly, as if to reassure her baby of its uniqueness. She sat down next to Lucy.

'Francis *totally* adores you,' said Lucy. 'Are you okay? I've never seen you like this. You two are so solid.'

'I don't know. It's just ...'

Before Olivia could finish, Saul appeared through the bamboo.

'Hello, ladies,' he said, 'what are you doing in the feng shui chalet? I wasn't sure I'd see you both before the *Brainwaves* launch in London. Are you looking forward to it? I'm telling you, Happy Helmets are going to be huge. Huge,' he repeated, spreading his arms wide. 'I smell money!'

'Really?' said Lucy. 'What does it smell like?'

'Freedom,' said Saul.

'And what does freedom smell like?' asked Olivia.

'Money,' said Saul.

'Okay, so total equivalence,' said Lucy.

'You'd better believe it!' said Saul. 'And you know what? I'm really happy that we're all going to be getting rich together, as part of a team, a really great team.'

He raised both his clenched fists and shook them, smiling fanatically at Lucy and Olivia.

'Wonderful,' said Lucy, wondering what was wrong with Saul.

'Ah, I think I hear another car,' said Olivia, releasing herself from the awkwardness of Saul's manic solidarity and getting up to see if Francis had finally returned.

18

No need to tie himself in knots trying to tie a knot in his tie. Over once, over twice, under and through the over and over, tighten, straighten – job done! Not quite right, start again. Was it better to be tied up or tied down? They sounded like opposites, but they were really the same. He often spotted that, opposites being the same. He hadn't worn a tie in donkey's years, but Dr Carr always wore a tie, and he wanted to wear one today to tell him, in person, about getting the job, not that you needed a tie to work in a kitchen; in fact, it would be considered an industrial hazard, dangling in the soup, sweeping the starters aside like an elephant's trunk, getting caught in the InSinkErator and then dragging you in after it – gobbling you up – or gobbling you down. Same thing. Ties in that sort of work-place didn't bear thinking about. Health and Safety would go bananas. He wasn't starting work until next Monday. The owner of the company had lost his son in a mental health tragedy and, in memory of his beloved child, he had created an opportunity for someone who had faced 'serious mental health challenges' to have a proper job in a supportive work environment, and Sebastian had aced the interview. The owner had said that he was 'the best possible candidate', and now he was dressing up properly to tell Dr Carr, because he felt proud of the work they had done together. Credit where credit was due, Dr Carr was a good man and the best bloody mind reader on the planet. It was literally as if your mind was a book written in Double Dutch and Dr Carr turned out to know Double Dutch, which everyone else thought was pure and utter nonsense. Dr Carr had got him from there to here in a trice. Three times a week for a year was a trice by any standards. 'An amazing transformation', that's what they had called it at the halfway house, halfway between there and here, but also halfway between here and there – not the first there that he had come from, not that again – but the far there on the other side of here from the there he'd started from, and which he hoped he had left behind for ever, after a long journey, a hard slog, a forced march, after the fall of Kabul in the documentary he saw, and a forced march through the Khyber Pass and there was only one survivor, an army doctor who had the honour of being presented to Queen Victoria in person, not on the phone, but in person. Dr Carr said it was very important to come in person. And it definitely helped, especially if you had a history of your mind and body not being in the same place at the same time, like he had. He used to have a really annoying, stupid fucking psychiatrist who said, 'Where did you go just then?' when he fell silent. She thought he had 'wandered off'. She didn't seem to understand that when his mind wandered off there was no you to say where you had been, because the first you and the second you were not the same and they were *not you anyway*. Or I, as he would now say. There were seventy-one gender preferences on Facebook, which was a blow for diversity but, as he had said to Dr Carr, he'd had enough diversity to last him a lifetime. What he wanted now was coherence. That had made Dr Carr smile. There might have been a time when he would have wanted to have been called 'Them and Us', or 'Every-Nobody', or 'Here It Comes Again', but now he said 'I' when he was talking about himself and answered to 'you' when someone addressed him, or 'he' or 'him' when he was being referred to, or 'we' when he was part of a group, or 'they' when he was part of a group that the speaker was not part of, or when he was referring to a group that he was not part of. Phew, got there in the end. Grammar was the ground everybody stood on to speak. Even if it was wrong grammar, it could only be wrong because there was right grammar there in the first place. It might sound ordinary not to have a special preference, perhaps boring in other people's eyes, but for him to be ordinary was a massive victory, like Trafalgar Square. Dr Carr had told him that Sigmund Freud had said that being well was 'ordinary unhappiness', which must sound like a bit of a let-down to a lot of people, and not make much sense, because they were pursuing their right to happiness. But that right was really a trick, because they should have been pursuing their right to ordinary unhappiness. It was wrong right, an opposite same. To Sebastian what Sigmund Freud had said made *perfect sense*. All he'd ever wanted was ordinary unhappiness – being caught in the rain, running out of money before the end of the week, being too shy to talk to the girl without wanting to kill himself; that sort of thing – anything, really, other than *extraordinary* unhappiness, diabolical torment, cruel and unusual punishment; episodes, one episode after another, bleeding into each other.

'No problemo,' he said to the mirror, like Arnie in *Terminator*. 'No pro-ble-mo.'

He had tied the knot. Job done! It was looking as if it wouldn't fall apart, or strangle him, which was another way of saying perfect. Dr Carr would be amazed. 'The perfect tie is a halfway house between disintegration and strangulation,' that's what he was going to say, like Oscar Wilde, or Jeeves, or someone like that. He'd been planning it for a while. Not everyone would get it, so he was keeping his made-up quotation for Dr Carr. He was much better now – 'an amazing transformation' – but he still had to be careful not to talk too much, not to be too cheerful or over-familiar, not to plunge in at the deep end. He was so relieved to have ordinary unhappiness that sometimes he wanted to tell the whole world, like someone in a musical who stands up and starts singing to the whole bus. If you weren't in a musical, though, instead of singing along, the other passengers would probably call the police. And what you had to keep a firm handle on was that you *were not* in a musical (unless you were in a musical).

He couldn't manage the Underground yet, although it was more direct, but he did love travelling to Belsize Park on the bus. As a sign that things were going his way, he got the seat he wanted at the top in the front. He was king of the world, master of all he could survey. In his imagination. They had talked a lot about his strong imagination and his talent – it turned out to be a talent – for connecting unexpected things. When he was six he had been on summer holiday to France with his fake parents and they all went to visit a very old church, and when he saw the rounded arches, he had said to his mum that he thought the church had been built by special dolphins who had leapt out of the ground and left arches hanging in the air behind them and that you could see that they had been playing and criss-crossing all through the vaulted cloisters; and he had broken into a run and thrown his arms out and spun around and shouted, 'Dolphins!' And his mum had hissed at him and told him to shut up and not make a spectacle of himself, and his dad said that dolphins lived in the sea and not to be so stupid. And they were both embarrassed by him and wished they had never adopted such a strange child and he was burning with shame and longing to be gone. And he'd sworn then not to think like that any more, but it went on happening in a separate part of his mind that he didn't tell people about, except for Simon when they started smoking skunk together, and then he only mentioned the bits that sort of exploded on to the scene. He had told Dr Carr quite recently about the dolphins, and Dr Carr said, 'What a beautiful idea!' and Sebastian had started crying and then he had cried so much he was worried he might not be able to stop. Now they called it 'the dolphin session', and they both knew what they meant by it. At the end of the Friday sessions, when they weren't going to see each other until the next Wednesday, Dr Carr often said 'I'll be holding you in mind' and Sebastian hadn't really taken it in as a kindness until a few weeks ago, and then he had said that it sounded like a cradle, and Dr Carr hadn't batted an eyelid and had said that the work they were doing was 'like a psychological cradle', and so he had got on the floor and curled up and sucked his thumb, to test the theory, and Dr Carr hadn't batted an eyelid (or battered an eyelid, like some people he could mention), just sat there and let him be in his cradle, because that's what he needed at the time.

This was his stop, his bus stop, or his Carr stop, as he called it. He liked to play with words, which was an improvement on words playing with him, like they used to, like the orcas in the documentary he'd seen, tossing a seal from mouth to mouth amongst the pod, letting it think it might get away, but then catching it again and hurling its bloodstained body through the air, to give it the feeling of despair, he supposed, although David Attenborough said it was practice for the baby orcas, and he was an expert on animals and a national treasure, and so it must be true as well, but Sebastian's mind had stayed in the seal's mind and he had to leave the TV room at the halfway house because he couldn't bear to watch. Some words like 'nothing' and 'vacuum', and phrases like 'burning flesh' and 'the devil is in the detail' and 'throwing the baby out with the bathwater', used to drive him mental every time he heard them, which meant that he heard them all the time. Even 'beyond' had caused him a lot of grief in its day, but now he had much more control over his reaction to things and he could use those words and phrases, if he needed to. There was no point in throwing the baby out with the bathwater. There! He'd said it and it hadn't taken him over. 'Throwing the baby out with the bath-water': no pro-ble-mo.

He was on Dr Carr's leafy street now, some of the leaves starting to turn yellow, but still thick and rustling. It made him calm just to be on the street. Whoops, he was fourteen minutes early. Walk to the end of the street and back, like the ads before a favourite programme. He had so much to tell Dr Carr. He hadn't seen him since Friday. He always had this dam-bursting feeling on Wednesday, with so many things to catch up on. Turn around and walk back slowly. Four minutes. He went down the side of the house and waited by the doorbell. It was all right if he rang a minute early, but when he rang five minutes early, Dr Carr wouldn't let him in, because he wasn't ready for him and the session had to be *contained*.

Dr Carr was standing by the door of his consulting room, as usual, smiling at him warmly.

'Notice anything different?' Sebastian asked, before they had even sat down.

'You tell me,' said Dr Carr, as he settled into his armchair.

'The perfect tie,' said Sebastian, enunciating his words meticulously, 'is a halfway house between disintegration and strangulation.' He pointed to the knot he had spent so much care assembling.

'I think that's a brilliant remark,' said Dr Carr. 'You used to feel that you might fall apart, but that if you trusted someone, you might be stifled by the closeness of the relationship, but today you've brought the perfect tie here, one that makes you feel safe without feeling constricted.'

'Yeah, yeah, contained,' said Sebastian. 'I knew you were going to use that word.'

'I don't think I did use that word,' said Dr Carr.

'Maybe not,' said Sebastian, 'but I thought it when I was standing outside … which is not the same thing,' he admitted, with a fleeting smile. 'I just wasn't in the mood for an interpretation.' He fell silent, like a disappointed child.

'As you may remember,' said Dr Carr, 'we sometimes used to hold back from making too many interpretations in one session, but since you've become stronger, I've felt that we could work more directly together with what you bring here, because you're now able to process it much better.'

'I just wasn't in the mood,' said Sebastian stubbornly. 'It was more like a Jeeves thing.'

'It did have the ring of a famous remark,' said Dr Carr, 'but I don't think Jeeves often said anything as insightful about the perfect human relationship, the perfect tie.'

'I got a job,' said Sebastian abruptly, ducking the compliment and drinking it in thirstily at the same time.

'Really?' said Dr Carr.

'Yeah,' said Sebastian, 'in a dungeon, I mean a kitchen.' Sebastian paused. 'That was a Freudian slip. I made one up as a joke and because you like them so much.'

'Thank you,' said Dr Carr, with a gentle laugh, 'but it also resonates with the tie knot, doesn't it? If the knot is too tight it constricts you, and if a kitchen is too confining, it becomes a dungeon.'

'It was a joke!' Sebastian shouted. 'I made it up! It's my bloody joke!'

'It was a good joke, and a clever trick to play on me,' said Dr Carr, 'but I'm just expressing concern about whether it has a meaning connected with things you've brought here today, or in the past.'

'Yeah, I get it,' said Sebastian. 'We mustn't throw the baby out with the bathwater.' He started to giggle uncontrollably. 'I'm sorry,' he said, after he had recovered. 'I just love being able to say that.' He breathed out slowly before resuming. 'I suppose my life has been no laughing matter—'

He started to crack up again. 'I'm sorry, I'm sorry, no laughing matter,' he managed, 'and I'm looking for some, well, some laughing matter.'

'Some good material,' said Dr Carr encouragingly.

'Yes, that's right,' said Sebastian. 'Seriously, though, I want to learn to make jokes, because people like jokes and they like people who are good at making them.'

'Well, I think it's wonderful that you're able to be so playful,' said Dr Carr. 'Not so long ago that wouldn't have even been a possibility.'

'Anyway, I got a job,' said Sebastian. 'You don't believe me, do you?' he asked, beginning to loosen his tie.

'Of course I believe you if you tell me you've been offered a job,' said Dr Carr.

'Yeah, I start on Monday afternoon.'

'In the afternoon?' asked Dr Carr.

'Yeah, it's in a kitchen, so they only need me to come in to clean up and prepare things for the evening. The owner said I was "the best possible candidate".'

'Well, congratulations,' said Dr Carr, 'that's really tremendous news.'

'I'm going to be gainfully employed,' said Sebastian, savouring the last two words and readjusting his tie.

After the session, on the way back to the bus stop, Sebastian felt that he was more like an apprentice to Dr Carr nowadays, as well as being a patient, of course. He wasn't just a patient, though. He could make deliberate Freudian slips, which Dr Carr had acknowledged was a clever trick, and they could work together on interpretations. Like the dolphins who had built the vaulted cloisters, they were collaborating on making a place where you could reflect quietly on what was really going on.

19

Francis ran the cleaver rapidly back and forth across the heap of dried liberty caps, chopping them into a coarse powder, which he then scraped on to the parchment paper next to the board. At a time when his thoughts were so often drawn to the vast and sometimes disturbing implications of fatherhood, of turning a love affair into a family, it was soothing to be engaged in such a practical and precise task. After drying his harvest of magic mushrooms in racks and dicing them up, he would scoop the powder into gelatine capsules, so as to make the dose as stable as possible. Mixing them up was a good precaution as the psilocybin content of each mushroom ranged from one quarter per cent to three per cent and encapsulating them helped reduce the indigestion they often caused. His arms and wrists were beginning to ache now, and it was time to switch to the finickity but less strenuous job of loading the powder into its little capsule. He needed a free day to deal with the magic mushroom assembly line. It was time consuming, not entirely legal and, as with cooking, he preferred to be left alone to follow his own rhythm and do what came naturally to him. He always gave George and Emma a bag of mushrooms; it was their land, after all, and he never lost his sense of gratitude and elation at being embedded in the middle of their wilding project.

Olivia was away as usual working in Oxford and London. She could often reduce her absence to three or four nights, but they still had to spend the core of the week apart. Exactly how their child would fit in to her migratory life was still not clear. He suspected that he would quite often be left holding the baby for a few days. Whereas Olivia might have to be in college, or at the British Library, he was the flexibly employed naturalist, wandering around a beguiling rural setting, counting turtle doves and Purple Emperor cocoons, putting rings on the feet of migrating birds, recording nightingales and checking the health of trees and deer, Exmoor ponies and Tamworth pigs. Part of him loved the idea of bringing up a child in the middle of this surge of regeneration, but he was also worried about the drastic loss of solitude. There was a lot of hazy talk about what enthusiastic grandparents Lizzie and Martin were bound to be, but they would only be available at the weekends and that would mean going up to London and becoming annexed to the magnificent Carrs. He had grown to love and admire Olivia's parents and yet there was something overpowering about their virtue and prosperity that strained his self-respect. He hadn't complained about it, and in a sense it was perfectly natural and convenient, but Olivia's decision to take their child to her big old home straight from the hospital, as if it were their child's true home, before they all went down together to her small new home (and his only home), had pissed him off. Why couldn't they go straight from the hospital to Willow Cottage and then, after a month or two, take the baby to meet its grandparents in their rambling old house? He was just saying – or rather, he wasn't.

For the time being, he had the cottage to himself. He had his fading solitude, but not the mental freedom he associated with solitude. The trouble was that when he was alone these days his thoughts were dragged back to California. Although it was only six weeks ago, his memories of the visit had the improbable depth of childhood recollections, as if he had lived with them for decades and they had played a deep role in his formation. No doubt this had something to do with Big Sur's precipitous Pacific landscape, and the clouds of Monarch butterflies and the smooth unfolding of the wilding project, and Hunter's house, which seemed like a concrete fantasy, something he might have dreamt before finding out that it existed. Above all, though, it was Hope's swimming pool that was pinned to his memory, like a beetle in a showcase, its black wings glinting with greens and petrol blues under a museum spotlight. He couldn't stop remembering every moment and every sensation that had led up to his agonising moral triumph in that sulphurous water. Hope was hanging from his throat until he said, 'I can't do this; it's just not fair', and then she dropped him, as if she didn't really mind either way, and swam off with a few firm strokes, changing the subject without a hint of reproach or regret. He was left to reproach himself, while regretting he had so little to reproach himself for. He had done nothing – or nothing much – except, it turned out, to surrender his sexual imagination to a woman he hadn't even fucked, although she had been willing enough. He was on the moral high ground, but only in the way that a 'zombie ant', invaded by the *Cordyceps* fungus, is forced to climb into the canopy and, after biting involuntarily into a leaf, is consumed by the parasite, which drives a stalk through its host's head to make a chimney for the dissemination of its spores. Francis was not an ant, of course, and the appropriation was not complete, but it sometimes took control of him at night, when he was not wearing his ethical armour or feeling his love for Olivia, but was almost entirely submerged in his unconscious, like a hippopotamus barely breaking the surface to breathe before returning to wallow in the silt and the reeds. He really must stop identifying with one non-human animal after another. He was a *Sapiens*, after all, and would regain mastery over his night mind – sooner or later.

Francis stopped loading the capsules abruptly, hoping to interrupt his obsessive recollections. He needed a walk, a cold, fast walk through the woods before it grew dark, which at this time of year would be in about two hours. He left the mushrooms behind, after putting the finished capsules into a Ziploc bag. As the world descended into catastrophe, the psychedelic renaissance had arrived just in time to catch its fall, thought Francis, with a half-smile, but also with the sense that there were dangerously few alternatives. Poets, the 'unacknowledged legislators of the world', were now the acknowledged casualties of literature; politicians seemed to be recruited exclusively from the locked wards of psychiatric hospitals, and protesters, in the absence of poets to write their scripts and politicians to legislate their demands, could only grow more strident and desperate as they vied for attention with the better funded organisations they were protesting against – Occupy Wall Street, for example, had not distracted Wall Street from its occupation. On the drive to San Francisco from Big Sur, Francis had seen a banner saying, 'Fuck You and Your Corporate Pride', without being able to catch whose corporate pride deserved to be fucked. Perhaps it was a universal denunciation. In any case, in the absence of poetry, politics and precise protest, there seemed to be little choice but to turn to psychedelics for a cure to a global malaise. Universities were now falling over each other to study the effects of psilocybin, and its therapeutic value for those suffering from chronic depression and destructive addictions was astonishing, far better than any manu-factured compounds. How could a pharmaceutical company, messing about for the last few decades, hope to compete with the expertise of fungi, which had been luring animals to disperse their spores for millions of years? Not only were the results magnificent but, by all accounts, there was an unusual atmosphere of collaboration between the university departments focused on this study, as if they were being guided by the psilocybin to form mycorrhizal networks, to fuse and transfer information, to branch and explore without losing a sense of shared purpose and basic unity. As he put the new bag of capsules next to the many other bags in a cool, dim corner of the larder, Francis had to recognise that if there were ever a call to promote awe, universal goodwill and personal breakthrough in West Sussex, he was unusually well placed to help.

Outside, a thin veil of cloud bruised the sunlight. The air was chill and the ground firm after several days without rain. Francis decided to cut across the open ground to the woods and then curve back home along the northern edge of the estate. He walked through the familiar and yet enduringly strange English savannah that had emerged from the wilding of Howorth. When he reached the woods, he caught a glimpse of the neighbouring land through the tangled branches: huge monotonous fields of winter stubble waiting for a shower of nitrogen and phosphates and pesticides and fungicides and herbicides and a rise in temperature to turn them into huge fields of monotonous blonde wheat. Isolated from the rest of nature, it required ever larger prescriptions of fertiliser, like adrenalin shots in the heart of an overdose victim. As he made his way among the first few trees, Francis heard a commotion deeper in the wood, in the direction of the field he had just glimpsed; the sound of shaking and cracking branches. He wondered if one of the poachers who were attracted by Howorth's abundant game had set a trap or wounded an animal with a crossbow. He pressed ahead towards the source of the disturbance and, after working his way around a thicket of brambles, came upon a full-grown fallow deer caught up in the wire of the boundary fence. Its thick neck was twisting back and forth, and its legs gouging the earth, pushing it deeper into the metal knot tangled around its palmated antlers. When it saw Francis, its frantic, glassy eyes stared at him with pure terror.

'It's all right, it's all right,' said Francis, 'I'm going to help you.'

He edged closer, trying to calm the tormented buck and to see if he could loosen the wire, but its agitation grew more violent as he approached.

'I'll be back,' he said, hoping his tone would sound soothing, or that at least his absence would reduce the poor animal's distress.

He crashed back through the narrow strip of woodland and started to run across the open ground to his house to fetch the wire cutters he kept in the garden shed. He was still jogging, but now short of breath, by the time he arrived in view of his cottage. Despite his longing to press on, he had to stop to take in what he thought he saw. Perhaps the urgency of his mission and the hours spent packing magic mushrooms had made him start to hallucinate, or perhaps Hope, in faded jeans and an elegant sheepskin jacket, was standing with her back to him writing on a notepad pressed to his front door, her slender wrist encircled by her silver and turquoise bracelet. It generated the fake nostalgia of recalling some-thing that had never happened and seeming like an ancient token of his love, rather than an object he had seen for the first time at Hunter's lunch.

'What the hell?' he said, more loudly than he had meant to.

'Hey, Francis!' said Hope, spinning around and smiling reproach-fully. 'What kind of a way is that to greet a friend?'

'I haven't got time for this,' said Francis, starting up again, 'there's a deer entangled in the boundary fence. It's in a blind panic. I have to set it free.'

He unlocked the shed and took the wire cutters from their hook.

'I'll help,' said Hope.

'That's not something I associate you with,' said Francis.

'Let's just save the deer and argue later, if you're still in the mood,' said Hope.

'Fine,' said Francis, in a tone that communicated the opposite.

When they arrived, the buck was further ensnarled in the wire, but also clearly demoralised by its futile struggle.

'Let me,' said Hope, putting a restraining hand on his arm. Her touch left him awash with chaotic desire.

'Shh,' she said, moving carefully towards the ensnared animal, pausing between each step. 'Shh …'

'Watch out,' said Francis.

Hope did not respond but took a further step, stretching out her hand and placing it on the buck's taut neck. She held it there with a quality of presence and compassion that Francis was surprised to see in a woman who he had tried to dismiss as a selfish opportunist. The deer moved its eyes, released from the fixity of relentless stress, and looked towards her, starting to breathe like a runner after a race, as if it knew that something was finished and that it could afford to rest. Without turning around, Hope reached back with her free arm and squeezed her hand twice in the air. As quietly as possible, Francis stepped forward and handed her the wire cutters. She turned parallel to the stag, leaning her body against it and continuing to soothe it with her voice while she cut the wires one by one. She left a single filament attached to the fence until she had unwound the metal tangled around its antlers and then, with one last cut, she released the buck entirely. It was by now so calm that it took a while to realise it was free. Hope gave it one last stroke along its back and then stepped gracefully away.

'You can go now,' she said.

Soon after she spoke, the buck turned abruptly, bobbed over a fallen branch and then, seeing an open path through the trees, put on a short burst of speed before pausing to look back at them. After this moment of connection, it set off again, cantering towards the open ground with its head held high.

'That was amazing,' said Francis.

'Do you still want to argue?' asked Hope, with a smile that made a perfect parenthesis for her lips, as if she had almost forgotten to mention how lovely they were.

'Maybe,' said Francis tenaciously. Now that the buck was free, he was free to be appalled that Hope had burst out of his guilty imagination and into his life, like a grand piano, whose faint music he had been overhearing from the flat above, crashing through the ceiling and landing at his feet.

'Maybe has a "maybe not" hidden inside it,' said Hope.

'Does it?' said Francis, kissing her lightly on the lips.

She pulled him forward and they started to kiss with more conviction.

'So,' said Francis, when they broke off, 'how come you're here? I still haven't recovered from our last encounter.'

'What's taking you so long,' said Hope, 'regret that we didn't make love?'

'I regret that we didn't; I would have regretted it if we had and, as it is, I regret that we came so close.'

'You're really into regret.'

'In your case,' said Francis, 'totally.' He felt her hands on his sides and imagined that he could understand the strange calm that had taken over the terrified deer when she touched him. Why did she have this tactile genius, and did she have a licence to use it?

'Didn't they teach you about non-attachment on the weekend workshop?' said Hope.

'They told me there would be exceptions – anything I liked or disliked, for instance. With the things I'm indifferent to, it's a pushover.'

'Indifference is not detachment,' said Hope.

'Yup, I heard that on the workshop as well,' said Francis, 'but don't pretend for one moment that you want me to be non-attached. Or perhaps you do, once I'm inside you. Is that what you are: an itinerant guru of Ultimate Paradox?'

'That's me!' said Hope. '*Paradox Dakini.*' She made the whooshing sound of a superhero arriving on the scene of impending disaster.

'Sure,' said Francis wearily. 'We should be heading back; it's too late to have a proper walk.'

He started to lead the way through the fallen leaves and broken branches.

'Seriously, though, how come you're here?' he asked.

'I was going to email you, but George and Emma told me that you were off the grid, so they drew me a map.'

'You're staying with George and Emma,' said Francis, struggling between alarm and excitement. For the past six weeks, he'd been thinking of Hope as an obscure torment on the far side of another continent, but now, if things went badly enough, she might end up in his bed in Willow Cottage. No, no, no, no; that was not going to happen, he insisted, noticing how hard he had to step on the brakes.

'Yes, your name came up at breakfast and we all said what a coincidence it was. Or you could say that it was serendipity, or synchronicity—'

'You have to pay extra for that sort of thing,' Francis interrupted. 'I travel in economy with the coincidences.'

'What about destiny?'

'That's strictly for pilots.'

'You must have some of those front-of-the-plane feelings,' Hope insisted.

'Maybe I do, but maybe I don't trust them,' said Francis. 'Or perhaps I'm just being difficult.'

'Oh, so, are we arguing after all? How exciting.'

They continued in silence for a while.

'The thistles are doing well,' said Francis, the naturalist, walking through the mass of dead brown stalks and sagging heads.

'Really well,' said Hope, as enthusiastically as she could.

'So, how come your parents called you Hope?' said Francis, playing with the front-door key in his jacket pocket and trying to counter his racing pulse with small talk.

'They didn't have any of their own, so they passed the problem on to me,' she replied. 'That's why I'm in Europe. I'm slowly dragging myself to my mother's house for Christmas. She has a whitewashed castle on a cliff in Portugal. The place is stunning; it's just the owner who's a problem. She's a selfish bitch and the main reason I decided never to have children.'

'Uh-huh,' said Francis, who was not concentrating properly. He really ought to tell Hope to go back to the Park and not visit him again.

'Do you want to come in for a cup of tea?' he asked.

'I'd love that,' said Hope.

He was reminded again of a zombie ant. Hope had clearly taken control of his language centres and made him say the opposite of what he intended. He must fight back.

'Are those what I think they are?' said Hope, stepping out of her shoes and discarding her jacket on the sofa.

'Yes, if you think they're magic mushrooms,' said Francis.

'Let's take some now.'

'I don't think that would be a good idea,' said Francis, tilting the guard to throw more logs on the fire, 'but I have some for you to take back to George and Emma. I'll go and get them and make some tea.'

'It's so cosy here,' said Hope, sitting sideways across the armchair and stretching her feet towards the rekindled flames.

Francis went into the kitchen and filled the battered, cream-coloured kettle that had amused Olivia on her first visit, a relic with a thick nozzle and a whistle. He put it on the hob and lit the gas, feeling that his polite but cool replies to Hope showed that he was getting on top of the *Cordyceps Californica* that was attempting to commandeer his mind and body. He dropped a teabag into the pot and put it on the tray with two mugs. There was still time to make this into an affectionate but decisive de-escalation of their charged and potentially destructive relationship. They had kissed, it was true, but not to have kissed would have been frankly hostile. He could still police the riot she had started by touching him. It was difficult for him to be on the side of the truncheons, the shields and the tear gas, but it would be vandalism to be on any other side. He loved Olivia and her family, and he was preparing to love their child. On this occasion, being a man meant stepping firmly away from his virility.

While he was in the larder collecting the mushrooms for Hope to take back to the house, the kettle started to whistle faintly, and Francis hurried to take it off the stove before it reached its shrillest note. He poured the water into the teapot, put the Ziploc bag next to the milk jug, picked up the tray and walked resolutely into the living room.

'Oh, for God's sake,' he said, standing in the doorway, 'put your clothes back on.'

'What?' said Hope. 'It's not like you haven't seen me naked before.'

'I've almost only seen you naked,' said Francis, 'that's why it would be refreshing to talk to you when you were wearing something – other than that bracelet.'

'I never take this off,' said Hope.

'How restrained of you,' said Francis. 'I wish you took the same approach to your underwear.'

'It was given to me by the only man I ever loved,' said Hope, sitting up and hugging her knees.

'What happened to him?' asked Francis, trying not to look at her and taking inordinately long to put the tray down on the table. 'Did he catch a chill snowboarding in the nude?'

'He drowned,' said Hope.

'Oh, okay, well, I'm sorry to hear that,' said Francis, feeling unjustly caught out.

'That's why I'm making a fool of myself chasing after you,' said Hope. 'I've been feeling numb for the last four years – until we met.'

'Oh, come on,' said Francis, 'you can't do that.'

'Do what? Tell the truth?'

'No, put that on me.'

'Don't you find me attractive?'

'Oh, fuck off. You know I do. That's why you've got to go. I can't believe you're sitting there naked, fishing for compliments!'

Francis dropped the bag of mushrooms on the sofa in front of Hope.

'I'm going to go upstairs and wait to hear the door close behind you.'

He leant over and kissed her on the forehead.

'I'll see you at Hunter's party,' said Hope.

'Oh, Christ, are you going to that as well?' said Francis.

'I promise to behave,' said Hope.

Francis gave her a final, despairing look and turned to leave the room.

20

Looking out from the window of his apartment in St James's Place, Hunter was filled with a hazy sense of depression, remembering how many times he had walked to school from his parents' flat in Mount Street, across Constitution Hill, which he could see through the leafless plane trees, its rain-soaked paths hurried along today by office workers, tramps, civil servants, tourists and, for all he knew, Westminster School children on their way to the morning service 'Up Abbey', or to double Chemistry, or to an expulsion interview with the Headmaster – he had managed to clock up three of those during his chequered adolescence. He hadn't thought of Westminster Abbey for a long time, although for five years he had gone there six times a week. He could still remember the chandeliers that hung by cords nearly invisible in the dimness of the morning service. They looked like glass bombs pointing down on the congregation, promising an explosion of light if they could only complete their descent to the stone floor a few feet below the tips of their scintillating bodies. Hunter would hide his most pressing homework inside his hymnal and pretend to sing while he tried to get on top of a Latin translation or a physics equation.

Sometimes, he used to take Queen's Walk, along the eastern boundary of Green Park, and look up at the buildings whose gardens ran to the edge of the path, thinking that they would constitute an ultimate London address. Now he was on the other side of the wall, on the top floors and, later that day, he would be giving a launch party fifty yards away in Spencer House, which also overlooked the park. And yet, despite this over-attainment of his teenage grandiosity, he still didn't feel as if he had arrived at his destination. On the contrary, a new destination that he couldn't yet make out clearly seemed to lie in the opposite direction, and the journey there seemed to begin with this strange feeling of unspecific sadness. It certainly included sadness for the hunger that had driven him to vault over the garden wall and turn himself from a voyeuristic pedestrian into a disappointed resident. He wasn't trudging his way to double Chemistry, but he did seem to be having some kind of history lesson: the history of how he had seen things at the time when he habitually walked back and forth across this park and the resulting mixture of revulsion and tenderness towards that former version of himself. At that time, he had been boiling with teenage conflicts which, although he would be fifty next year, didn't seem to have simmered down until quite recently. The temperature had started to rise when he was fourteen, and by the time he was fifteen he had demanded that his parents let him become a weekly boarder at Westminster, so as to get away from their moronic company and their intrusive enquiries. He still often went back home between four and seven to raid the fridge, steal alcohol and money and take his mother's Valium from the medicine cabinet. His school bedroom in Busby's gave on to a flat roof that overlooked Big Ben and the Houses of Parliament; a view he still had, in a more remote form, from his roof terrace upstairs. In the summer term, on hot days, when he was in a 'private study', supposedly working on his A levels, he would spread blankets out on that terrace, and smoke joints, watching the hands of the world's most famous clock take a staccato measure of his wasted time. The appearance of idleness was of great importance at Westminster (although an 'essay crisis' was allowed, since it issued from a collision between personal laziness and a universally resented authority). In reality, the cult of idleness had to be accompanied by secret bouts of hard work in order to stay in a school determined to keep its place at the top of the league table, delivering more students to the world's best universities than any other in the country. Sometimes, Matron would stick her head out of his study window and ask, as swirls of hash and tobacco smoke dispersed over the division-bell area, if Hunter had been smoking.

'Absolutely not, Matron,' Hunter would say, barely able to disguise his annoyance at being interrupted while he admired the clouds that he was Rorschach testing through his wrap-around Ray-Bans.

His roof terrace also provided a fire escape for Busby's, leading on to the high, sloping roof of Church House. There was a flat area at the top of a set of metal steps, girded on three sides by some simple rusting railings. Hunter found that it was just possible to hook his feet under the lowest bar of the railings and lean backwards along the slope of the roof, lying at a sixty-degree angle, held only by the pointed tips of his black leather boots. The challenge was to smoke an entire joint of Afghani Black in this position, against the steep, smooth slate tiles, with nothing, if he lost his foothold, to interrupt his headlong rush into Great College Street, more than a hundred feet below. Excited by this discovery, he invited his gang of reckless and clever friends to join him on the roof. After demonstrating the dare, he hoisted himself up, clasped the dirty and corroded iron bar and clambered back on to the flat area.

'Who's next?' he asked, holding up a pre-rolled joint.

To his surprise, there were no takers. He had crossed the line from bravado to something unacceptably sinister that lay beyond the presumption of invulnerability among these self-professed daredevils, who never tired of driving cars over the speed limit without a licence, or jumping from high rocks into seas of uncertain depth, or swallowing random pills sold to them by strangers at festivals.

Where had his internal inhibition been? Hunter wondered, taking another mouthful of coffee from a broad thin cup and looking out on the dreary winter scene. Lucy was still in bed. There was no doubt that the strange flood of sadness he was feeling came not only from being in his rarely used London flat and experiencing it as a kind of umpire's chair between his old home and his old school, between his past self and his present self, but also from living with Lucy's illness, which had made him temper his megalomania and look seriously into the idea of moderation for the first time since his raging adolescence. At first, it had just seemed too tactless to wolf down cocaine in the presence of a woman who was abstaining from carbohydrates. Lucy was already lying upside down on a steep roof of undeserved misfortune and, far from wanting to hand her a joint, he wanted to lift her back to safety. He still wasn't sure where his old appetite for high risk had come from. For a long time, he had imagined that his misguided audacity on that rooftop was an early sign, not yet fixed on its proper target, of the daring investment policies that had made him a billionaire with the *Midas* fund. When clients told him that the name of his fund was 'kind of weird', or even 'inappropriate', because King Midas had not been a happy bunny when he watched his food and his daughter turn to metal, Hunter would restrain himself from pointing out that he had absorbed all the Greek myths by the age of eight, and simply replied that he was the one taking 'the Midas hit' for them and that it was only their investments that would turn to gold. And in a sense, he had taken the Midas hit. Love of power and money had acted as a proxy for love itself, until Lucy had suggested a more direct path.

Although his phone was on silent, Hunter saw the screen light up and the word 'Jade' appear.

'Hi,' he said.

'Hey, Hunter!' said Jade, as surprised and delighted as ever to speak to him. 'I'm sorry to call you so early, but Cardinal Lagerfeld's office is pushing for him to come to the party tonight. I wrote to you about it last week, but you didn't get back to me.'

'Did his parents call him Cardinal, like Ellington's parents called him Duke, or did he call himself Cardinal, like Prince called himself Prince?' asked Hunter.

'No,' said Jade, laughing a little more than necessary, 'he's a real Cardinal. He was involved with the *Capo Santo* deal.'

'I thought that was the little Abbot who came to *Soleil*.'

'Father Guido. It was, but the Cardinal was the guy with the legal team.'

'They were a pain in the ass,' said Hunter. 'They almost wrecked the deal. Is Guido coming?'

'You'd better believe it,' said Jade, 'he's way excited. He's coming by train, or donkey, or on foot, or on his knees, I'm not sure, but he left Assisi about a week ago.'

'Okay, we'd better let Cardinal Ellington come along,' said Hunter, 'or it might be awkward for Guido. I love that guy and so does Lucy.'

'Did she enjoy the immunotherapy meeting with Dr Seaford?'

'It was great,' said Hunter, 'and it ties in with what she is doing at *Epi,* working with the natural defences of plants.'

'Right!' said Jade, who appeared to be even more passionate about Lucy's longevity than Hunter, or Lucy herself. 'It just makes so much sense, working with the body instead of against it.'

'Sure,' said Hunter, 'bar the odd amputation, antibiotic, transplant, anti-viral medication …'

'Okay, so maybe I was rushing ahead,' said Jade.

'I think I'm going to try one of the *Capo Santo* programs before Lucy wakes up,' said Hunter. 'I never got around to testing it out. I was too busy with *Focus* and *Concentrate.* I could really use a mystical experience this morning and I'd like to see whether Cardinal Ellington has ripped us off or not.'

'Enjoy!' said Jade, in her go-to-bed voice, just in case Hunter had forgotten that she was always there for him.

'I suppose we must support Lucy,' said Martin, 'but this *Brainwaves* thing …'

'I know, darling,' said Lizzie. 'Look on the bright side, there might be a placebo effect.'

'Oh, there'll certainly be lots of effects. We've been shooting electric currents through the brain for some time. I used to have to watch. And we've been surrendering parts of ourselves to technology ever since we hit someone with a rock rather than a fist. It's the credulity and the voluptuousness of the surrender …'

'What if it works?' said Lizzie. 'Maybe there are brain-wave patterns that induce desirable emotional states.'

'That's what I'm afraid of,' said Martin. 'There are already so many ways to confuse pleasure with well-being.'

'You're such a puritan,' said Lizzie, resting her hand on Martin's shoulder and giving it a squeeze.

He got up and they both cleared away their coffee cups and the rest of the breakfast things, carrying them over to the sink.

'I thought there was something odd about Francis last night,' said Martin.

'Maybe he's just staring into the crevasse of parenthood,' said Lizzie.

'Maybe,' said Martin, 'it was definitely a crevasse of some sort.'

Lizzie gave Martin a sympathetic but firm look, managing to show that she understood, but was opposed to further speculation. 'I enjoyed meeting Hunter. It turns out he's been in analysis for quite a while.'

'Yes,' said Martin, 'he mentioned that to me as well.'

Martin had spoken to Hunter and Francis at some length over dinner about what Lizzie called 'the bee in Martin's bonnet': the way in which psychotherapy as a treatment for the most serious mental illness was denigrated by those who thought that it belonged to some fanciful realm beyond the proper objects of scientific enquiry: brain mapping and biochemistry.

'The fanciful realm of emotion,' Martin had said to Hunter, 'of symbolic language, psychological conditioning and cultural context ...'

'Hang on a moment,' Hunter pretended to object, 'culture is invited to the party, once it's been atomised into "memes", to give it the boost of making its particles rhyme with "genes".'

'Yes, the "meme" is probably the luckiest break for civilisation since the invention of gunpowder,' said Martin. 'The idea that emotion and psychological conditioning should be rigorously excluded from science or included only as far-flung provinces of a Celestial Empire whose capital is the Large Hadron Collider at

CERN belongs in a satire by Swift but, sadly, he's not around to write it.'

'I agree,' said Hunter, the agreeable guest. 'Science is a subset of human nature and not the other way around. It has its own oppressive sociology of funding and peer review and publication and profit, and it shares all the emotions of rivalry, intuition, conformity, anxiety and generosity that inform every other field of activity.'

'At the beginning of my career,' said Martin, 'I spent a good deal of time in hospitals run by psychiatrists who were more or less unsympathetic to my approach. One of the patients whose incarceration was renewed year after year under the Mental Health Act of 1959 complained that he had Christ-like nails driven through his feet, not through his hands but through his feet. The psychiatrist doing the rounds explained as patiently as he could – he was not a cruel man, but it was rather exasperatingly obvious – that this claim was proof that the patient was hallucinating and therefore that it was the correct decision to keep him in the hospital. The patient turned to me, knowing that I had an interest in the workings of the human mind, and said, "Some of these doctors don't seem to have ever heard of a metaphor."'

'That's hilarious and tragic,' said Hunter.

'Mainly tragic,' said Martin.

'Are you a fan of Ronald Laing's?'

'It was hard to be an unreserved fan of Laing's,' said Martin, 'he was so incredibly drunk; but he did show moments of genius in analysing the dynamics running through schizophrenic families, and his wild and sometimes misguided experiments have to be understood in the context of the world I was just describing, where incarceration and sedation and at times barbaric treatment were seen as the only possibilities.'

Martin would have expected Francis to contribute more to the discussion, and it was during this exchange, when Francis was leaning in and nodding and appearing to listen, that Martin had noticed something uncharacteristically distant and inauthentic about his presence.

*

'I suppose you're wildly excited to be seeing Lucy tonight,' said Lesley. 'She must be even more tantalising now that she's shacked up with a billionaire.'

'My sister tells me she's blissfully happy with Hunter,' said Charlie.

'My sister would probably have lied just to torment me,' said Lesley.

'I know,' said Charlie, reminding himself that one day he really must stop understanding Lesley, and break up with her instead. 'I'll just have to settle for the kind of sister I have, my ally in all things.'

'Anyway, it's not Lucy's happiness I'm concerned about,' said Lesley, 'it's your fantasies of happiness at her side.'

'I'm not so confused that a woman being delighted by her existing situation, as well as unavailable, acts as an aphrodisiac on me,' said Charlie, pleased not to be strapped to a polygraph.

'Oh, because you're all so *psychoanalysed*,' said Lesley. 'I'm sorry, I'm sorry. You know this subject makes me irrational and you know that it's only because I love you so much.'

'Sure,' said Charlie resignedly, 'but could we have a go at enjoying this party tonight.'

'My lips are sealed,' said Lesley, zipping them up with her right hand and throwing away the key.

The world is information, and life is an arrangement of information that enables it to grow, replicate and achieve some level of interactive sensitivity with its environment – that much was obvious, at least to John MacDonald. Man was clearly destined to build machines far more intelligent than Homo sapiens. They would become the 3-D printers of the future, in turn building any further machine that the species desired, made out of an informed rearrangement of atoms, which, to all intents and purposes, were in limitless supply. Humanity would be released from the resource anxiety that afflicted men and women less visionary and scientifically rigorous than John. In the rudimentary stages of the escape from planet scarcity (or Planet Scaremongering, as he liked to call it), there might be some value in the kind of information gleaned by *Brainwaves*, but only while sentimentalists remained attached to the biological substrate that evolution had handed down, with a brain that had not wavered from its three-pound and fifteen-billion-nerve-cell format for over a hundred thousand years, despite the explosion in knowledge that had taken place during this period of cerebral stagnation. Although that seemed to show that the capacities of the mind were not entirely inherent to the design of the brain, and that the mind had been able to evolve without changing the physical basis of its existence, John had plans for upgrading that antique vehicle to something altogether more potent, while keeping it aligned with the interests of the human race – in so far as they could be imagined at this early stage of The Greatest Upgrade in the History of the Universe.

It was a frustrating but unavoidable fact that he would need a great deal of money to make that transition happen and it would involve a deeper collaboration with *Digitas* than he had originally envisaged, but he had a plan for getting what he needed later today at the launch party.

Father Guido could not resist lowering and raising the brown and purple blinds of his hotel room one more time, using the remote control on his bedside table, while doubting that this was an entirely proper pastime for a Franciscan Abbot. He was not simply giving in to the childish pleasure of playing with a toy that had never been in his possession before, since the act of raising the blind had become entangled in his imagination with the miraculous power of Our Lord when he raised Lazarus from the dead, although, Father Guido reminded himself, Christ had not raised and lowered Lazarus three times; in fact, he had rather bided his time before raising him at all. Guido placed the remote control firmly back where he had found it and promised himself not to touch it again until nightfall, which, at this time of year, was quite soon enough to soften his renunciation with the promise of an imminent return to pleasure.

Cardinal Lagerfeld was staying in the honoured guestroom of the Apostolic Nuncio, in his magnificent Residence overlooking Wimbledon Common. Father Guido had been given a room in the

Hospitality Inn, around the corner, overlooking the car park of the Hospitality Inn. In some ways, this visit to England was a sad occasion. The Blessed Fra Domenico had died during a cold snap at the end of November, only a couple of weeks ago. He had been found by Manfredi with a 'beatific smile' on his face, in the hut where he had spent thirty years of austere silence. Cardinal Lagerfeld was giving a Solemn Pontifical Mass of Thanksgiving for the life of the Blessed Fra Domenico in the private chapel in the Apostolic Nuncio's Residence, and then descending on the Brompton Oratory to perform another Solemn Pontifical Mass, but combined, on this more public occasion, with a sermon to console the faithful that the brain of the greatest mystic of the modern era had been scanned just in time and that Fra Domenico would not only be interceding for them from the supernatural realm, in the usual fashion, in response to their petitionary and intercessory prayers, but would also be available in the form of the *Capo Santo*, which promised to plunge the owner into the profoundest mystical state by replicating the Blessed Fra Domenico's neuroimagery and stimulating the mystical centres of the brain. One hundred Special Edition *Capo Santo* helmets, signed by His Eminence, would be on sale after the Mass. With no time to spare, he and the Cardinal would then be rushing over to Signor Sterling's *Brainwaves* launch party at the Palazzo Spencer, which belonged to the family into which the lovely Princess Diana had been born, a truly beautiful and virtuous woman. What a day! He must set off to the Residence – but first, thought Guido, reaching eagerly for the remote control, he had one last task to perform.

Everyone has cancer all the time; that was the perspective that Lucy had been given in her immunotherapy meeting with Dr Seaford. Those diagnosed with cancer had immune systems that had failed to eliminate the cancerous cells efficiently enough to stop them from growing dominant. Once a brain tumour formed, it sent out chemicals to suppress the immune system everywhere, as well as finding ways to disguise its own abnormality. T cells, the infantry of the immune system, gradually became exhausted by the long-term presence of a tumour. The tumour, however, was not a homogenous entity, it was a mixture of cancerous cells and other cells whose immune defences could be boosted.

Immunotherapy was potentially the most exciting development in the history of oncology. Its collaborative rather than adversarial approach created a new set of odds for the patient. Whereas a surgeon would have to remove the entire tumour to cure the disease and would only think that it was worth 'buying time', considering the risks of surgery, if ninety per cent could be cut out, the immune system just had to be stronger than the cancer by fifty-one to forty-nine per cent in order to achieve a cure, a cure which was a self-healing, rather than a burning, a poisoning or an excision. Dr Seaford had kindly agreed to include Lucy in his immunotherapy trial, starting in January. He had managed to get a few doses of the startlingly expensive Ipilimumab. Brain cancer was the most underfunded cancer in the country, because its small patient population usually made Big Pharma unwilling to participate in trials. As one of Seaford's assistants had told Lucy before the meeting, 'The problem is that with other types of cancer, like breast and colon and prostate, survivors do a lot of fundraising, but with brain cancer, there just aren't that many of them around, and I'm not sure you want to roll them out, if you know what I mean.'

'Well, here I am,' Lucy had said, giving him a defiant stare.

He had tried to amend his tactlessness by saying that he normally worked with glioblastoma patients and that Lucy's situation was not as grim, but she was shaken and as she sat down to the meeting a small seizure clutched at her right leg.

Some of the shock of her initial diagnosis had dissipated over the last year, but there was still a basic sense that as a thirty-five-year-old woman she was out of step with conventional mortality. The teenage years of anxiety and grief, which had sometimes made her life close to unbearable, were far behind her, and the failing faculties and spreading pains, the fatigue and the arthritis, the increasingly limited possibilities of redeeming a disappointing life – the veiled kindnesses of old age that might encourage a person to join the queue for death with a certain eagerness – had not yet come her way. Her desire to 'end it all', in so far as she had ever had one, had been at a record low when she received the news.

And yet, although she would be embarking on an immunotherapy trial at the same time as her best friend was embarking on motherhood, she still felt immensely lucky to be surrounded by so much love. She was also encouraged, as a patient, to be living at a time when oncology might be about to enter a revolutionary change rather than just make incremental refinements to its old attacks on the 'emperor of all maladies', as the famous oncologist Siddhartha Mukherjee had called it. Whether a revolution was about to occur or not, she must, as she had often discussed with Francis, resist the lure of optimism as much as the lure of terror and 'rest in not knowing', as he put it. Amazingly enough, that was what she was doing now, looking out of Hunter's windows at the darkening park, perhaps more at ease than she had ever been, not just with her tumour, but with being alive.

Saul and Chrissy Prokosh sat in the bar of Dukes hotel, which Chrissy had told Saul was 'one of the world's best', according to the *New York Times*.

'Better get used to it, baby,' said Saul, clinking his prodigious, frosted Martini against Chrissy's cloudy yellow margarita, while raking up a handful of nuts from the silver bowl on the elegant table between them.

'This was Ian Fleming's favourite bar,' said Chrissy.

'And this was his favourite drink,' said Saul, taking his first gulp. 'Boy, that is a great Martini.'

'So, why should I get used to the "world's best"?' said Chrissy, half coy and half challenging.

'Because I have plans,' said Saul, draining the rest of his drink and fake shuddering as it slipped down his throat. 'Can I get another one of these?' he asked a waiter who was passing.

'Plans? I thought you had to wait until your contract expired,' said Chrissy, leaning forward, 'so you could get away from the long and vengeful arm of Hunter's legal department.'

'I'm putting out feelers,' said Saul, 'preparing the ground, so that when we make our move, there'll be things in place, but it's all legally watertight.'

Chrissy raised her glass.

'To getting used to it,' she said, sinking back in her dark blue armchair and giving him an admiring smile with just enough wickedness in it to remind him that he wouldn't be in this enviable position without the relentless pressure she had put him under to act like a man.

'So, what's it like making love to a pregnant woman?' Hope asked, amazed by the domed and indented ceiling of the Palm Room in Spencer House, like a curved honeycomb which, to her enhanced visual centres, seemed to be dripping gold.

'Realistic,' said Francis. 'Thanks for asking; it makes this situation even more relaxing than it is anyway.'

'Would that make us virtual, *if* we ever made love?' said Hope, destroying his defensiveness by pressing her leg lightly against his.

'Totally,' said Francis. 'When they move on from *Focus* and *Relax* to the *Brainwaves Flirt* series, they'll be begging us for a scan.'

'You make it sound so romantic,' said Hope, breaking contact.

'There's another effect,' said Francis, trying to disguise his devastation at the interruption of the erotic transfusion between them, 'to go back to your first question about sex with a pregnant woman, or at least one you've made pregnant – I don't claim any general expertise – it's like a painter being shown a canvas that no longer belongs to him, hanging in a house that never belonged to him, in a place of honour, over the fireplace – important and lost at the same time. There's a mixture of intimacy and usurpation. Some women get post-natal depression; some men get pre-natal depression.'

'Lucky I'm here to cheer you up,' said Hope, restoring contact.

'Yes,' said Francis, delinquently grateful. 'I'm not sure that it was a good idea to take quite so many mushrooms, although those golden palm trees look pretty great.'

'I love the ceiling, too.'

'Yes,' said Francis. 'We really ought to circulate.'

'Our hips or our tongues?' asked Hope.

'You're impossible,' said Francis.

'Who is that?' asked Hope, amazed by the vivid contrast between the red face, white hair and glacial blue eyes of the figure in front of her grasping a glass of champagne from one of the circulating staff. 'He looks like a neon man who swallowed a French flag.'

'I see what you mean,' said Francis. 'From Olivia's point of view, he's more of a *bête noire* than a *tricolore*. His name is William Moorhead ...'

'Oh, him ...'

'He's just been thrown out of the University of Riyadh.'

'So, how come he's looking so unhappy?'

'He left in disgrace, for emptying a hip flask of whisky into his lemonade at a party and then hitting on the wife of a fellow academic. Standard behaviour, you might say, but he was spotted by the deputy head of the religious police and the wife was a devout Salafist who despises alcohol and worships her husband, the Vice-Chancellor. Moorhead was lucky to escape lashes and prison. Apparently, his line is, "I forgot to change my SIM card at the airport."'

'Ho-ho-ho,' said Hope.

'Ho-ho-ho,' said Francis. 'He's spent his career as a public intellectual pouring scorn on all fields of human enquiry that are not susceptible to the scientific method, without applying the scientific method to itself, saddling us with "missing heritability", generated by genetic dogma, not by evidence; "dark matter" generated by the need to balance equations; multiverses, also without a shred of evidence, generated by a Many-worlds interpretation of quantum theory. It was great when empiricism displaced ignorance, but now mathematics has usurped empiricism ...'

'Baby, you're so intellectual,' said Hope, resting her palm at the base of Francis's spine. 'That's just one of the things I like about you. Remember the sleeping snake coiled here.' She spread her palm over his sacrum. 'And when it wakes up it shoots up the spine,' she went on, running her hand up the centre of his back, 'and strikes at the base of your skull and your whole mind explodes into light.' She ran her nails through his hair towards the crown of his head.

Francis closed his eyes and felt the firework display inside the sky of his skull and then inside the dome of the sky and then in a pulsing expansion of coloured light exploding in all directions with no limit.

'You can't,' mumbled Francis, still vaguely tethered to the fact that he was at Hunter's party surrounded by dozens of people, including Olivia and Lucy and Martin and Lizzie and George and Emma and Hunter and Saul – the list went on – who might see this strange scene and be amazed by his dumb ecstasy. 'You mustn't.'

'Sorry,' said Hope, quickly removing her hand.

'No,' said Francis, 'don't stop.'

She put her hand back with a quiet sigh, and ran her fingers through his hair again, provoking another burst of light in Francis's imagination and, for all he knew, everywhere.

Olivia was resting on the green velvet cushion of a golden chair, watching Bill Moorhead through the doorway, beneath the palms. She remembered the room well from her tour of the house, when she and Lucy had been taken by Jade to admire her choice of location for the party: that astonishingly gilded space, with palms on the principal columns, which fanned into the ceiling and then reappeared in miniature in the inner frame of the golden mirror above the fireplace and in the legs of the sofa and chairs designed for the room. The architect, whose name she had forgotten, had been inspired by Inigo Jones's plans for a royal bedroom. Palms were a symbol of marital fertility. She had the fertility down, although marriage wasn't something that interested her or Francis. Still, perhaps he would lose his head and propose, if she could stagger across the threshold.

Moorhead was grabbing a glass of champagne from a passing tray. He drank it with the abandon of a man recently ejected from a dry country, called the waiter back and exchanged his empty glass for a full one. The waiter clearly made some remark, which left Moorhead staring indignantly at his back.

'There you are!'

'Oh, hi, Luce; I was just having a rest.'

'Laying down your burden,' said Lucy, sitting down next to her.

'I'm looking on the obesity crisis with renewed compassion,' said Olivia. 'Look who's drinking at a reckless pace in the Palm Room.'

'Oh, heavens, as I live and breathe, is it not Sir William Moorhead?' said Lucy, pretending to fan herself with the agitation of an aspirant bride in a BBC costume drama.

'It is indeed that sad gentleman,' said Olivia, playing along, 'much oppressed by his tribulations in the Orient.'

'Tell me about it,' said Lucy. 'He's been emailing Hunter over the last two days asking him for help in getting a job at Google. He wants to be their Spokesman for Public Discourse on Science and Technology.'

Lucy and Olivia were caught in one of the fits of laughter that had swept through their friendship over the years.

'I think Hunter should endow the Sir William Moorhead Prize for Premature Denigration,' said Olivia, 'rather than introducing him to Silicon Valley.'

'Yes, I'm sure he was a member of the Stop Continental Drift Society,' said Lucy. 'In fact, he was probably at Galileo's trial, probing the sincerity of his recantation ...'

'Still,' said Olivia, with one of the sudden waves of sympathy that seemed to be preparing her for the unrelenting demands of motherhood, 'it's difficult not to feel sorry for him. I mean, look, he's obviously panicking under all that smugness.'

'Stay strong,' said Lucy.

'Sorry, I must have testosterone on my amygdala again,' said Olivia.

'That's just the sort of explanation he would approve of: putting magnanimity on a sound physical basis,' said Lucy. 'Oh, by the way, just to test the strength of those mercy hormones, guess who I just saw?'

'I'm flooding my bloodstream,' said Olivia. 'Who?'

'Hope.'

'What? Why is she here?' said Olivia. 'Was she with Francis?'

'Not really. She was talking to Hunter, and Francis was standing nearby, but in his defence, he seemed to be much more interested in the ceiling than in Hotel California.'

'Yes, I think he decided that the exceptional architecture called for an exceptional dose of magic mushrooms, but what's she doing here at all?'

'Well, she is a friend of Hunter's and it is his party ...'

'True,' said Olivia, 'it must be my ...'

'Hormones?'

'Right!'

'They sort of explain everything, along with genes and quarks and, well, everything, especially RNA.'

'Now you're just being trendy,' said Olivia.

'Okay, everything explains everything,' Lucy conceded. 'Let's hold that beautiful thought.'

'Where did you see them?'

'Through there,' said Lucy, pointing at the Palm Room.

'Why are you staring at that waiter?' asked Charlie. 'Do you remember him from Broadmoor?'

'No,' said Martin, relieved that his son had overreached and allowed him to tell the truth. 'He just looked a little lost, that's all. As you know, it's one of the shadows of my profession that I can't entirely stop interpreting.'

'I do know,' said Charlie, 'but you've got much better at disguising it.'

'Stop flattering me,' said Martin, laughing.

'You're like a constitutional monarch. You may have strong views, but you're not allowed to give anything away.'

'I'm sure the Queen and I could have hours of conversation on that particular topic – if either of us were allowed to discuss it,' said Martin.

Francis heard the ominous appeals for silence that precede speeches and bolted up the stone staircase, against the advice of various people who seemed to think he must be longing to hear Saul's promotional musings on *Brainwaves*, a subject that had already stolen days of his attention in Big Sur and *Plein Soleil*. Given the strength of the mushrooms and the scorpion's nest of his conscience, Francis would have been driven into hiding whether there had been speeches or not. In a sense they were welcome, since he could now search for solitude in less crowded rooms, especially since all the people close to him would feel compelled by politeness to listen while Saul and Hunter were unveiling the technology of consciousness.

Once upstairs, Francis passed through the thinning population of guests loitering in a magnificent red silk room, with a green and gold ceiling of shallow domes, that he would normally have taken time to be enchanted by. On this occasion, the opportunity for promiscuous visual pleasure offered by every carving, every painting, every window pane glowing with reflected chandeliers, every detail, down to the serpentine pattern of golden metal entwined around the door handles, was being usurped by an emotional urgency that drove him deeper into the house, as far away from other people as possible. Eventually, he came to a smaller, intensely decorated room. The pieces of furniture that had been made specifically for the room were already cordoned off and occupied by polite notices requesting visitors not to touch them, but a caterer's chair was still available for Francis to rest on. A couple stood in the bay window speaking quietly, and a man who seemed to be straining to give the impression that he was no stranger to such surroundings was squinting at the neoclassical decoration as if he had been asked to authenticate it, but was in no rush to lend his authority to the anxious owner. Otherwise, the room was mercifully empty. Francis calculated that it must be directly above the Palm Room where he had sat with Hope earlier in the evening. He was distraught from the recklessness of their conversation (not to mention the recklessness of the behaviour that had accompanied it), and by the fact that he seemed to have become addicted to her touch. It was a drug that created its own anguish. He hadn't been anguished before he met her and then suddenly been relieved by her touch; he had become anguished by discovering her touch and the bleakness of its absence. In fact, it was deeper than that, they seemed to be part of the same organism, rather than individuals who had chosen to enter into some kind of relationship. As an ecologist, he was always going around saying that life occurred in a world of processes and not things, but he had been thinking of biology, not love, and he was somewhat taken aback that the fervently mutual life he had been observing with binoculars and analysing in soil samples and talking about with passion, while he catalogued the wilding of Howorth, had suddenly broken into what he had secretly persisted in regarding as a private sphere. Far from being a private sphere, it turned out to be a tropical ecosystem over which he had no individual control, and in which, perhaps, he had no individual existence. No, he really didn't want to have that thought. It was all very well to chop a carrot mindfully, acknowledging the shop and the van driver and the farmer and the farmer's children and the microorganisms in the soil and the seed and the history of the plant and the rain and the clouds and the evaporating oceans: the endless sprawl of interdependent causes and conditions, but being the person who was holding that awareness with practised logic and easy inclusiveness was quite another matter from feeling like a microorganism in the soil of another process in which his own decisions and judgements were devoured and dissolved. The mushrooms were not helping, if the idea was for him to preserve any sense of control, or they were helping, if the idea was to see what a waste of time it was to cling to that illusion.

Oh, shit, the connoisseur was homing in on him, with the pedantic smirk of a man who is always ready to take a masterpiece off the hands of the ignorant fools who happen to own it.

'Christopher Spandral,' said the connoisseur.

Francis seemed incapable of saying his own name and simply stared.

'As you probably know,' said the connoisseur, rushing past the obvious historical facts, 'this room suffered some damage during the war, but rather wickedly, I have to admit that I actually prefer—'

'I'm sorry,' said Francis, 'I don't want to be rude, but I've come here to be alone. I've just had some rather overwhelming news.'

The connoisseur nodded, with a slightly raised eyebrow that indicated that in his day he had been no stranger to fierce emotion, but that he had stamped on that spitting cobra long ago, without being in the least surprised to see it flaring up impressively in the lives of lesser mortals. He slipped from a room that had ceased to amuse him; while at the same time the couple who had been whispering in the bulging, pregnant window, chose to wander off, leaving Francis unexpectedly alone. He closed his eyes to deepen his solitude, but instead of the darkness and peace that he craved, he found that his eyelids had turned into hectic and vivid screens. He seemed to be hurtling through a V-shaped space towards an infinitely postponed convergence, rushing past charged but indecipherable clips from a cutting-room floor, subliminal advertisements for products that didn't exist and were impossible to desire.

'To hell with that,' said Francis, opening his eyes without dispelling his unease.

He was in trouble. It turned out that Hope was going to see her mother in Portugal in order to persuade her to leave her considerable fortune to *Not on Our Watch,* a consortium of rich environmentalists that was buying up thousands of square miles of Amazonia, in order to preserve them and their indigenous inhabitants from predation. She wanted him to help run *Not on Our Watch.* She wanted him to go with her to Eastern Ecuador where they had one of their bases, since Ecuador was the first country to have included The Rights of Nature in its constitution. Francis was longing to go with her, to make love on the equator, among the swirling info-chemicals, with the full heat of the world weighing down on them. She said it would be a richer life, not a double life; that she would be sharing him, not stealing him, but, in the end, he didn't even know if the story of the bracelet she had told in his cottage was true. He wavered between paranoia and adoration – variants of credulity – without finding anything he could believe. At the most mundane level, he was unclear how he was going to run an Amazonian non-profit while looking after a newborn child in a cottage in Sussex.

'Oh, so that's where you are.'

'Oh, hi. Hi, yes. Sorry, overdid the mushrooms a bit.'

'I see,' said Olivia. 'Is that why you're hiding up here?'

'Yes. All quite full-on downstairs. It's nice to see you. Sorry.'

'Are you all right?'

'Ultimately, yes, but I've got to metabolise rather more psilocybin than I bargained for.'

'Is that all? Because George and Emma were saying that Hope Schwartz is trying to steal you away to run some Amazonian project ...'

'No, no, no; I mean, yes: there is an Amazonian thing that Hunter is involved with and Hope and lots of rich people ...'

'And how are you going to be involved?'

'Technology,' said Francis boldly. 'Drones are going to patrol all the land owned by *Not on Our Watch* and they'll have sensors to detect pollution, gold prospecting, deliberate fires, and so on.'

'Hmm,' said Olivia. 'And you're going to process all this information with your Nokia Brick while living off the grid in the ecological Langley of Willow Cottage.'

'Well, I suppose I'll have to compromise,' said Francis.

'What other compromises are you planning to make?' Olivia asked.

'None that I can think of,' said Francis.

Other guests started to wander into the room.

'I'll see you downstairs,' said Olivia, 'when you've metabolised.'

'Yup, definitely, just need a while to get my head straight.'

What was he doing? He did not want to live a divided life. On the other hand, he already was. It was divided by his overwhelming attraction to Hope. There was nothing wrong with the attraction; it was grasping at Hope that was splitting him in two. He mustn't be distracted by his yearning for Hope, but he also mustn't be distracted by his loyalty to Olivia. Resolution couldn't lie in siding with either part of the divide; it must be deeper than that.

He tried to pull himself together and concentrate. The way out was not to constrict the underlying feeling of attraction, but to expand it. As he allowed its full force to rise up in him, it seemed to push Hope aside, like the bud on a tree pushing aside its sticky scales as it breaks into flower and opens to the sun.

What a feeling.

He still wanted to fuck her, there was no getting away from that, but for the moment he didn't have to shield himself with guilt when he could open himself to something even more thrilling than her touch.

Phew. Okay. Back in the saddle. See how long that lasts. Better get back down to the party.

'Hey, Saul,' said Hunter, calling over his friend. 'Great speech. I wanted to make sure you know that before I sack you.'

'Sack me?' said Saul, chuckling. 'You always had a twisted sense of humour. The speech was great, right? You just said so.'

'It was adequate,' said Hunter, 'but the reason I'm sacking you is because I've seen the email trail between you and John MacDonald.'

'That is a private email exchange, at a private address on a personal device,' said Saul. 'Whatever you think you found by hacking my emails, which by the way are totally exploratory, is inadmissible and I can sue you for violation—'

'No hacking, Saul. MacDonald sent me the whole exchange and wanted to know if I would make a better offer. I could. So, we've signed and you're out.'

'Hunter, it's not like it looks. These inventors are sometimes so on the spectrum, they're *off* the spectrum, if you know what I mean. Out there. They need special handling—'

'Saul,' said Jade, 'Chrissy is standing in the hall flanked by two security guards. She's not looking happy, more like a shoplifter being handcuffed in Macy's in front of her children. The longer you delay this, the longer she's going to be having that feeling and the more she's going to hate you.'

'Hunter?' Saul pleaded.

'Get him out of the building,' Hunter said to Jade.

'Hunter!' said a delighted William Moorhead, moving into the space vacated by Saul and Jade. 'What a truly magnificent party; the best possible setting, perfectly organised and what an impressive crowd. Talking of which, I was wondering if you could put in a good word for me with some of your pals at Google. There's a position there that I think would suit me rather well and help keep the roof on Little Soddington.'

'Jesus,' said Hunter, 'have you still got that place? Shouldn't you downsize after the divorce? Isn't there a Very Little Soddington Manor? Or a Tiny Soddington Manor?'

'You mustn't hit a fellow when he's down,' said Moorhead.

Hunter put a hand on Moorhead's shoulder and addressed him with apparent tenderness.

'Listen, William, ever since I heard a Google exec say, "It is our intention to manage the knowledge of the world," I've been longing to clip their wings. That's far too great a weight for a single corporation to take on. Although you would clearly be a liability to any organisation that employed you, I can't just pick up a rusty nail file from the pavement when I clip those giant wings, I'm going to need a chainsaw.'

Hunter slapped Moorhead rather too hard on his shoulder and walked away without giving him the chance to reply.

Plagues were sweeping across the world: Ebola, sweating blood out of West Africa; rabid dogs roaming and foaming in India; superbugs crawling up hospital walls. If you thought about it, thought Sebastian, hospitals were really for looking after germs, not people, to make sure that they learnt how to survive all the antibiotics known to man. You were never going to get human beings who survived one hundred per cent of the insults thrown at them, but these superbugs were entering a realm of immortality. We were preparing them to be the gods of the next era, when humans were dinosaurs. The real point, though, like the tip of a syringe, like a syringe giving you a flu jab, was that this year there was a very nasty flu virus doing the rounds and a lot of his workmates had been struck. They were bedridden now, with superbugs parachuting from the ceiling into their compromised immune systems. Mr Morris, whose son had taken his own life in a mental health tragedy, used the word 'colleagues', but Sebastian couldn't handle that. It was more than he could bear to think he was important enough to have a 'colleague'.

Once you had a colleague, you might end up with 'an opposite number' and, once you had an 'opposite number', you might get cancelled out, like being eaten in a video game, or like anti-matter – which he wasn't quite clear about, but it didn't sound good, did it, from the point of view of matter? And nowadays he did take the point of view of matter, although at one time he had probably been more anti-matter-minded.

'My opposite number in Washington,' said Sebastian to himself, in his super-posh voice, checking out Eric's suit in the mirror again, but then Washington seemed so far away that he got a bit upset. 'My opposite number in Dalston,' he said, to make it less frightening, but in the same voice, otherwise it would be cheating. Dr Carr said that they were his voices and that he was learning to have a more playful relationship with them.

There was no disguising it, he was feeling extremely, extremely nervous. Mr Morris had called that morning to say that so many of his 'colleagues' had been struck down by the flu that he was going to have to ask Sebastian to help serve the canapés at tonight's event. He said that Sebastian had been a valuable and reliable 'member of the team' washing the dishes, and that he had 'complete confidence' that Sebastian could 'step up to the plate' and help with the canapés tonight. Sebastian had become very confused for a moment because he was still thinking about the dishes and ended up picturing himself stepping on a plate of canapés, but Mr Morris brought him back to his senses by saying that he was having Eric's suit couriered over to the venue, because Sebastian and Eric were 'roughly the same fit'.

'Roughly' was one way of putting it, although in fact it was quite slippery and slithery getting into Eric's suit and also, since the shoulders sloped off the end of his shoulders and the sleeves practically came down to his knuckles, it was in fact totally the wrong fit. He looked like a boy who was in a uniform that would fit him in three years, like the one his fake mum bought him, saying there was no point in wasting money. But then Carol, who was very, very nice, had taken some of the tissue paper from the coat hanger and worked it into the shoulder pads and managed to raise the sleeves by a couple of inches and make the shoulders look as if they belonged to him.

About lunchtime, his nerves had got so bad he'd thought of taking some of his old meds. Dr Carr had said that he was doing really well without them, but that it was all right to keep them at the back of the medicine cabinet as an insurance policy. They had been talking a lot about the side effects recently. He had told Dr Carr all about the dry mouth and the dullness and the weight gain, and the tremors, but they had also discussed some long-term studies – he was always online, reading up on his meds. Dr Carr was careful not to be negative about the meds, because he knew that compared to an episode, they were like a packet of cigarettes and a tub of ice cream in the park. It was the studies that were negative, showing that anti-psychotics lowered people's life expectancy, which wasn't good – unless you wanted to kill yourself, of course. 'The exception that proves the rule', as people liked to say. But even if you wanted to commit suicide, they weren't much good, because they didn't kill you outright, they just caused cardiovascular complications, and other stuff, that made your life, on average, shorter. Lots of people wanted to live for a long time, and quite a lot of people wanted to kill themselves, but you really had to look long and hard to find people who were gagging to make their lives shorter and nastier, on average, over quite a long period. Not that lots of people didn't manage to do that.

Carol had told him that all he had to do was hold out the tray and smile and say, 'Would you care for a canapé?' When the tray was empty, he should go back and get another one. He'd already done that three times now, but he still got super-tense each time he left the kitchen. He also had to know the ingredients of the food he was offering, because allergies were the biggest thing in catering now, and you had to be able to say that there were no peanuts in the smoked salmon, or someone might foam at the mouth and suffocate on the floor, like that poor boy at his birthday in a restaurant on the news. This time his tray had asparagus tips on it with tight little belts of special Spanish ham and some black napkins in the corner and a shot glass full of toothpicks. Gabriella, who was very nice and very cheerful, had some black seaweed cones with some shredded veggies in them, and John had some tiny pancakes with stiff cream and caviar (but no peanuts) and some lemon wedges. The special ham was called *Jamon Iberico*, which was a bit of a tongue twister, but he memorised it by thinking 'jam' 'on' and then, as he was wearing Eric's suit, but it was Spanish ham, 'erico'. The 'Ib' was a bit random, but he'd just have to remember to stick it in.

And so, he set off into the stone hall tucked in behind John and Gabriella, watching their every move. In the hall there was a huge statue of one of those beasts that was half horse and half man, like in *Harry Potter*. In the old days it might have totally thrown him to see a magical beast crouched at the foot of the stairs, but as he knew it was on Harry's side, it was sort of okay. In fact, it definitely would have thrown him in the old days. 'Might' was a funny word, because it meant strong and it also meant uncertain. Same opposites.

He knew they had to separate, and it was quite difficult, but then, as if she could read his thoughts, Gabriella turned around and winked at him and whispered, 'Go Sebastian!' in a way that was really encouraging. She was such a warm person, he wished he could live with her.

The next thing he knew he was standing in front of a tall, gaunt man in a bright red dress with a huge cross hanging on a chain around his neck. Camp as Christmas, but live and let live, right? People in glass houses. Who was he to complain? He could have done without some of the comments about his appearance over the years, so he wasn't about to say anything about the dress, just stick to the script.

'Would you care for a canapé?'

'What is it?' asked the Chinese-looking gentleman with a French accent who was standing next to the tranny.

'Jam on Erico and asparagus,' said Sebastian.

'After you, Monseigneur,' said the Frenchman.

'Ah, *Jamón Ibérico*,' said Monseigneur. 'It was always used in Spanish homes to catch out Jews who had made a false conversion;

or a whole leg would be hung in the kitchen window to show that such people were not welcome. A great tradition.'

He impaled the asparagus firmly and popped it in his mouth.

'I'm good,' said the Frenchman, which Sebastian thought was quite boastful and not really relevant.

'Is it your first time serving?' asked Monseigneur with a waxy smile.

'Yes,' said Sebastian.

'Well, you're doing very well, my son,' he said, impaling a third canapé. 'Now, you must take these away, or you will tempt me to eat them all. Such a great tradition, *Jamón Ibérico*.'

And then it was as if he didn't exist and Monseigneur continued to talk to the Frenchman, ignoring Sebastian completely, like when his father hadn't looked up from the paper when he came down to breakfast in his giant school uniform.

'As you can see, I didn't have time to change out of my vestments,' said Monseigneur, 'which makes me a very conspicuous target, but whether, in the age of terrorism, a priest needs to have bullet-proof clothing is another question. You say they would look identical.'

'Indistinguishable,' said the Frenchman. 'The ceramic filaments can be interwoven with silk, or any other fabric. It's a new tech-nology we've developed from our ceramic armour. You could try it out with the College of Cardinals to begin with and, of course, His Holiness.'

'Incredible, incredible,' said Monseigneur, who was obviously a bit of a shopaholic.

Sebastian moved into the enormous room, but before he could make much progress, he became enthralled by a pair of golden lions with vine leaves bursting from their ears and bunches of grapes hanging inside their wings. They were supporting a great slab of pinkish marble with their heads, and Sebastian felt that they deserved a rest, but if they flew away the whole table would collapse, which would freak everybody out completely. He imagined supporting the marble on his own back, while the lions went out through one of the big glass doors and swooped and glided around the park for a while. He could probably only last a few minutes under that sort of strain. While he was staring at the lions, quite a few people seemed to have had a go at his canapés because when he looked down at the tray again, there were far fewer than before. He had to pull himself together and set off across the dark blue carpet with its complicated patterns that were easy to get lost in if you didn't concentrate: splayed cream flowers with red centres and red flowers with cream centres, entangled with twisting stems, like an exotic garden where Aladdin might be hiding at night. A lad insane. David Bowie. He needed a Ziggie on the terrace to calm his nerves. He had to get across the rug before it dragged him down, with all its tangled associations and its tangled vines clutching at his ankles. He headed for the big glass doors where the rug ran out and there was a solid wooden floor, but it was like the Khyber Pass, with people picking off his canapés one by one. He couldn't stop, because he had to be the sole survivor, like the doctor who was presented to Queen Victoria in person. He was seeing Dr Carr in person tomorrow, thank god.

Made it. The wood felt much better. Mr Morris had complete confidence. There were three canapés left. Perhaps they were his colleagues and they were all survivors together. 'May I present Sergeant Jam on Erico, Your Majesty,' he imagined saying to Queen Victoria, 'who comported himself with the utmost valour in the Khyber Pass.' And then he heard a voice saying, 'Can I have one, please?' And he looked down and there was a very pregnant lady with a very nice face sitting on a golden chair.

'Would you care for a canapé?' said Sebastian, zooming back to the task in hand.

'Yes,' she said, laughing, but not in a humiliating way, more like they were sharing a joke, because she had just asked for one.

'You'll need two,' said Sebastian, 'one for you and one for the baby.'

'Oh, thanks, I'm really hungry.'

'Or you could have all three, if you're having twins.'

'Well, I'm not having twins.'

'You could pretend you are, so I can take the empty tray back to the kitchen.'

'Do you want to sit down?'

'I don't think I'm allowed to,' said Sebastian.

'Well, the people giving the party are my friends, so I think I'm allowed to invite you,' said Olivia. 'You look like you need to take the weight off.'

'I do,' said Sebastian. 'How did you know?'

'I know the feeling,' said Olivia, resting her hands on her bulging tummy.

'Thanks,' said Sebastian, sitting next to her, with his tray tilted at a dangerous angle.

'Okay, you've persuaded me,' said Olivia, taking the last canapé. 'For my fictional twins.'

'That's a relief,' said Sebastian, with a smile, resting the tray flat on his knees. 'I think this is the most beautiful room I've ever been in.'

'It used to be the dining room.'

'The dining room,' said Sebastian. 'Imagine having that many friends!'

'Well, the house was built as a temple to love, hospitality and the arts.'

'How come you know?'

'I was given the tour before *Brainwaves* decided to take it.'

'Love, hospitality and the arts,' Sebastian repeated. 'Not bad.'

'Yeah,' said Olivia, 'not bad. I'd like science to get a look-in.'

'Maybe science is an art. Like psychoanalysis is a mixture of both,' said Sebastian. 'What's wrong, did I say something stupid?'

'No! It's just that both my parents are shrinks and I think they would agree with you.'

'Well, actually, I was quoting something my doctor said.'

'Hey, Seb ...'

Sebastian and Olivia looked up and saw another waiter standing beside them.

'John,' said Sebastian.

'You should get back to work, mate.'

'Sorry, it's entirely my fault,' said Olivia. 'I was feeling a bit strange and I asked Seb to sit with me. He's been very kind.'

'Oh, okay, right, great,' said John, and moved on.

'Thanks,' said Sebastian.

'I told you I had your back,' said Olivia. 'Still, you probably ...'

'I know,' said Sebastian. 'What's this party for, by the way?'

'A *Brainwaves* product. Its nickname is Happy Helmets.'

'What?' said Sebastian. 'You put on a helmet and you feel happy?'

'It helps,' said Olivia cautiously.

'I imagine everyone would want one of those,' said Sebastian, getting up.

'I think that's what they're counting on.'

'Well, I haven't put on a helmet, but I feel much better now,' said Sebastian.

'So do I,' said Olivia, 'nice meeting you.'

'You too. You're a very nice lady.'

Sebastian set off back to the kitchen, eager to fetch another tray. He used to think the world was full of monsters, and obviously there must be a few of those lurking around, but there were so many good people, like Gabriella and Carol and Mr Morris and Dr Carr and this lady he had just met. It was enough to make a grown boy cry.